"This high-octane thriller subtly but clearly illustrates the linkages between environmental protection, social justice and human welfare. It presents a compellingly plausible look into our future."

Guy McPherson, author of *Going Dark*.

"You can't stop thinking about climate change. You're appalled that the world continues to burn oil and cut down rainforests with apparent abandon. And you're frustrated at what seems like a timid response from the environmental movement. Then you'll find this book cathartic. A ripping yarn on a background of international intrigue that brings big issues to life."

Erik Curren, *Transition Voice*

"Reading like a docudrama, William Flynn's compelling and fast-paced account of the destruction of the Indonesian rainforest takes you to the heart of a hidden world of environmental activism that gives the book its title.

Crisscrossing a militarized Indonesia, the main characters engage in a fight that threatens to bring the country to the edge of civil war ... if the military and the police don't catch up with them first."

Kurt Cobb, author of *Prelude*, a peak oil novel, and frequent contributor to *The Christian Science Monitor*

DIRECT ACTION

W. R. Flynn

First Edition

Correspondence for the author should be addressed to:
wrflynn54@gmail.com

Manufactured in the United States of America
CreateSpace, Charleston, SC

Also by W. R. Flynn

Shut Down
Buck
First Journey
Stone Warriors

"If man doesn't learn to treat the oceans and the rainforest with respect, man will become extinct."

Peter Benchley

"What we are doing to the forests of the world is but a mirror reflection of what we are doing to ourselves and to one another."

Mahatma Gandhi

ACKNOWLEDGEMENTS

These are the people who contributed to make this project a reality. I hope I haven't overlooked anyone.

First, I want to thank my dear wife, Deborah, who kindly gave her inspiration, proofreading skills and patience. Without her support, writing this novel would have been impossible.

My sister, Patricia, performed the final editing making the work publishable.

My daughter, Alison, edited the manuscript from start to finish helping me decipher the complex oddities of our common language.

My good friend and fellow English teacher, Jerry Kalapus, proofread the first draft of this work and offered priceless encouragement. The advice he provided was essential to the successful completion of this novel.

Lastly, I give thanks to Tom Newberry, Jesse Vella and the other good people who helped make this work a reality. You know who you are and I thank you.

CHAPTER ONE

When David Reseigh's cell phone began to vibrate he wiped his muddy hands off on the sides of his faded blue denim jeans and dug it out of his right front pocket. Sweat was dripping off his angular ruddy face so he tucked his chin down and held the touch screen out in front of his chest. He caught the small band of shade his lean, fat-free frame cast in the warm, midday May sun.

He squinted at the device and tapped in the code which unlocked the screen. Then he touched the text notification shortcut. The international code for the incoming message showed sixty-two. It was from Indonesia, sent from a number he did not recognize. David presumed it was from a friend of his, Azka, a reporter from the Jakarta Post. He sometimes used a different phone. If not from Azka it was from someone close to him.

He tapped it open then enlarged the attached image. The picture was fuzzy, but the message was clear. The image was that of a note. It appeared to have been written by hand on standard plain white copy paper. The words were in both English and Indonesian. It had been nailed securely to a man's forehead, just like the other three from the day before. They, too, had been sent by text message from an unknown Indonesian number, possibly a cheap disposable phone Azka occasionally used. All four notes had announced the same warning, as if they'd been printed by the hundreds like unfolded handbills: "Stop the Destruction."

"Hey, Gary!" David turned and yelled to his close friend and fellow environmental activist, Professor Gary Jackman. The seventy-two-year-old nuclear physicist from the University of California, Berkeley, had somehow remained unmarried and childless. He claimed staying single made it easier to conduct research. They generally used their first names when other scientists or environmental activists weren't around.

While an eighteen-year-old undergraduate, David had taken up bicycling as a way to help him recover from a costly, physically destructive journey into illegal drug abuse and he never turned back. It started while he was in high school with occasional alcohol-fueled weekends partying with buddies who enjoyed smoking pot and sniffing lines of cocaine. It wasn't yet enough to adversely impact his high grades or stunning test scores. He took his high school counselor's advice and applied to a number of top-level universities. He was accepted into Berkeley on a full scholarship. He started out his first year at 4.0, but by the time the young student from Daly City was a sophomore at UCB his health and grade point average had both decayed. It was entirely due to the lost weekends spent wasted on drugs with his old high school buddies.

One Monday morning in the middle of the fall semester, Gary, then David's physics professor, pulled him aside after class and verbally ripped him apart. He told the bleary-eyed student that he didn't care one bit if his home life was a train wreck. "Mine was, too," the professor said. "You graduated from high school at age sixteen, you have an IQ of over a hundred and fifty and, from what I understand, you're committing suicide by spending your weekends high on cocaine and alcohol. Meth's next. Then you're dead. I know the high price of following the path you're on. You're not working, your family is poor, you're on a full scholarship, so how can you possibly afford this? I believe you're selling the crap."

David turned away and headed to the door.

"I'm not through," the professor continued. David stopped. "Even worse, I think you're selling that poison to other students. As one of your mentors, and as a friend, consider this meeting your first and final intervention. What you're doing will destroy not only you but others around you. From this day forward if I hear so much as a rumor of you continuing along this road to ruin I'll make it my personal mission to have you removed from campus. And it'll happen that day."

David gazed out the door and off into the distance with a thousand yard stare, as stoners often do.

"Look at me, damn you," the professor demanded. He spoke loud this time, up close, a foot from David's face. Passing students shied away. He was well inside the young student's comfort space when their eyes met. "I want to help you because you're falling apart fast, both physically and mentally. I refuse to sit back and allow that to happen to a young man with such great potential. I believe what you need first is a regular fitness program which will direct your mind toward more positive pursuits," the professor suggested. Then he continued in a compassionate voice as David's eyes moistened.

"Listen. I really do want to help you. A group on campus, students and professors alike, we ride road bikes each weekend, rain or shine. Many have backgrounds much like yours. There's not a silver spoon among in the crowd. I want you to join us this Saturday. I have a spare Trek hybrid you can use. It's older and a bit heavy, but the exercise will do you some good. It'll work until you can buy a decent road bike of your own should you choose to ride regularly with us."

David began to sob like a four-year-old boy, right in front of the students hurrying by the door to his lab at Campbell Hall, the university's new physics and astronomy building. He placed his head on

3

Professor Jackman's chest. David quietly told him he was sick of the drug use and the cruel hangovers and that he'd be honored to accept the offer to ride with his group.

And did he ever. Each weekend starting that first cold and rainy Saturday. His newly discovered love of bicycling never faded, nor did his personal debt to the professor. In no time at all his youthful energy was directed at keeping pace with the others in the informal campus biking club. He eventually became fast friends with them all.

David also began eating properly and regained his health. Before long he was back in shape, his grades had recovered, and his old drug buddies from high school grew tired of his distant manner and stopped calling him. He further endeared himself to Professor Jackman and the others by gaining a profound love for the outdoors and a growing sympathy for anyone who defended nature, no matter what the approach.

While David stared at his phone Professor Jackman was a distance away and unaware of the brutal message he had received. Alongside the slow-moving river Professor Jackman was on his knees, in the mud, yet an easy shouting distance away. He was clearly uncomfortable in that position. The narrow leather belt holding up his tan cargo pants strained, barely containing his forty-one inch waist. His back muscles resisted with varying levels of pain after each and every twist his torso made. Long scraggly white hair covered his collar and all but the two bare patches reaching far above each temple. It gave him the weather-beaten appearance of an old hipster, or maybe a stereotypical old physicist featured in a black and white horror film from the fifties.

The idea that he should begin a serious fitness program had started to cross the professor's mind more and more lately. The back surgery five years ago had taken a toll. While recovering he had to place his love of bicycling in the Berkeley hills on hold. During that time his muscles atrophied and his waistline grew. With a number of research projects piling up he became buried in his work and put fitness on the back burner. Now he was paying the price.

For the past four days the two had been collecting water and mud samples from shallow pools alongside the Columbia River just west of Kennewick. It was four miles south of the Hanford Nuclear Reservation. They had two more days to go, then they would be finished collecting data for the project. He planned to relax and recover for a few days when it was done.

Concerned Earth Scientists, better known in the environmental movement as the CES, had hired Professor Jackman to independently verify that the radiation in the river was at an acceptable level. Department of Energy scientists had recently announced, as they had every spring for the past three decades, that the radioactive material known to be leaking underground near the Hanford site, a short distance upriver from where they were working, remained minimal and had not impacted the river. David and Gary suspected otherwise, so did CES.

CES allowed Professor Jackman to hire an assistant. His first and only choice was Doctor Reseigh, now an environmental scientist, who readily agreed to join him. The professor treated David like a son, and David enjoyed working with him. In addition, since both of them were flying to Jakarta a few days after the field work portion of the river testing project ended, it gave them both an opportunity to plan for that journey. "Just a second," Gary said.

"They got another one," David said, without waiting.

"Another what?" Gary replied. After a short pause he continued, "You mean number four?"

"At least four," David replied. "The day is still young."

Gary removed his plastic gloves and picked up his bulky aluminum sided testing case by the handle. He walked toward David while unbuttoning his red flannel shirt with his free hand. His eyes scanned the ground below through thick wire rim eyeglasses, careful not to trip on the occasional jagged stones punctuating the muddy riverbank. Concerned about his costly phone, which filled one of his front shirt pockets, he set the aluminum case on a dry patch of ground and approached closer to David. Anyone with the right knowledge and equipment could eavesdrop through cell phones, whether on or off, so the two were careful to not discuss sensitive topics near their devices. He gently draped his mud-spattered denim shirt on a particularly large rock. Then he whispered softly as he rubbed his free hand on his pants.

David barely heard him over the swishing noise his hand and pants together made. "Walk with me a minute." Professor Jackman said and pointed at his shirt. He then made the universal hand to ear gesture indicating he was faking a phone call.

David knew the routine. He placed his own phone in his canvas tool bag which was a few paces from Gary's shirt. The two men silently walked along the shore a safe distance away from their phones.

"The ball is finally rolling," Gary quietly said after they were twenty steps away from their smart phones. Anyone interested in what the two discussed regarding the true purpose of their upcoming trip to Indonesia could no longer eavesdrop. What they had to discuss was too sensitive to be shared with anyone.

"They nailed the note right onto the guy's head," David said. "Take a look."

"Just like they did to the other ones. Good God, does it have to be so damned gruesome?" Gary asked while he stooped over and rooted around inside his case. He extracted a small glass container, walked a few steps to the river, and kneeled in a patch of mud.

"Like they say, my friend: When all else fails, take direct action. For the past fifty years the mainstream environmental movement as a whole has been working within the system doing things the comfortable way, the easy way, the inoffensive way. With men and women in fancy suits meeting in high-rise modern office buildings they've built quite an imposing empire. Using full-page newspaper ads, slick television commercials and recruiting movie stars to raise money was the sensible approach, the only way to promote environmentalism without offending their corporate donors. They raised tens of billions.

Oh sure, there've been a few dissenters who called for a more active approach, but almost everyone considered them crazy radicals, really out there on the fringe. I've had to struggle to keep my mouth shut about their corporate approach to environmental activism countless times. But when you add it all up, look where it's gotten us."

"I know," Gary said. "Dead forests. Dying oceans. Melting ice-caps. Soil depletion. Methane releases. Radioactive oceans. All of it. Everyone in the world will suffer unless someone does something about it, and soon. The Earth is dying right before their very eyes and all they do is focus on raising money for their offices and salaries. The mainstream environmentalists are playing right into the hands of big business. They have all along, too, like good boys and girls."

"Exactly," David said. "The so-called crazy radicals have been right all along. Working to save the environment with all those idiotic feel-good, traditional methods was a waste of time and money. Five years ago you and I would have called the radicals nutcases, and terribly divisive to the common mission. How wrong we were. In fact, Gary, we became the enemy. Our actions only served to hasten the destruc-tion of not only the forests, but the groundwater and everything else. That's why I've hooked up with that new group in Sumatra, Direct Action. They're making things happen and it's about damn time. They've shut down two mines in the past month alone."

"Students, activists, common workers and the Islamist radicals all working together to stop the destruction of the Indonesian rainfor-ests. It's hard to believe."

"Don't forget the leftists," David said. "They're organizing like they did back in the fifties and sixties. Rumors are some sympathetic soldiers and sailors are getting involved. That'll make things more than just a little interesting. Everyone's set aside their differences for the greater good. They can resume killing each other, or not, after they win this one. And I couldn't care less as long as the rainforests survive. At this point my compassion and concern is for the forests and the wonderful life they hold."

7

"I'm not James Bond," Gary said. "If you don't mind, I really don't want to meet any of them."

"You won't. Your only contacts are me and my darling Killarney schoolteacher, Shannon O'Connell, who you'll finally meet on the first day of the conference. She'll arrive around ten in the morning. Schools in Ireland are closed during July and August, but she managed to get a two-week break approved for the conference. Her talk Sunday on the ecology of Killarney National Park will be one we won't want to miss. After my trip there last fall I must tell you it's the most beautiful place on Earth. I'm really not exaggerating. Have you ever been there?"

"I took a month-long break from protesting against the Vietnam War and hiked through that park back when I was a college student. It was part of a grand tour of Western Europe. I'll never forget the absolutely breathtaking view from the top of that mountain just south of that park. What was its name?"

"Was it possibly Torc Mountain?"

"Yes! That's it. After that we camped overnight in the Gap of Dunloe. I remember it took us forever to find a place to pitch our tent. The ground was quite rocky. Sheep and dung were everywhere. And the famous Ireland rain. It wouldn't let up, except it let up the morning we hiked Torc Mountain."

"I enjoyed the drive around the Ring of Kerry. Shannon's used to the crazy way the Irish drive so she drove. I wouldn't dare."

"My companions were frightened out of their minds. I'll never forget it. One called the road the Ring of Scary because of the tight curves, cliffs, crazy drivers and that constant tailgating. Our bus driver didn't calm anyone when he told us that if we crashed it could be days before anyone found us."

"It's odd being in such a safe, peaceful place," David said. "Even in this day and age the cops in Killarney don't carry guns. It's an incredible part of the world, that's for sure, and she is as beautiful as that emerald land of hers."

"After hearing you tell me so much about her, I can't wait."

"Me, too," David said. "But don't let the fact that she's a pretty red-headed secondary school biology teacher tone down your respect for her capabilities. She's one tough woman. Her family tree is filled with tales of revolution and resistance. It's in her blood, so to speak. So rest your nerves, my only contacts are you, the reporter, the silent moneyman, and my lovely Irish girlfriend. Again, you'll only meet Shannon. If I hadn't attended that climate change conference in Cork three years ago we wouldn't have met."

"Lucky you."

"Lucky us. She's brilliant, an incredible asset," David said. "And she's becoming an avid bicyclist. I'll never forget the way her blue eyes lit up when she saw my favorite road bike, my Look 695, which I packed with me on that trip to Ireland. A month ago I told her I'd buy her one if she married me."

"What'd she say to your new Look bicycle idea?" Gary asked.

"She said I had to buy her the bike first, and she'd think about it. So I did. She's still thinking, but we now have plans for a fall bike ride all over Europe. We may do it as soon as our Indonesia project is up and running."

"You still haven't shared your plans for me."

"Your role at this point will be to provide operational cover and help carry cash. That's all you need to do, at least for now. Things could change, as you well know, and if you want out, all you have to do is tell me. Remember, our role in this project is narrowly focused. It'll have to stay that way. The Direct Action organization is eager to get moving. All they lack is decent funding."

"C'mon," Gary said. "They must have some sort of local fundraising."

"Oh, they have local fundraisers. But the economic slowdown has really hammered Indonesia. They call it the world's fifteenth largest economy, but you wouldn't know it when you're driving outside the biggest cities. Little of the national wealth trickles down to the farmers or workers. In fact, a huge slice is syphoned out of the country.

"As long as we keep our mouths shut and share our game with no one we can have a truly dynamic impact. For us, everything is safe as long as the project remains compartmentalized. It's why nearly all that we'll ever be doing is helping to finance these guys. If someone asks you about Direct Action while we're at the conference just shake your head and call them a bunch of radicals or crazy kooks."

"They assured us after you made your first cash delivery last month that they were planning to make an initial bold statement, generate a message the bastards would listen to." Gary said. "And they certainly have."

"I'll say so," David agreed. "Right before the conference, too. The media rarely covers these routine academic affairs. Maybe this one'll be different."

"I wouldn't be surprised. Are you sure it's safe for you to receive those text messages?" Gary asked while scooping mud into the glass container. "I'm totally down with what we're doing, don't get me wrong. But, man, this is all new to me. I'm concerned, even nervous about us somehow getting tied in to this, uh, escalation."

"Absolutely safe," David replied. "Hundreds, even thousands of people have received the same picture by now. They've sent it to dozens of Indonesian reporters, a long list of foreign reporters in Jakarta, as well as a zillion student activists. Plus the staff of Walhi, every number on the contact list at next week's meeting in Jakarta as well as everyone who's anyone at Big Green, you know, the Sierra Club, the WWF and your favorite, the big guys cutting our current paycheck, Concerned Earth Scientists."

"By now it's in my email, or a text, no doubt."

"No doubt. As we discussed, as a political figure, the chief financial officer for Preserve the Rainforests, I'm apparently on the long list of those receiving it straight from Direct Action, well, from the ones in the trenches doing the dirty work so to speak. But as a simple, everyday scientist and researcher, you're not. However, by the end of the day someone will have forwarded it to you. You'll see. Heck, by now it's probably on the BBC website," David said.

"Like I'll feel better when that happens."

"Hey, relax, Gary. We're safe. Seriously, I'm just another phone number on someone's list. And the phones they use are sold in stores everywhere. Plus I'm told they're destroyed after each message."

"Still it's hard to believe the game is on," Gary said. "It's just that I'm a scientist, a radical on some issues, perhaps, like many of my colleagues, but still I'm only an academic, not a true radical activist. All I do is pay dues to CES, maybe write a paper now and then or occasionally share my leftist ideology and philosophy with the students. That's all. I'm not used to all this cloak and dagger stuff, especially the dagger part. I mean, I can barely jog twenty feet without my back acting up. Maybe I should start biking again or join a gym."

"It's a bit unsettling, I agree. But as we've discussed so many times over the past couple of months, we have no other choice. In fact, I'm going to pass the picture along to some friends of mine. I'll even send it to some reporters I know so some clown at the NSA won't wonder why I kept it to myself, if it gets to that. In fact, I'll pass it along to you right now."

"Just what I need," Gary said while he brushed mud off his pant legs.

"It would raise suspicions if I didn't."

"You're probably right," Gary replied, focusing intently on scooping out another muddy sample. "I just wish we didn't have to do it the hard way."

"You and me, both," David said. "But look where all those years of traditional executive room environmental activism got our movement, and our planet."

"Yeah, lovely radioactive wastelands like this. Let's finish up here, UPS these off for testing, and then get ready for our flight to Jakarta. The conference this year will be one we don't wanna miss."

"Sounds good."

"This is your first trip to Indonesia. Are you prepared for your presentation on the Fukushima radiation leaks and its impact on Pacific Ocean fish populations?"

"Yes," Gary said. "I wouldn't miss it for the world."

"It's odd, Gary. Everyone there will be listening to you and your colleagues present your groundbreaking study, but in the back of their minds they'll probably be focused on news reports about Direct Action. And we'll be involved in all of it."

CHAPTER TWO

The focus of the academics, scientists and assorted rainforest advocates as well as the various environmental groups gathered in Jakarta was to bring worldwide attention to the destruction of the Indonesian forests and, in particular, the Sumatran rainforest. At least that was the public message, the one the press releases and public statements shared. In reality it was a huge fundraiser, the biggest of all for most of the environmental groups present. For the dozens of business executives sequestered in nearby hotels, it was an opportunity to write millions of dollars of grants thereby demonstrating to the public their concern for the environment. Plus the gifts and grants would load their bottom lines with hefty tax deductions.

Each year the conference focused on a specific environmental cause. Last year it was the looming extinction of the polar bears. That gathering had been held in Murmansk, Russia, not in the dead of winter, but in late June when it was often warm, sunny, short-sleeve weather twenty-four hours each day. The year before that it had addressed the environmental damage caused by hydro fracking. That conference had been held in Fargo, North Dakota. Again, it was held in June. But that year those gathered stayed in the hotel four days longer than planned due to a huge flood.

The most prestigious environmental groups were represented this year at the Jakarta gathering, which was being held in the Marriott Hotel. It was near downtown, less then an hour from the international airport. In addition to the world's most influential environmental groups the event featured official representatives from the Indonesian government's environmental advocate, the Directorate General of Forest Protection and Nature Conservation, better know by its Indonesian acronym, PHKA.

A small group of scientists and activists from Walhi, an Indonesian environmental group dedicated to saving the rainforest, or, rather what remained of it, had submitted a paper which they would present. They argued that the only way to protect the remnants of the nation's biodiversity was for the remaining rainforests to be converted into national parks under the protection of the United Nations. Of course to accomplish this the People's Consultative Assembly, which most referred to by its acronym, the MPR, would have to move fast. The forests were vanishing. It would require taking decisive action before the end of this summer or next. But there was little hope of that happening, particularly in light of the politically powerful army's past participation in protecting forest clearing operations throughout Indonesia and in particular those on Sumatra.

A wide array of smaller environmental groups had a presence there, too, including Concerned Earth Scientists, the influential organization Professor Jackman belonged to. All conference attendees were properly vetted by the organizers to minimize what they called, "distractive elements," thereby helping to ensure a calm, more productive approach to the greater cause.

Not to be left out, a host of international corporations had a presence, not at the conference itself in the form of displays and open forums, but in private gatherings held in nearby hotels. The idea was to share with the specially invited grant-hungry scientists, environmentalists and environmental groups the extent of their various green, renewable approaches to their various business models. In the eyes of many at the conference, working closely with, rather than against, international corporations offered the best long-term path to a worldwide environmentally friendly and sustainable future.

Some of the smaller, more radical groups who were specifically excluded from the annual gathering disagreed. They called it the annual Big Green fundraiser. But the organizers geared the event toward soliciting and selecting research papers which would be presented at the conference and later published in a future issue of the quarterly Journal of Environmental Sciences. The idea was to ensure that a more sober-sounding, less confrontational tone would result and be easier to present to grant-giving governments, companies desiring some green credibility in the marketplace and, most importantly, the media. The suit and tie approach was a time-tested process that worked well, particularly at raising money. The WWF, for example, expected to pick up a cool twenty million dollars in grants at this conference alone, thereby increasing the size of its war chest to nearly one billion dollars.

CHAPTER THREE

"I don't have much time left," Chuck said to David, as he stood staring through wire rim glasses at the Golden Gate Bridge. The tinted, floor-to-ceiling windows on the main floor of his four story home on Vallejo Street offered a postcard view reaching beyond the bridge and across the bay to Alcatraz Island. From the top floor the view was even more spectacular.

The solid steel-framed Georgian home was built nearly a century ago. After dozens of earthquakes the decorative exterior bricks which reached all the way to the roof hadn't sprouted a single crack.

The eight bedroom house was furnished almost entirely with ornately carved dark hardwood, most likely imported from some-where in Southeast Asia. The floors and the commanding circular stairway near the entry were made from similar tropical hardwoods.

With his long black silk robe and black stockings he could have been mistaken for an elderly Spanish friar. The thinning band of closely-cropped white hair reaching from above one oversized ear to the other contributed to the image. The haze-tinted sun, now nearly orange, reflected off the top of his head as he stood near a north-facing window.

"I'm told the pancreatic cancer is winning. But it's graciously granting me an additional six months, according to my doctors. I'm planning on five years, regardless of what those overpaid morons tell me. However, in case they're right, I'm asking you to accelerate your efforts to help me with this project of mine. It's important that I put my remaining time to good use."

"Of course," David said, staring at the old man's reflection in the window. David wore his usual travel clothing: a faded denim shirt and crisp beige cargo pants. It was late May and he felt inadequately dressed for the weather. He was still cold, even though he hadn't walked far. A fifty-two degree evening in San Francisco somehow chilled the bones like a thirty-five degree evening anywhere else. Some day he'd find out why. Maybe it was as simple as an odd mix of the shifting wind and humidity.

His new tan hiking boots, which he removed as soon as he entered, were left on the inside mat by the door. His single piece of luggage and the carry-on backpack containing all his documents and notes were with Gary. His tan expedition hat had been hung on a hook next to the front door by one of Chuck's two short and stocky Nepalese bodyguards. Judging by the perspiration on their faces when answering the door, they had probably been lifting weights in Chuck's home gym. The two now sat near the door on heavy wooden chairs reading books written in their Himalayan language.

He decided to dodge the subject of Chuck's health. "What exactly do you have in mind?"

David sat across the glass-topped coffee table from one of the wealthiest men in the energy business. He marveled at the immense power Chuck represented as a captain of the energy services industry. He was known professionally as Charles Henry Simmons, a leading investment banker for a global network of natural gas and oil service companies. Many of them he owned outright. Only a select few friends got away with calling the tall, slender man, Chuck. David was one of them. Everyone else used all three names, usually preceded with the word "mister."

Chuck then shot a whispered question. "Where's your phone?"

"My colleague, Professor Jackman, has it. When his taxi dropped me off four or five blocks from here I gave it to him along with my luggage. I'm meeting the professor at the airport around nine. The flight departs at midnight, but that new passport exit control procedure takes forever, so we have to arrive three hours early."

"Good. I'm glad we don't have to rush for a change. My phone's in the handgun safe on the kitchen counter so we can speak freely. If it wasn't for that loser son of mine calling me all the time I'd leave the damn thing there. At forty-seven he still lives off the allowance I give him, but I'm digressing. You should know my fantastic Gurkha bodyguards sweep this place electronically every week. They've found four listening devices, two in the past year alone. They or the guards before them have checked this place religiously for the past fifteen years. I suspect it's a competitor of mine scrounging around for information, but it's impossible to prove who it was. They probably pay off the maid or who-knows-what. Oh, and the guards store their phones in the safe, too. Anyhow, here's what I would like you to do," Chuck said. He coughed twice and took a sip of his red wine. David took a sip from his, too, and waited patiently while Chuck collected his thoughts.

The clever and imaginative oil tycoon then spoke for twenty minutes outlining in general terms how he intended to use David to move millions in cash and gold to help fund a radical movement dedicated to preserving what remained of the Indonesian rainforests, starting with Sumatra.

"I've gathered up some cash and gold coins for you to bring with you on this trip," Chuck said. He leaned over and opened a black leather briefcase which had been occupying the open space on the table between their wine glasses. "Instead of Eagles it'll be Krugerrands this time. I suggest splitting the cash between the two of you and letting the professor set the roll of coins somewhere among the testing equipment in his checked luggage. It'll be nicely hidden in plain sight among the electronic components and all that other metallic clutter your professor friend carries. I've smuggled cash and gold across borders many times. It's not all that difficult. When you arrive in Jakarta be sure to pass it on to your Indonesian connection as soon as possible. It's a bit more than last time but nowhere near what's coming if things go well. I want this money to go directly to the local people hitting back at the bastards who are destroying the island."

"It will."

"Furthermore, I'd like you to return here in ten days. I'll have more for you. Much more. Several million, probably. But shipping the next load will be a bit tricky. Bear in mind I'm an old hand at this sort of thing. I'll let you know the details when the time comes. Be prepared. The method of shipment will surprise you. If you don't mind I'd rather you not know the specifics until the last minute."

David thought a moment. "Today's the twenty-fourth. So that'll be June fourth. My flight should arrive in San Francisco at nine in the morning that day so I'll be able to make it here around noon, maybe earlier."

"Make it noon. I'll expect you. Have the taxi drop you off at your apartment on Geary and walk the distance, or hoof it here from your office on Van Ness as you've sometimes done in the past. Again, don't ever call or email me. The cameras around my home record everything, but I delete the data every few days. Wear a hat and dark glasses anyhow in case they're subpoenaed for whatever reason. I hope you don't mind me repeating all this."

"Some things bear repeating. I'll be here the fourth of June, at noon."

"Perfect. Make up some excuse to return to Pekanbaru on the morning of June seventh, which means you'll have to fly back the night of the fifth, one day after arriving here in San Francisco."

"I'll think of something. Thankfully, my position allows me to travel pretty much whenever and wherever I choose. As long as I don't squander funds, and the PTR budget is properly managed, everyone's happy."

"Good."

"It's funny, Chuck. My office and travel budget is nearly the same as my salary. After holding this position for the past five years it's still four thousand dollars a month, each. It's basically a stipend. With executive salaries getting out of control where would they find a replacement?"

"In many ways you're like a saint, David. When this cancer finally kicks my ass you'll never have to be concerned about money again. In the interest of due diligence, a year ago I had a little background research done on you."

"I wondered if you had," David said with a grin, which Chuck returned. The old oil tycoon looked a decade younger when he smiled like that.

"I like what I've discovered, too. Especially the part about that wonderful transformation you underwent during your early university days. But let me get to the point. You should now know that I've directed my attorneys to establish a trust fund based in the Cayman Islands with you as the sole beneficiary. It'll pay you plenty and your monthly stipend will be five figures, not four. Inflation adjusted, too."

"You don't need to do that, Chuck. I'm happy living the life of the poor wandering environmentalist."

"In time your attitude will change so don't argue with me about this. I've made up my mind about it and that's that. Plus it'll come in handy if you have children." Chuck then aimed his somewhat bent and bony right forefinger at David and continued with an even wider grin. "If you feel so strongly about staying poor I trust you'll donate it properly."

"Thank you. I don't know what to say."

"Start by telling me in general terms how it's going for you over in Indonesia."

"Like I mentioned earlier, I've established a good sympathetic contact in Jakarta who was able to move the cash last time. He assured me he'll do the same this time. I believe he's trustworthy and reliable. He's assured me he has solid connections with Direct Action, but at this point I have no way to verify it other than the pictures."

"What pictures?"

"I have them on my phone. They might be in the media by now," David said.

"You mean the notes nailed to those guys' heads?"

"Yeah."

"It was on the television news."

"I'm confident this contact of mine has solid connections with the underground radicals. Plus he has a position where he can access people and places without too much scrutiny."

"I hope so, but I really don't want to know any specific details about him. All I want is results. I want the destruction stopped. It absolutely must stop. I fully realize it's a long shot. But if even a remnant can somehow be preserved, and the plantations destroyed, the forest has a small chance of recovering to its natural state. It could recover like the Amazon did after a huge section was ruined back in the fifteenth century, or whenever it was."

"We'll do everything we can. Money is really the key, the missing element for them."

"David," Chuck said, stepping around the table and moving closer, off to the side some. He placed his large hand on the younger man's shoulder. "I'm fully aware of the hard work the environmental movement's done in the past, including your group, the PTR, Preserve the Rainforests. You are, too, I'm sure. It's been your life's work, well, since not long after graduating from college. But let me share something with you. All the well-intentioned environmentalists like you have been duped by the likes of people such as me and the others in the energy industry. We privately laughed at environmentalists during the years of your bitter boycotts, protests and letter writing campaigns."

"We must have caused some good," David said. "What about the tens of millions in fines and the laws we got passed. What about the lawsuits we filed and won? They must have hurt."

"Oh, sure, we were all slapped with fines and headline-grabbing restrictive laws and regulations. None of that mattered to us. We couldn't've cared less. There were no laws anywhere in the world that we couldn't figure out a way to work around. Not one. And the lawsuits and fines meant nothing to us. All that pointless environmental activism was, at most, soft background noise. It was all just nonsense, hardly rising to the level of annoyance and it actually served us well in a roundabout way. The public in general thought we were controlled by the various governments and working for the common good by providing needed energy. However, as you are fully aware it's brought humanity to the brink of catastrophe, and I'm not only talking about the looming extinction of the life in the forests, but of humanity itself. If we stay on our current path humanity will be doomed. David, it's time for action."

"May I ask you a question?" David said.

"I may not answer, but you can go ahead and ask me anything you wish."

"Why focus solely on the forests? Why not take action against genetically modified crops or Arctic drilling or a dozen other destructive activities?"

"I made the greater part of my wealth financing and providing equipment for those who drilled for oil and gas. They did a damn good job of extracting all of the easy-to-get hydrocarbons out of the ground. Now the low-hanging fruit, as we called it, is all gone. Get this. I'm now being asked to finance and supply all kinds of crazy projects. They're all over the fringes, in the Arctic, deep water, tar sand operations, that disgusting fracking and this or that other hare-brained idea. But all of them added up can't come close to powering humanity. The decline rates of the super giant fields are too high. Each year it seems some oil producing nation becomes a net importer of oil. Obviously the number of countries exporting shrinks each year, too. The worldwide conventional oil production plateau that was reached in 'oh-five undulated some, as anyone can easily read on those world oil production charts. And it remained essentially flat, or essentially stable, for a decade. Then the decline began. Now look where we are. Seven dollars a gallon here. Gas lines are an hour long in San Francisco and in European cities even longer. Twelve bucks for four liters in the old world and traffic's still bumper to bumper at five p.m. in London. That's why the damn fools are cutting the rainforests. It's not about mining or clearing land to grow more cooking oil, coffee and tea. That's only a small part of it."

David sat still politely as the elderly icon of the oil industry collected his thoughts a moment.

"The real reason we went into renewable energy some years back was to appear green and eco-friendly. It had nothing whatsoever to do with carbon dioxide or other greenhouse gasses. It's simply politically popular these days to harvest green energy no matter how much damage it causes. It gives the industry a happy face, nothing more. Hell, we sponsored all those alternative energy ads everyone watches on their televisions. We created a public opinion that freed us to do whatever we wanted in order to get more energy, especially biofuel energy. No one in North America, Asia or the EU would dare vote against a ten percent palm oil biofuels mandate. If the public only knew that the wars America wages are fought only to protect energy industry profits they'd revolt."

"Some people know," David said, unable to resist, implying he was well aware why the USA wages war.

"And we've done an outstanding job of coloring anyone protesting as kooks. Anyhow, we merely pretend to make more fuel when

23

we refine biofuels, especially corn and palm oil. It costs more energy to make that kind of liquid energy than we get out of it. If anyone ever bothered to add up all the energy used on the plantation they'd find out how bad it really is. Consider planting, fertilizing, harvesting, paste production, shipping that crap to Rotterdam or Anacortes or Finland, and then finally refining it into biodiesel, they'd find out it's a net energy drain, or damn close to it." Chuck paused and smiled at David. "I'm sorry. You already know this stuff is a net negative on energy. I'm afraid I may be repeating myself, and worse yet, preaching to the choir."

David returned the smile. "It's okay. You're not repeating yourself, Chuck. Each time you speak I learn something, gain more insight and become more committed to what we're doing. But why me? You must have contacts everywhere."

"Why you? I'm only one man and can't do it all. Because of all those Bloomberg interviews I do I can't go outside without some idiot snapping my picture. I'd fly there right now and spread the cash around myself if I thought I wouldn't be recognized. Since I read about your work, then called you here to meet with me, I've become truly inspired. For that I thank you from the bottom of my heart. It's a feeling of excitement much like when I was in my twenties earning my first millions wildcatting in Texas." Chuck stopped, removed his glasses and wiped his eyes. "It's now time for me to pay back for the damage I've caused, either directly of indirectly."

"Yes, but now ..."

Chuck waved a hand across the table toward David. "I'm still earning millions shipping oil and natural gas supplies to Sumatra. Hell, if it wasn't me doing it someone else would jump in. And when I die they will. You watch. I'm partially responsible for this grand mess we're in. I believe when the forests are gone, and they will be within a decade the way we're heading, it'll soon thereafter be game over for humanity. You and your organization helped bring me to that realization, as I've told you before. I've made the decision to direct my final spear at those responsible for the vicious wave of burning. I'll then let God direct His spear at me, or not, however He sees fit."

"There will be bloodshed. Not just the four men a few days ago, but I'm talking about triggering raging street battles, maybe even a civil war. It could run into the thousands."

"Yes. I understand all that. A half million died in the sixties during that Indonesian civil war. I hope it doesn't come to that. But if we just sit on our asses and do nothing then the Four Horsemen will saddle up. Imagine the blood that will flow when that happens. It'd be millions. If that's allowed it'll be partially my blame. I have one last shot at keeping them in their corral where they belong and I fully intend to take it."

"I'll do everything I can for our project," David said. "I have a funny feeling we'll have no shortage of supporters, not only among environmentalists, but more importantly, among common Indonesians. The economy's hit them pretty hard. From a practical perspective few of them want to see foreigners destroy what remains of their land. My contact is quite adamant on this point. He tells me the army's demoralized and weaker with the recent budget cuts. That'll help since they can't adequately respond to every disturbance on Sumatra, at least not as effectively as they've done in the past. They've got their hands tied with Muslim radicals all across the country and with leftist revolutionaries on Java and Borneo. Our timing couldn't be better. The Indonesian army has just had its budget slashed to half of what it was before their oil peak back in the nineties."

"It'll get weaker each year, too, and the officers know it. They're probably getting concerned. It might even reach the point of a coup attempt."

David thought about that a moment. "And don't forget, with the recent wave of nationalizations, particularly in the mining industry, they're on a path that'll eventually lead them to where Argentina and Zimbabwe are: right on the bottom of the list of who receives foreign investment and military aid. This will serve to slow to a snail's pace any ideas of a forceful foreign response to whatever Direct Action has in mind."

"I agree," Chuck said. "Our timing couldn't be better. But it also means you'd better be extra cautious. If things get ugly I'll do what I can, but unfortunately you'll be mostly on your own."

CHAPTER FOUR

When David approached the dozens of inspection booths and the uniformed passport control officials at Jakarta's Soekarno-Hatta International Airport he wondered for a moment if Gary's heart was pounding as fast and as hard as his. And if so, how long would Gary's old ticker keep beating? It wasn't the seven thousand dollars cash in his carry-on, nor was it the nine thousand dollars in Gary's. As long as they carried under ten thousand dollars each there was no need to declare the cash. It wasn't even the ten thousand dollar cashier's check payable to Walhi that concerned him. It had been written from the bank account of Preserve the Rainforests a week ago. The PTR donation was a routine annual grant from his organization in support of international efforts on behalf of one pro-environmental cause or another.

What had been bothering David was Gary's declining health. He hadn't been taking very good care of himself since his back surgery a few years ago. David made a mental note to take occasional walks with Gary. It was the least he could do. However, the immediate concern was passing through customs and officially entering Indonesia with their nonimmigrant research visas.

For the past year a hard currency crisis had gripped the world's financial system. India, Indonesia, Pakistan and many other struggling nations had recently restricted the importation of bullion in an effort to protect their national currencies. The roll of undeclared gold Krugerrands stashed inside Gary's locked aluminum testing case wasn't a serious issue. It was well under the one kilogram annual limit. If the officials found the roll the worst that would happen was he might have to complete another form.

The cash, the check and the gold could be easily explained due to his position as the CFO of PTR. They both planned to remain in Indonesia with Shannon for ten days. That included the conference as well as a side trip to Sumatra to take pictures, test river water and to learn more in order to better raise awareness of the ongoing ecological destruction of the tropical island. That was routine, hands-on work, typical of the CES, PTR and the rest of the assorted environmental groups.

But it took money. And cash or gold worked best. The Krugerrands they carried, although somewhat unusual to carry, were accepted anywhere on Earth. Traveling with some cash was not unusual among researchers and scientists, too, particularly those heading into places where bribe-hungry officials were common and banks were scarce.

Their cover story, attending the conference and studying the Sumatran rainforest first-hand, was well rehearsed and, he believed, watertight. What made David nervous was the following morning's breakfast meeting in the Marriott's Executive Lounge with Azka. He was a young news reporter with the Jakarta Post and David's sole connection with access to the recently formed, shadowy militant group, Direct Action. If the Indonesian government discovered David's role as a primary funder of the radical group it would mean a lengthy prison sentence or worse. It was a risk he was prepared to face but it rattled him more than he thought it would.

His association with Azka went back two years when PTR first decided to more actively deepen its contacts with local environmental activists in Africa, South America and throughout Asia. David, who had been a salaried staff member since graduating from UC Berkeley ten years earlier, was assigned to expand their grassroots contacts in Sumatra while others performed similar work elsewhere.

He met Azka at a protest march in Pekanbaru. They quickly discovered they shared a common perspective regarding the preservation of the forests and soon became close, trusted friends. Pekanbaru was located near the epicenter of the recent forest burning. More importantly, it was the home of both a growing Indonesian student protest movement struggling against the destruction of the nation's rainforests and an underground campaign striving to drive western interests out of the country. The two activist groups realized they had a mutual interest in preserving the last of the rainforests and, as a result, a loose, quiet alliance was forged promising mutual assistance on this one issue. Azka, a devout Muslim with trusted friends and contacts throughout Sumatra, also had extensive links among the growing student environmentalists on the ravaged tropical island.

Azka's press credentials granted him free access throughout much of the hotel, much of any hotel, for that matter. So even as a non-guest he had no trouble getting past the two doormen at the entrance of the Executive Lounge. The cash and Krugerrands would be discreetly passed to him outside, after the two sat together, shared the latest news from Sumatra, and laughed at a few jokes while eating their eggs and toast.

It was past midnight and the queue moved fast with only one flight in the passport control room. The official waved David forward. She saw the United States passport in his hand and accepted it with one of hers. Without a word she removed the completed landing card and placed it on her small desk while sliding the proper page of his passport into a digital card reader. She then glanced without expression at her computer screen. "What is the purpose of your trip to Indonesia?"

"Business. I'm attending the International Conference on Environmental Pollution and Prevention. It starts tomorrow at the Marriott."

She may or may not have paid attention to what David said, it was tough to tell. Happily, she was also no longer interested in whatever her computer screen revealed and focused her attention on flipping through the pages of the heavily inked passport, pausing here and there to read an entry or exit stamp.

While she did her duty he again read the bold type, red-lettered warning, "Death to Drug Traffickers," which proclaimed the dire message to all travelers on the bottom of landing cards. It struck David as strange that the Indonesian government would hang someone for smuggling a bag of heroin yet encouraged people to destroy the rainforests and thereby, eventually, risk killing off the entire country.

She flattened the passport exposing page twenty-one, which was only partially filled with the stamps of previous journeys to sub-Saharan Africa, South America and Asia. "How long will you stay?"

"Ten days," David replied. "I'm flying to Pekanbaru immediately after the conference. I'll be in Riau Province for a week. Then I fly home, to San Francisco."

"Enjoy your stay," she replied, then stamped his passport and each half of the landing card. She tore the white card in half and placed the right portion inside his passport and placed the other one on a growing pile on her counter. She handed David his documents with a blank, expressionless face, typical of passport control officials all over the world. "Next!" she said, and went through the same routine with Gary while David waited not far away.

"Now we get our luggage and hop the hotel shuttle," David said. "Badda bing."

"Badda boom," Gary said.

The two walked the short distance to the luggage carousel. "The tough part's almost done," David said.

"It'll be nice to get out of this airport," Gary said as they stood near the silent and empty stainless steel merry-go-round. "Place gives me the creeps."

"Relax. Piece of cake," David said as the shiny carousel started moving triggering the thumps of cascading suitcases. He glanced across the spinning steel at two hard-faced young soldiers carrying assault rifles. They stood moving their eyes everywhere at once, maybe four or five paces from one another, not thirty feet from them. "At least we have some decent protection here at the airport."

"No shortages of cops or soldiers in Jakarta, at least there wasn't last time I was here. But I'd feel much safer in bed, under my covers," Gary said. "That's my first objective."

CHAPTER FIVE

Forty minutes later the two men stepped out of the Marriott Hotel shuttle bus and approached the front entrance. Fifteen meters from the heavily tinted glass front doors they were confronted by a series of zigzagging red stanchions which herded all arriving guests towards a wide white tent under which was a collection of uniformed men with handguns standing at attention.

"Set your luggage on the table, please," one guard said while his eyes stared ahead from under his perfectly angled tan beret. "Laptops, too. Place everything in your pockets on the table as well. We need to search all of your bags before you are allowed into the hotel."

"Sure." Gary placed his oversized hard black suitcase on one sturdy steel table. Without a word David did the same for another guard on the other end of the table. It was one a.m. and the four armed men whose task was to rummage through every bag and suitcase that entered the Marriott appeared to be sleepwalking or, more accurately, sleep standing, while they made their routine search for weapons and explosive devices. Two overhead cameras silently recorded it all including the passing of the hand-held metal detector wands over every centimeter of their bodies.

"Enjoy your stay," they said after determining there was no dangerous contraband in any of their bags.

"Thank you," Gary said.

As they neared the hotel door Gary turned to David. "The government officials at the airport pay no attention to us at all. We grabbed our checked bags and out the door we went. Then we get to the hotel and these goons toss our bags like we're entering Fort Knox."

"Except they missed the gold coins in my testing case and ignored our cash," David replied.

"That was a happy surprise."

"They're only interested in finding bombs and guns. Stuff like that. We don't look like terrorists. Well, at least I don't."

Gary shot him a playful hard stare.

"They're only paranoid about another terrorist attack like the ones in the nineties," David continued. "The guards could tell we're here for the conference as soon as we walked up. Our bags were searched for show so that the overhead cameras would record them doing their job. This hotel has been bombed twice. They should be concerned."

David smiled as kind cool air smacked him in the face when he entered the hotel. The newsstand on his right displayed the previous day's Jakarta Post. A gruesome image of a dead laborer stared out from above the fold. The headline article announced in bold black letters, "Forty-Two Killed in Sumatra Violence."

"You're right," Gary said. "They do need to be careful these days."

CHAPTER SIX

Gym bag in hand, David walked through the glass door and quickly darted to the corner window table Azka had secured ten minutes earlier. The young scientist was in serious violation of the hotel's dress code which required those dining in the Executive Lounge to be attired in business casual, at a minimum. His snug, red, calf-length running pants and black, tight-fitting short-sleeve fitness shirt, each displaying a tiny white Nike logo, revealed nearly every muscle on his upper body as well as a few on his lower. That may have been the reason the two young Indonesian women stationed at the entry let him through the door.

"It's really great to see you, Azka, my friend," David said with a genuine mile-wide grin. He shook Azka's outstretched hand. "Selamat pagi, I should say."

Azka saw David and stood up in front of the small dining table he'd been assigned. "I'm happy to see you, too, David, or should I call you Doctor Reseigh while I'm in the hotel?" Azka could have been mistaken for a waiter with his neatly pressed black slacks covered past the pockets by a pristine, loose-fitting white button-down. His shiny black dress shoes tapped the floor under the table. He had been working as a reporter for the Jakarta Post for seven years and had witnessed the daily English language newspaper expand from a circulation of thirty thousand copies when he hired on to forty thousand copies. It was one of the few major newspapers in Asia whose print circulation had been increasing.

"I'm fine with David," he said as he placed the black vinyl bag on the empty chair across from Azka and sat near the window, ninety degrees from his friend. The chair he chose was partially hidden by the white tablecloth. That meant his workout clothing would be less visible to the staff. David glanced a second over his shoulder and out the tall window at the city below. "Nice view."

"Downtown Jakarta is the other direction. If the air wasn't so hazy we could see the airport from here," Azka said.

"Not today, I suppose," David said then patted his bag. "I've brought you a gift from America."

Azka smiled and nodded once. "We can talk a moment about it after breakfast, which I already ordered. You're having toast and a vegetarian omelet, the same thing I'm having. I suggest a healthy walk afterwards. Based on your appearance I presume you've been running. However, after sitting on the plane for twenty-four hours you could probably use more exercise, maybe some fresh air."

"Excellent suggestion. We'll get a few streets away from the hotel and its cameras. You and I have a lot of news and gossip to catch up on, and some exciting things are going on that will certainly sell a lot of copies of your newspaper."

"I can't wait," Azka said. "You travelled with your friend. Is he joining us?"

"No way. He's still asleep. That reminds me. I forgot my cell phone in the room. Anyhow, he has a presentation at noon and he'll be with his fellow scientists preparing as soon as he gets up, probably around nine. I need to talk with him before he gets to work."

Azka raised the left sleeve of his white shirt a few inches with his right hand and glanced at his watch while the waiter appeared out of nowhere and set the steaming eggs in the proper place before the two and placed a tall pile of wheat toast right between them in the center of the square table.

"I ordered eight slices," Azka said to David. "Two for me and six for you, which you'll probably need after running this morning."

A slender, good-looking man dressed similarly to Azka appeared. "Anything to drink?" the well-groomed young Indonesian waiter asked in perfect, British-accented English. He then gazed a bit longer than he should at David's shirt.

"Black coffee for me," David said.

"Green tea, please," Azka said. "And water as well for my colleague and me."

"Anything else?" he asked sneaking another two-second stare at the front of the black exercise shirt.

"No," David replied. "That will be all, for now."

The waiter smiled a little more than he needed to, mostly at David, then flashed his eyebrows and left, Azka leaned closer to David and softly spoke. "I usually leave my phone at the office unless I'm covering a story, which today, I'm not. The hotel doesn't know this, but the conference isn't news, at least not yet. However, with my press credentials I can go just about anywhere, which is why the guards out front allowed me to pass through. Once we get outside we can talk freely. It's now seven."

"We'll have plenty of time."

"Your friend must be exhausted if he's getting up two hours from now."

"He earned the rest. All that research he's been doing and the excitement of his first trip to Indonesia has really worn him out. No matter how tired I am, when I travel to Europe or Asia I always rise before sunrise and jog outdoors or run the treadmill for a while. I do the same when I get home. It's the only cure for jet lag known to man. Some scientist proved it a few years ago."

"Really? I thought there was no way to overcome jet lag. What scientist did this study?"

"I did."

Azka laughed while David smiled and bit off another quarter piece of toast, his last slice of the fast depleted pile.

"Anyhow," David added while swallowing a fork full of his fast vanishing omelette, "today I didn't feel in the mood to deal with that platoon of soldiers out front. So I went to the hotel gym. The treadmill was free and I hopped right on it. A forty-five minute run, a quick shower, a shave, and voila, here I am."

"Busy guy. By the way, David, they're not soldiers, they're private security guards hired by the hotel."

"How can you tell the difference?"

"They dress much like soldiers so you can't tell them apart until you get close. Private security guards aren't allowed to wear any patches on their shoulders, berets or chest, unless it's the company name, but many don't do that. Soldiers also carry a rank insignia on their uniforms. Next time you enter the hotel, check it out. Anyhow, the soldiers are spread way too thin to bother with hotels, especially foreign ones. They're too busy fighting the Islamists on Sumatra and communist bands on Borneo and in the mountains of Kalimantan."

CHAPTER SEVEN

After breakfast the two took the elevator to the lobby and walked outside. They were greeted by the muggy morning sunshine which, surprisingly, was hardly impacted by the haze from the fires raging hundreds of kilometers to the north. It was already hot.

"Protesters," David said. "Maybe fifty, or so. Are they here because of the conference?"

"Yes," Azka replied. "They can't be here for any other reason. The signs demand that we stop destroying the rainforests."

"More soldiers out front today than last night, too."

"Let's get away from here where we can talk," Azka said.

"You lead the way."

"The Trisakti University campus is only ten minutes away. Let's go there, maybe buy some fruit drinks from a vendor, then find a place to sit a while in the shade."

"Fine. Isn't that where the riots back in the late nineties began?"

"Yes and no," Azka replied. "Same university, but it has many campuses in Jakarta. The shootings you refer to, the ones that led to the riots, which eventually led to the fall of Suharto, occurred on a different campus, but not too far from here."

As they walked by the Ritz-Carlton Hotel there were about thirty protesters out front on the sidewalk. A few carried signs written in Indonesian, the other short crisp messages scrawled in English were clearly directed at the conference attendees. "Stop the Burning," read one. "No Palm Oil," read another. Looking on were a handful of serious-faced soldiers, or maybe they were private security guards carrying rifles and outfitted in green military attire in an effort to appear tougher. It was hard to tell from a distance. If so, it had the desired effect. No one came close to them. David still couldn't tell the security guards, soldiers and police apart. He made a mental note to solve that mystery by lunchtime, but it was soon lost and forgotten in the tangled web of his thoughts.

In front of the small campus Azka bought two dragon fruit drinks and quickly found a nearby, yet somewhat remote, shaded bench on a wide wooded path. The two men sat. David closed his eyes and stretched his legs out halfway across the paved walkway nearly tripping the closest of two slender young women walking past, their arms loaded with books, their heads, but not faces, covered by black scarves.

"Whoa! Sorry," he said.

The two students darted aside, giggled, and continued walking without a word.

When the coast was clear David spoke. "Take a peek inside the gym bag. It's yours."

Azka did. "Wow. Thank you. We shall put it to good use."

"There's a ten thousand dollar check payable to Walhi inside, too. I don't want anyone to know it came directly from me to you. Could you please discreetly pass it along for me?"

"Sure. I'm stopping by their Pekanbaru office shortly."

"I would like to have the bag back."

"I'll buy a shirt from that market," Azka said, tipping his head to the west, toward a shopping center. "They'll provide me with a bag for the shirt. I'll put this money and the coins inside with it."

"I can't believe they're still handing out a plastic bag with each purchase."

"One battle at a time, David."

"Right. Yesterday gold was selling for thirty-four hundred dollars an ounce. That and the cash adds up to fifty thousand dollars. It should be enough to get things moving, for a while at least."

Azka unzipped the bag and directed his eyes inside while David smiled. "Wow."

"Put it to good use, my friend. The man funding this operation is wealthy and reads the news. He told me he wants to use the last of his life to, and I'll quote him without paraphrasing, 'leave a positive meaningful impact before I die by doing whatever I can to save the planet from humanity. Cost is no objective.' His words, not mine. If there are positive results I'll be back soon with a larger payment."

"It'll be distributed by dark. By the way, have you read the news in the past two days?" Azka asked with a grin.

"No. Between the plane ride and the nap afterwards there's really been no time. But I read the headline when I entered the hotel at one. Something about a wave of killings on Sumatra."

"There's more. The night before last four thousand oil palm trees were cut down. It's on page two of the Post. They hit, I mean, we hit, a remote CSPO plantation. Like certified sustainable palm oil or not certified makes any difference to the orangutans. Screw 'em. All plantations are targeted."

"Nice work. Anyone arrested?"

"Not yet. However, the pressure to arrest someone, anyone, is growing. The Direct Action leadership is becoming more cautious. As I understood, the initial plan was to pay off the seriously underpaid night watchmen, tell them it would be wise if they were to go guard somewhere else for a few hours. That idea was risky, too dangerous, to me.

But the boots on the ground know the situation better than anyone, as they say. Apparently they found it risky, too, and changed the plan. According to the news from Sumatra, the forty-two killed included six security guards. The nailed notes are really starting to intimidate the workers. Fewer are showing up for work. Many guards are quitting, too. Those who remain have received hefty bonuses and pay hikes."

"What else?"

"Oh, there's more. My Muslim buddies really showed their stuff last night. It was on the Post's news email system. Twelve workers on a cutting crew were found dead in the forest. Broad daylight. Notes nailed to the forehead of one, just like with the others. No witnesses. No one saw or heard a thing. Their heavy equipment, bulldozers, trucks, storage building and barracks, all of it set on fire."

"I really hope this works."

"Money has always been a problem, but not the entire problem. It's also about jobs. Millions of Indonesians make their livelihood from either cutting the forest or working on plantations."

"That's too damn bad. Let 'em find work somewhere else."

"I agree, and they're now starting to. It's not like we haven't tried everything else. All the environmental activism over the past six decades has produced absolutely zero results. In fact, the destruction has only accelerated. It's gotten so bad even the palm oil processor, Wilmar, has booked a room at the Ritz. They're planning to dish out grants to select conference attendees."

"You must stay clean, Azka. Keep away from any trouble. Your only connection is to me. It can easily be explained because we go back a long time. Remember, without this link the operation falls apart."

"Will do."

"My girlfriend is arriving tonight. She and I are flying to Sumatra the day after the conference. I want her to witness first hand the devastation. I wish you could meet her."

"One day I will, for sure. We shall all share a toast, a dragon fruit toast to our success."

"She has a gift for you, but I'll hand it to you tomorrow morning in the Executive Lounge, same time. It's on a memory card. No bag will be needed."

"What is it?"

"Simple directions explaining how to construct a magnet bomb, the kind a guy on the back of a motorcycle can reach over and easily attach to the door of a moving car. The beauty of it is that most of what's needed can be quietly stolen from a farm or even bought at a hardware store without raising any eyebrows."

"Those plans are available online, too, so I'm told."

"Yes, they are. And everyone who accesses those nut-job websites explaining how to make kitchen explosives gets added to a bad-boy list."

"Good point."

"Plus these are from her uncle. He's Irish, and a very good friend of the IRA."

"So? What's that supposed to mean?"

"That means they'll work every time."

CHAPTER EIGHT

"Hotel room service," the friendly female voice said after quietly knocking twice.

A moment later the door to the twelfth floor, southwest corner room of the Ritz-Carlton opened a crack. The luxury hotel was located right across the plaza from the Marriott. It was where most of the corporate donors were staying. The hotel was close to the conference, but far enough away so guests, particularly those representing universities and environmental organizations, could discreetly arrange for their supposedly anonymous grants.

Hemminki Kokkonen, the assistant director of public relations for the Finnish palm oil refiner, Neste Oil, opened the door the rest of the way. When he offered a friendly smile to the pretty young woman a man's arm shot past her. She moved aside, fast. Then she gently closed the door in one, smooth, well-planned motion. Hemminki's chest was ignited by a sudden, sharp, explosion of pain from the razor-sharp stiletto. He fell, first to his knees, then flat on his back, just inside the door to his room. He gasped for air a few seconds before losing consciousness.

He didn't even feel the nail pierce his forehead. The note it secured was different this time. The words on the standard-sized white copy paper read, "Direct Action." The man, dressed as a woman in a housekeeping uniform, left the room placing a "Do Not Disturb" placard on the door handle.

Without a word the woman dressed as a maid pushed her cart to the next room on her floor and knocked. It was occupied by a guest named Danny Wong. He was the assistant CFO of Wilmar International, the world's largest oil palm tree plantation operator and trader. He had no false illusions about silencing the seemingly endless avalanche of shrill voices from the environmentalist movement with his grants. It had worked every time. All he expected to do with his anonymous handouts over the next few days was distribute enough cash to tone down the most pointed rhetoric, somewhat, and thereby let Wilmar Corporation continue to do what they did best: cut and burn the last of the rainforest and grow renewable oil palm trees without the distracting daily drumbeat from those annoying activists constantly accusing his company of killing the rainforests. In his mind Wilmar was transforming the rainforest, putting it to good use for the benefit of its stockholders.

While the man in the housekeeping uniform stood by the wall, just away from the view of the peephole, the maid knocked on his door. "Hotel room service," she said.

CHAPTER NINE

After meeting with David, Azka hopped on his small scooter and snaked his way through the heavy traffic straight to his office at the Jakarta Post on Palmerah Barat. The bag containing his new white dress shirt, the gold coins, and the cash was locked in the helmet-sized compartment under his seat. It was six kilometers from the Marriott but traffic was light so getting there took him only ten minutes. It was ten thirty. He was a half hour early for his shift. He parked in a row of several dozen other small motorcycles and scooters in the newspaper's fenced and somewhat secure parking lot. He thought a second and decided to take a chance and leave the bag where it was, for now.

He walked to the main entrance of the old colonial-style building and flashed his identification card to the familiar security guards at the door. He brushed right past them after a quick greeting and went inside bypassing the long wood table where visitors' bags were searched. He jogged up the broad center stairs and slowed to a fast walk when he turned right.

His boss, Fajar, was busy talking into a cell phone. He saw Azka in the hallway as soon as he approached the glass door to the press-room. Although in his late fifties, Fajar was as fidgety as a fifteen-year-old on his first date, except it went on all the time. Skinny as a straw, the energetic newsroom manager still had a thick head of white hair, which would have matched his baggy shirt, but it was dyed to a bizarre shade of dark red. It was a shade nature hadn't granted anyone through old fashioned genetics. His hair was combed curi-ously to one side with a precise part, furrowed a few centimeters to the right of top dead center. Held in place by spray or gel, the coiffure featured an array of equally precise waves, reminiscent of an extinct fashion once popular prior to when television was first invented.

The desks inside the room were visible through the hip to ceiling clear glass windows to anyone passing by in the hallway. The space below the windows had been wainscoted with a veneer of dark hard-wood. The dozen skinny-legged steel desks were arranged in neat rows. Most were occupied by men and women busily tapping quietly, yet intently focused at their laptops, occasionally gazing at docu-ments and other papers scattered in their midst. None of the desks were personalized with name placards or family photos. They were shared, occupied on a first-come basis in a tradition that went back decades, except for the large desk in the corner.

It had windows facing front, to the busy intersection below. For twenty-five years the corner space had been Fajar's, but he hadn't personalized it except for a prominent framed picture of his wife. He had survived two owners and seven chief editors. He intended to keep the desk at least another twenty-five years by staying on top of the latest news as it developed.

"Azka!" Fajar shouted while fanning a hand at him. He abruptly ended his call and aimed his smiling face at his young reporter. "I'm so glad you're early. Come to my desk immediately."

Azka made a direct line to his boss, as all reporters did when summoned by the man in charge. "Selamat pagi, Fajar. What do you have for me today?"

"Pagi," Fajar said. His voice had dropped in volume to a level inaudible to potential eavesdroppers. "You're flying to Pekanbaru immediately. Things are heating up on Sumatra. Our office in Pekanbaru needs a good reporter there immediately. That is you."

"What's going on? And when did we open an office in Pekanbaru?"

"We haven't opened an office there. But we should with all the unrest."

"I haven't read any news from Sumatra today. What happened?"

"It's not so much what happened. It's what I suspect will happen in the coming days. This new group, Direct Action, claims they murdered two guests at the Ritz this morning. Knifed them in the chest, notes hammered into their heads, just like the others who got it on Sumatra. The police suspect the guests who were murdered were planning to hand out donations to environmental groups holding a conference at the Marriott next door. Apparently Direct Action just kicked things up a notch."

Azka felt his pulse quicken. It was enough that it would have easily been registered by a lie detector. "Did they catch anyone?"

"No. The last time the door to either room was opened was for the maids. Each time the cameras recorded one maid going inside, then she left the room a few seconds later."

"C'mon. Maids? That can't be right."

"The police have no suspects, no witnesses, no evidence other than the videos, the nails and the notes. They're not telling us what the notes say, but I'll know soon. I've put the screws to a few police department contacts who owe me for not printing what they are doing on the side."

"I have to go home and pack a few things. I can be ready in two or three hours, be at the airport by three."

"No time for all that. You can fly with what you're wearing. I have a ready-pack for your laptop, phone, toiletries. If you need more clothes you can buy some when you arrive. Use the paper's credit card."

"Leave right now? I have two articles to finish."

"Finish them on the plane and email it all to me when you land," Fajar said. He handed Azka a packet of papers. "Your flight leaves at two. Here are your plane tickets, hotel reservations and some walking around cash as well as a credit card. Every rupiah is scrutinized so think twice before you use the card and, as usual, track all the money you spend. In fact, I expect you to return most of the cash. A taxi will be here in twenty minutes to take you to the airport. If you had a wife and kids I would let you kiss them goodbye before you leave, but you don't, which is part of the reason I picked you. Plus you know Sumatra better than any of our other reporters."

"I do have a few contacts with the students at the university and I know the leaders of Walhi in Pekanbaru and Medan."

"Yes, I know all that. We all do. But you're not going all the way to Medan. I want you where the action is, right on the front lines of the burning forests."

"Yes, sir," Azka replied. He had no time to stash the cash and gold locked under the seat of his scooter so he had to decide fast what to do about it. "Let me get ready."

"Just be at the front door in fifteen minutes," Fajar said.

Azka went out the side door leading to the parking lot and jogged to his scooter. He removed the bag, and jogged back inside the building, again flashing his card and a big smile at the guards, who smiled back as they waved him through. They were used to seeing the busy reporters run in and out of the building. He called the hotel and left a message with David on his room's voice recorder letting him know he'd be waiting for him at noon, two days from today, in Sumatra at the plaza where they first met. He added jokingly that he'd give him a tour of the Post's new office in Pekanbaru, which didn't exist.

His reporter travel bag had a convenient Velcro compartment that was designed to hold important papers and reports. He filled it with assorted documents related to his work and sandwiched in between the pages the two packets of cash. It wasn't perfect but it would do. Since it was a domestic flight there was nothing illegal about traveling with a large sum of cash. However, to remain discreet it would be important to keep it hidden. The roll of Krugerrands went inside the bulky bag, too. He planned to check it as luggage and hand carry his camera equipment through the passenger inspection station. The officials there would be scanning and searching for weapons and explosives, as usual, so the cash and coins shouldn't pose a problem.

CHAPTER TEN

While Azka was preparing to board his flight three white US-made SUVs were meandering close together down a dusty rutted dirt road not far from his destination. The visibility was down to less than a half kilometer due to the thick smoky haze caused by the burning of the forests throughout central Sumatra. It was impossible to tell if it was a sunny day or not, but it was unusually hot, as humid and muggy as the tropical island ever got. They were about a two-hour drive west of the airport. The drivers and reporters couldn't wait for this inspection tour to be over and done with. Although most of the others felt the same, none dared to say that in front of the top-level executives.

"An army checkpoint," the hired Indonesian driver of the lead vehicle said to the four executives in his SUV. They were from Wilmar International, the large palm oil producer, refiner and trader. "Looks like we have to stop a minute."

"No one said anything about army checkpoints," said the youngest one seated next to the driver. The four were from Singapore and therefore spoke perfect English.

The rented white Chevy Tahoe they were in was the first in a caravan of three identical American SUVs, all driven by unarmed escorts hired from the same Pekanbaru security company foreign executives favored. The first two vehicles each seated four representatives of Wilmar International, all eight of whom were visiting the site of their newest oil palm plantation.

The two white-haired European men and the much younger yellow-haired woman in the middle SUV were various vice presidents while the fourth passenger in that SUV was a man, her thirty-something Dutch executive secretary. The passengers in the rear vehicle were a group of three Singaporean reporters as well as a public relations executive secretary from Wilmar.

"What the hell is the army doing stopping us out here?" asked one of the Singaporean executives.

"We'll find out in a moment," the driver said as he slowed and prepared to pull over as far as he could. "They're signaling for us to pull to the side of the road and stop."

The three SUVs parked in a neat row on the left side of the road. The three drivers' windows dropped at the same time.

"Everyone out of their vehicles," one of the four men in military uniforms shouted in broken English. All carried military rifles, but there were no military vehicles nearby.

"Where are your army vehicles?" the driver of the first SUV asked as he opened his door.

He waved the barrel of his Indonesian-made Pindad SS1 assault rifle in the general direction of the driver and gave another command. "No talking."

Everyone got out of the SUVs and silently milled around them a moment. They observed a fourth vehicle, a battered old Toyota, pull in behind them. It was an isolated area. No one else and no other vehicles were in sight, although through the filthy air it was impossible to see very far.

"Stand on the other side of the road," the vocal one ordered. "We need to check your vehicles."

As soon as they lined up, the four armed men moved near the SUVs, as if to proceed with a routine search. Instead of entering the SUVs, they turned and opened fire, peppering the fifteen with a brief, loud cascade of ammunition. The four walked casually among bullet-ridden bodies. They crouched to carefully inspect them. They had to be certain the occupants of the SUVs were all dead. One of them, a driver, moaned and opened his eyes. A bullet to the head silenced him. More rounds were fired at four others found unconscious, yet breathing.

While the Toyota pulled past, between the SUVs and the strewn carnage, one of the armed men reached inside his camouflaged shirt and pulled out a sheet of standard sized copy paper which he flung on the ground. He then slung his rifle on his back and reached into a front pocket and extracted a five-centimeter-long nail.

He stood before one of the dead white haired European men, the one with the paper lying by his chest, and spoke to his three comrades, as well as to his friend driving the stopped Toyota. He addressed them in their own language, Minangkabau. He held the nail up and asked them all, "Any of you guys got a hammer?"

CHAPTER ELEVEN

"Shannon!" David said across the main floor of the Marriott, just loud enough for her and to turn a few additional heads, as well. He walked toward her with a smile that lit up the lobby. "You're right on time."

"David," she replied and hurried to him, offering a big hug. Shorter than the average Irish woman, she had to rise up on her toes and reach high to place her arms around David's neck. One of her feet then rose as if to explore the back of her lover's legs. David playfully swatted it down.

"Careful, dear, we don't want to upset anyone. Some frown on public displays of affection around here."

"I forgot," she replied with a sheepish grin. "There'll be plenty of time for that, later."

"I can hardly wait."

"I can hardly wait either. But first I brought something for you. I'll give it to you after dinner."

Shannon's straight, light brown hair was nearly the same color and length as David's, maybe with a touch of red under the sun. It was cut very short, as it had been since they met, a few centimeters on the back and sides, a bit longer on top. A modest-sized green stone, possibly jade, adorned each of her pierced earlobes. With her blushing cheeks highlighting her already reddish complexion it might remind someone of Christmas cheer. David bent over some and whispered softly into one of her exposed ears. "The instructions?"

"You are so romantic. But yes," Shannon replied, whispering as quietly as she could in her thick Gaelic accent. "And more."

Shannon's sympathy for oppressed people began when she was young. She grew up in the small town of Cahersiveen. It was a coastal community located in County Kerry, near the western tip of southwest Ireland on the Iveragh Peninsula.

Her home town was once famous for being the eastern terminal of the first transatlantic telegraph cable. The small fishing village also possessed a long history of revolutionary fervor. In the center of town, on West Main Street, the An Bonnan Bui pub and hotel, which her uncle owned, was decorated with posters demanding a unified Ireland. In fact, the Catholic church she attended while growing up was named after Daniel O'Connell, the famous Irish nationalist leader who was born there. The Daniel O'Connell Memorial Church of the Holy Cross is the only Catholic church in Ireland named after a layperson.

As a child she would take long hikes throughout this rough corner of Ireland with her father and his older brother. They would pause now and then to point out this or that site where Irish nationalists had ambushed a British foot patrol, or a place where British soldiers had slaughtered an Irish family in retaliation. Anyone hiking through the mountains and hills in her remote part of Ireland will occasionally encounter low rows of large stones. They were once used by Irish revolutionaries to secretly observe patrolling British soldiers. It was a proud part of Ireland that could only be occupied by the use of ruthless force.

She saw the same thing occurring on Sumatra and she found it upsetting. Much like the British had done to her homeland, foreign invaders in the form of multinational corporations, were enslaving the island's population and destroying the land. She knew very well that simply asking them to stop, as the environmental movement had been doing for decades, wouldn't work.

"The economic slowdown is slamming everyone hard," David said. "The lines for gasoline and diesel in Jakarta are two hours long. Little sightseeing this trip, I'm afraid."

"Same back home. With most British troops off fighting all those idiotic American wars, as usual, my uncle and his buddies in County Kerry are saying the time is ripe for Irish reunification. My uncle's favorite club is back in business."

"I read on the news that there had been some explosions in Ulster. I hope he's okay."

"Oh, I'm sure he is. He's got a job working on a farm not far from the border. But it's a cover so he can do what he does best for the cause."

"I wish him the best of luck," David replied. He was a bit surprised that he, a mix of French, German and who-knows-what-else, by birth, had acquired a sympathy for the Irish nationalist cause. Up until meeting Shannon he hadn't given a second thought to the seemingly never-ending struggle for a unified Ireland.

"Thank you," Shannon said, then spoke louder, in a normal volume. "I need to get checked in. Then I need a nap, unless you've got something planned for us."

David smiled. "I may have some time free."

"Maybe you could come to my room and edit my speech for tonight. A teacher could find a few things others might overlook."

"I won't stay long. Then afterward you can rest. Would an hour be okay?"

"I can't think of anything I'd rather do. Well, maybe a quick shower, first."

"Let's make it happen," David said as he took her carry-on bag and the two headed toward the check-in counter. "Professor Jackman, my colleague, will be dining with us at five thirty. But first, the two of us want to attend a presentation on tactics and strategy at three."

"Sounds like fun. But I'll have to miss it, if you don't mind. I couldn't sleep a wink on the long flight here and need a short nap."

"No problem. I speak at seven, so we'll all meet for dinner. It'll be good for you two to get acquainted."

"It'll be nice to finally meet Professor Jackman."

"He's a bit of a radical. So unless you want to get eaten alive, avoid controversial politics."

"Me, talk politics?"

"You would never," he said with a smile. "That's another reason why I love you, Shannon."

"I love you, too, David," she replied and pinched where his spare tire would be if he had one. "I'll tell you all the reasons soon."

CHAPTER TWELVE

The door to the conference room was manned by two security guards. Each was armed with holstered hanguns, their black leather belts festooned with an assortment of other mean-looking gear. They didn't search the guests one by one as they entered, and as other guards had as guests first entered the hotel. But everyone was eyed suspiciously. Some were pulled aside while another quickly waved a wand over their bodies. David and Gary easily made it past the two toughs and took the two last open seats in the back of the packed conference room.

The three representatives from the World Wildlife Fund were giving a ninety-minute presentation on tactics and strategy. It had started ten minutes earlier, at two p.m. They had missed the introduction, but David knew two of the speakers from past events. The third was the new CEO, someone unfamiliar to David and Gary.

"It's the new guy, Larson," Gary whispered. "The one speaking. Guy makes six hundred grand a year, plus expenses."

"Six hundred thousand US dollars a year. No wonder he speaks and looks like the CEO of Exxon," David whispered back, then he fingered his necktie. "I bet his suit alone cost more than my monthly salary. I got this yellow tie from a street vendor this morning. Pure silk. See? It even says so on the label. Cost me two bucks. I bet his tie cost him two hundred."

"Two bucks?" Gary asked as he reached over and fingered the tip of the cheap yellow silk hanging from David's neck. "Hmm. I would've guessed it cost you at least five. I've had this old brown tie since the seventies and it's still good as new."

"I was going to ask what decade it was from," David said. He playfully elbowed Gary in the ribs. "I haven't seen one that wide in a very long time."

"Watch it, buster. That Australian outback shirt you're wearing is not appropriate for a business-attire event even with a silk tie draped in front of it."

"Clothes are low on my priority list."

"I can tell," Gary said, and smacked David in the ankles with his cane. "Mud stains on your pant cuffs. That's classy. Listen to this. I just found out what Larson earns from a fellow professor I bumped into out in the hallway. It's outrageous. After three decades as a loyal member of the WWF I'm going to stop paying my annual dues and ask to be removed from their board. Two of my colleagues are quitting the board, too. But to avoid any disruption we're going to wait until we get back home. I'll stick with the CES. They funded my Fukushima radiation study and paid for my hotel and airfare here. Their head office is in Seattle, not far from the UW campus. Their furnishings are military surplus and the outside walls of their building are regularly painted by whichever drug gang is in charge of the street. It changes monthly. I can assure you no one there's earning close to a hundred grand."

"You know, Professor Jackman, I don't see his name on the speakers list," David said.

"It's not. He's a surprise speaker," Gary replied, still whispering. "But this high salary nonsense really annoys me. When I joined, back in the eighties, the CEO of the WWF made about the same as I did.

Now they've gone completely corporate. In a year or two they'll probably be earning seven figures."

"Yes, it's a disturbing trend. But I thought you'd been a member since Lincoln was president," David said and laughed softly.

"No," Gary replied. "Since my secret favorite, Andrew Jackson."

"Wait a minute. You're on their board of directors. How could you not know what the CEO makes?"

"We're honorary members only. They pack the board with dozens of celebrities, scientists and academics then keep us all in the dark about everything. Our names appear on their letterhead and we receive an annual check for a few grand. That's about it. They do it to lend credibility, and it works. I believe we've been duped. They only used us to help raise money. I'm not very happy about this."

"I have a pretty clear idea what he's going to say," David said. "More of the same. Fundraising. Membership drives. Fundraising. Letter writing. Fundraising. Boycotting. Fundraising. Lobbying elected officials. More fundraising. I get sick to my stomach even thinking about it. Whaddya say we blow this lecture. You can catch up on some reading or take a nap. Shannon's probably still sleeping. I want to greet her in the lobby when she comes down from her rest. I'll grab a chair by the elevators and wait there while I read a few newspapers."

"You are a wise man, Doctor Reseigh," Gary said as he quietly stood, steadying himself on the way up with his carbon fiber walking stick. "You've certainly got your priorities squared away."

"Thank you, Professor Jackman," David stood and replied, gently holding one of the older man's elbows. "You're no slouch, yourself. Speaking of priorities, we have a few minutes to spare. How about we stop at the Blu Martini bar for a drink."

"That's a wise suggestion," Gary said as they made it through the door without disturbing the talk. "Tea only. You know I don't drink anymore."

"Of course," David said and directed Gary toward the bar, conveniently located on the lobby floor. "Some day I may follow you in your teetotalling footsteps. But not today. It'll be whiskey, for me. Since my presentation isn't until tomorrow evening, and I've got it practically memorized, I have no need to further prepare. So if you don't mind, I may make it two."

They walked right up to the bar and took two stools. The dance music blasted through speakers affixed to every nook and cranny of the ceiling. The place was empty of customers, probably because the main conference speaker was still talking. Just about everything in the room was glassy and glitzy, as if it had been made in the nineties, right before the Nasdaq bubble burst. Assorted blue tones illuminated the room. The ceiling, the tiled entry, the upholstery and everything else, except the mud-brown carpet, was a different shade of blue, too. But the back wall, the deepest blue of them all, reflected severely against the mirror set behind the standard display of booze bottles. That was where both men now gazed. Gary was lost deep in a thought about some aspect of the Fukushima disaster. David was seemingly daydreaming about something, too, but it was the bartender's slacks that he focused his eyes on.

"What would you like?" the short, slender young male bartender asked the two men as he polished a glass while standing a few meters to one side. When there was no reply he came close and leaned forward across the bar. He asked again, this time in a friendly soft whisper. When there was still no reply from the momentarily daydreaming men he rose to his toes and addressed only Gary. "Hello, there. What would you like?"

In the mirror David hadn't yet noticed the man's face, which was now turned toward Gary, but was instead calculating through the application of simple math and physics his observation that the bartender's tight-fitting black dress slacks would split open if he was a millimeter larger across his rump. The handsome and slim bartender had on a starched, dark blue button-down dress shirt. But if David had been asked later what color the shirt was he probably wouldn't have been able to recall. His focused gaze and observation continued.

Gary shuddered, as if hit by a low voltage shock. "Green tea and a glass of ice water, for me."

"You want your tea in a glass of ice water?"

"No, hot tea and a glass of ice water."

"Okay. And for you?" he asked David who had completed his initial observation and was now addressing the tight fitting situation from a new angle. His face blushed some as he directed his attention to the bartender's face. A quick wave of recognition swept over the bartender and he broke out in a sweet smile. He raised an eyebrow. "Hey. I remember you. You've finally changed out of your sweaty gym clothes. See anything you like back here?"

"Give me a second."

The waiter from the executive dining room, now working as a bartender, then stared at David a few seconds longer than needed while slowly widening his smile to reveal two rows of perfect white teeth. "Now what exactly would you like, young man? I have everything a man like you would ever want back here."

"A shot of whiskey would be fine. I don't care which brand."

"JB?"

"Sure. And a glass of water on the side."

While the bartender prepared the drinks Gary turned to David with a serious expression and whispered while aiming an extended thumb at the bartender. "Do you want me to keep Shannon busy after your speech, you know, show her the town in case you might find something better to keep you busy?"

"Cute one, Gary. Kind of you to offer, but I'll pass."

"Okay," Gary said, again flicking a thumb toward the nice looking bartender while he precisely poured a shot of JB. "If you change your mind, let me know. We're buddies. I promise not to tell a soul."

"Gary, please."

"Here you go. Tea and JD," the bartender said.

"Thanks. Let's grab a table," David suggested as he stood, eager to create some distance from the bartender without hurting his feelings.

The bartender overheard David and didn't waste a second, eager for one final chance to get to know him better. "Are you two from the environmentalist conference?"

"Yes, we are," Gary said. "We're both scientists."

"I love science. Hey, it's crazy what happened across the street at the Ritz this morning, isn't it?"

"I haven't heard any news all afternoon," Gary replied.

"Me neither," David said. "What happened at the Ritz?"

"Two of their guests were murdered today."

"Murdered?" Gary asked.

"Right in the hotel?" David asked. "With all this security how is it possible?"

The bartender summarized what little he knew and embellished some to make the story more interesting, as if it was necessary. He filled in what he didn't know with rumors and guesses, as people often will. "The rumor is they were stabbed by a maid. Then she hammered notes to their heads with nails."

"Nails?" David asked.

"Yes. Nails. The police won't confirm it, but I was told by a friend who works at the Ritz that the notes had two words on them: 'Direct Action.' Be careful, guys. Stay away from those maids. They're tougher than they look. The police say the two that got killed were here for the conference."

"Thank you for the information," David said.

"Seriously. Watch yourselves. Someone might be killing environmentalists."

"Thank you for your concern," David said. "Please excuse us."

"I'm here until seven, you know, if you want to talk or something," the bartender said to David. "Maybe you might want someone to show you around town?"

"I really appreciate your kind and friendly offer," David said with a half of a smile. "But I'm busy tonight. And tomorrow I'm flying to Sumatra. Maybe some other time."

"Sure. You have an email address?"

"Yes, I do," David said. "But my fiance would be upset if I gave it out, uh, socially, if you know what I mean."

"Oh. I get it. Well, if you change your mind, my name is Dani. I'm always around, filling in for someone skipping a shift. I practically live in the hotel. If you want to find me, just ask anyone. In the meantime, let me know if you or your friend needs another drink."

"Thank you, Dani. I probably will. In fact, go ahead and pour me another one now," David said. He downed the last of his first shot in one sip, then smiled as he placed the empty little glass on the bar. Dani reached for the bottle and poured David another drink, JB, right to the rim. He then returned the smile and added a seductive stare. David took a deep breath and walked away to sit by Gary at the corner table he had selected.

"Nails," Gary said as soon as David sat. "It's barbaric."

"They're trying to frighten the bastards away, that's all. You got any better ideas?"

"No," Gary said. "I suppose they do have to drive home the point that they're serious."

While Dani continued glancing adoringly at David, David glared at Gary through squinted eyes and a sour expression. "Drive home the point?"

Gary scratched an annoying itch somewhere below the back of his neck and replied. "No pun was intended."

"If I sit in this blue room much longer it may impact me psychologically," David said as he surveyed the bar. He caught a smile from Dani, who stared and swayed some to the loud music, his head cocked at a not unpleasant angle.

"It appears as though our lovely bartender has high hopes in that regard."

David tossed down the rest of his second shot. "Let's get out of here. I have to catch up on the news. And you, my friend, could use some study time as well as some rest before dinner."

"How right you are," Gary said. The two walked toward the door of the bar, Gary somehow now stepping easily without the need for his cane or an elbow assist from David.

"Hey!" a voice called out from inside the bar. "You never told me your name."

Gary paused a moment and grinned at David. "I'm Gary. My colleague is David. Doctor David Reseigh."

"Thank you, Gary," Dani said, then he waved and smiled. "I hope to see you soon, David."

"Say goodbye to the nice man, darling," Gary whispered to David.

David gave Gary the usual hard glare. Then he turned to face Dani before walking out the door. "Nice to meet you, Dani. I hope to see you around, too."

"See?" Gary said as soon as the two walked out of the Blue Martini. "Now you've made a new friend. That's exactly what'll happen when you smile and treat everyone nicely."

"You. Go to your room and stay there. It's too dangerous for me to hang around you with your twisted matchmaking. Go get some rest. Shannon and I'll see you in the lobby at seven. Then we'll decide where to have dinner."

CHAPTER THIRTEEN

They met in the lobby and decided to dine in the hotel's second-floor Pearl Chinese Restaurant rather than risk walking around at night in search of something better. With the army, the police, the protesters and possibly stray members of Direct Action out and about it might not be a good time for a small group of westerners to take an evening stroll in Jakarta.

For dinner the three enjoyed a local favorite: spicy beef rendang over white rice with a separate presentation of assorted vegetables. Their dinner conversation centered on the local cuisine and culture. David's cell phone, which he pointed at once or twice, was prominently placed near his dinnerware as a reminder to avoid mentioning the smuggling operation.

"I believe we may have a new waiter," Gary said with a grin, eager for the opportunity to tease David one more time.

David saw Dani pass by the table and he shrank in his chair. But it was too late. "Hi, David. How are you, Gary? Your first waiter was needed at home. Since I practically live in this hotel he asked me to cover for him. I'll be your waiter for dessert."

"Nice to see you again, Dani," Gary said.

"Likewise, Gary. David, is this beautiful woman the lucky fiancee?"

"Fiancee?" Shannon said. David shrank a bit more. "That's news to me."

"Just joking," Dani said. "I meet so many guests it's hard to keep them all straight." The true reason he worked such long hours was that for him the hotel was the safest place in town. More than a few times he'd been pushed around, threatened or punched in the head while on the streets of Jakarta. In the Marriott he was safe, even protected by other staff and guards.

"How do you know their names?" Shannon asked Dani.

"He was our bartender this afternoon," Gary said.

"Our bartender?"

"Yes," David answered. "We stopped in the Blue Martini bar this afternoon for some whiskey."

"Some whiskey? In the middle of the afternoon?"

"I didn't drink all that much," David said, painting himself deeper into the corner.

"That much? I thought I smelled whiskey on your breath. Were you drunk when you came to my room?"

"Of course not ..."

"He only had two shots," Dani interjected with a sensational grin and a television minister's body language and poise. "That's nothing for someone his size. Plus the bar was busy, plenty of scientists around. I make it a point to get to know my customers, especially if they're academics. Scientists are excellent tippers."

His effort to protect David by fudging the scene in the bar was charming. David nodded approvingly at Dani.

"Okay," Shannon said. "I happen to know what too much drinking can do to a person. It's been a curse against my people for generations. It truly frightens me."

"This is a Muslim country," Dani added. "Drinking is highly frowned upon. Therefore, guests rarely leave the Blue Martini tipsy."

"It's been ages since I've seen David enjoy a drink," Gary said. "He's essentially a non-drinker."

"Well, David?" Shannon said, her tone of voice considerably softened.

"I was really upset about the Larson character, the new CEO of the WWF."

"I haven't heard of David getting that upset since the time he told me the story about macaques being used by beggars on Jakarta street corners. They were wearing human baby masks. A woman held one of the poor animals by a short chain leash. Every one of the monkey's teeth had been pulled so it couldn't bite anyone."

"Those macaque acts are illegal now. But I wouldn't mind if someone pulled out a few of Larson's teeth," David said.

"Well, tell me, David. What is it that makes you so upset with him?" Shannon asked.

"He spoke this afternoon, a surprise guest. What jacks me up is that the guy earns three-quarters of a million dollars running an environmental organization."

"Plus expenses," Gary said. "Imagine what his office is like. I bet it's truly opulent."

"Donald Trump would probably feel right at home there. Larson earns damn near a million a year if you add it all up. All the bastard thinks of is fundraising," David said. "I couldn't take another minute of it. I had to walk out."

"Nearly a million dollars!" Shannon said. "That's preposterous. If I run into him I'll give him a piece of my mind. When does that bar close?"

"One a.m.," Dani said.

"First, how about we have some dessert?" Shannon suggested.

"Great idea," Gary said. "Then let's drop by the bar after David's presentation. I think by then I'll need a drink, too."

"Can't wait," Shannon said. "I might get lucky tonight. Maybe Larson'll be there."

For dessert they shared a sumptuous plate of local fruit including mangosteen, rambutan, papaya and star fruit.

"This papaya is absolutely wonderful, David," Shannon said.

"Yes, it is," David said. "However, I prefer the mangosteen. We don't get it like this in America."

"I've never seen it before," Shannon said.

"The maitre d' has assured me the fruit they serve in this hotel is only grown on old, well-established plantations."

"I bet they all say that. But for tonight, I don't give a hoot," Gary said. "I just want to enjoy my dessert."

"And it appears as though you are," David said as he quick swiped a piece of jackfruit off Gary's plate with his fork.

"Hey," Gary said with a snarl while waving his butter knife like someone might flash a switchblade. "I don't want to have to bring out my less peaceful side. But I will if you jack any more of my jackfruit."

"Shannon, watch me jack Jackman's jackfruit." David aimed his fork in Gary's direction and gave it a twist.

"I'll run this blade through your throat."

"David, knock it off," Shannon said. "You, too, Gary. Come now, boys. I'll ask the waiter to bring more, if you like. And David won't be able to speak tonight if he has a fork sticking out of his neck."

"I bet I could still speak. But it might not be quite as understandable. How about a truce, comrade."

"Deal."

Dani appeared. "Anything else for you three?"

"Anyone?" David asked.

"Not me," Gary said. "That was the best dinner I've had in my entire life."

"It was right up there in the top ten, for me," Shannon added. "But I can't eat another bite."

"Charge it to my room," David said.

"Yes, sir. I already know your room number," Dani replied with a smile. David instantly blushed and Shannon tossed him a quizzical expression.

"Tomorrow," Gary said, "I'll cover breakfast."

"I'll remind you of that," David said as he stood. "It's six thirty. I have to meet with my colleagues and do a last minute preparing. You two may want to grab seats now. That way you can get up closer, maybe even claim some front row seats."

"Let's go right now and secure three," Shannon said to Gary as he elevated himself from his chair with his cane. "You need a hand?"

"No. I'm fine, thanks. I can't wait to hear your presentation, Doctor Reseigh. This will be the high point of my trip."

"I hope whoever shows up listens closely."

CHAPTER FOURTEEN

The brightly lit main conference room was filled to capacity. About half of the conference guests were older white men, some from Europe, others from North America. The rest were an international assortment of men and women, young and old, including four teenage boys from Nigeria. This morning they had shared a horrifying tale about how their ancient tribal village, once surrounded by lush forest, had vanished this past spring under tall waves of sand dunes.

A delegation from Sumatran mountain villagers filled the front row. The eight men in beige sarongs and four women in colorful traditional dresses sat in the front. Gary and Shannon guarded David's chair and sat in the two remaining front row seats at the end, on the speaker's right.

The room illumination was done with little thought. The dozen soft lights mounted at face level on each of the dark-stained hardwood walls tried but failed to brighten the white ceiling far above. Two plastic-covered rectangular light boxes shined down on the guests from the ceiling. They did so too brightly, as if they had been designed to be used in oversized suntan booths. Men with receding hairlines would be wise to apply sunscreen if they sat inside the room for long.

The two hundred and forty attendees were seated fifteen across on cushy chairs, each covered with a pristine polyester white fabric. The old orange wall-to-wall carpet stared up at the gaudy rectangular lights in stark, Halloween-like contrast to the sixteen rows of black cloth topped tables. The room was split by two off-center aisles. Jammed near the podium were young Asian men, reporters, most likely, each busily adjusting this and that on their tripod mounted cameras. Their complex digital devices would record every word David spoke and could document each itch he scratched. With that in mind he placed his hands flat on the podium as soon as he got there and, other than to flip the pages of his speech, that's where they remained the entire time he spoke.

He would be allowed fifty minutes for his presentation followed by a thirty-minute question and answer period. The attendees each had a copy of his speech, some translated into their own language. The attendees who didn't understand English would follow along, reading and listening politely. The schedule was tight and the moderator had warned the speakers to stay within their allotted time. The main speaker at the conference was the executive director of Walhi, Doctor Zaqi. He would approach the podium at precisely eight thirty, ten minutes after David's presentation ended.

After introducing himself to the scientists, environmental activists and others attending his presentation Doctor Reseigh dove right in. He quickly outlined the current scope of the destruction, offering a few oral jabs at those who profited or benefitted from the carnage. Then he delivered a carefully worded conclusion.

"The rainforests throughout the world are nearly all destroyed. We saw it coming many years ago and, despite the environmental movement's best efforts, the destruction hasn't slowed at all. In fact, over the past decade it's accelerated. But we're all aware of this so I won't bore you with the gory details. The long list of extinct insects, birds, mammals, plants and trees is much too long to recite here. The long list of endangered life forms now shrinks while the list of those extinct grows longer. We're all aware of this. It's information you can easily access online. So I'll move on to summarizing what Sumatra will be like in three years, if we allow the destruction to continue.

"In three years central Sumatra will be nothing but one large oil palm plantation shared like medieval kingdoms by a handful of multinational corporations. The entire island'll be nothing more than an army-guarded farm adding nothing whatsoever to the world's need for energy, serving only to further enrich a tiny group of wealthy stockholders in Singapore, North America and Europe. Twenty percent of the island's tropical rainforest still stands, but that remnant, too, will soon vanish by saws or in flames.

"So what can we do about it? Do we remain on the path we've walked for decades? Or do we try a new approach? There's not one person here who can honestly tell me the combined actions of the environmental movement as a whole has done anything whatsoever to stem the wholesale devastation.

"Recent news reports are suggesting that members of the local population on Sumatra and elsewhere may be taking matters into their own hands. That's an expected, natural development. The only surprise is that it took so long to happen." Some in the crowd stirred as he said the words. Others whispered to those sitting nearby, a few others shaking their heads in disbelief. Doctor Reseigh continued after a short pause, noticing that a few among the group from Sumatra seated before him were stifling understanding smiles and nodding in agreement with him. David nodded back stoically in their direction and made a mental note to speak with them before the evening was through. "In conclusion I'll leave you all with one simple and final thought. As scientists, academics and environmental activists it is our holy obligation to do more than simply prepare studies and report our findings to one another. And, as we all know, what we've been doing over the past many decades, unfortunately, hasn't done more than scientifically monitor the destruction, step by step. I urge all of you in the strongest way possible to think outside the Big Green box and explore other, more creative ways of protecting what little remains. Thank you very much."

The Sumatrans stood up and clapped loudly while a distinctly polite applause spread to the back of the hall. Shannon stood, too, joining those seated alongside her while at the same time helping Gary to his feet. The colorfully attired indigenous delegations from Papua New Guinea, Nigeria, Bolivia and Brazil who were seated in the two rows behind the Sumatrans rose up cheering and clapping loudly. A rhythmic clapping soon developed, drawing the less enthusiastically applauding western academics to join in as well. The thunderous applause went on for a full two minutes punctuated by an assortment of shouts. David stood nervously at the podium. It was not at all the response he had expected. The moderator was dumfounded. He finally stepped up alongside the podium with his arms raised. The crowd quieted and finally took their seats. As if on cue dozens of delegates' hands rose up high, eager to ask David questions as if he were a rising rock star.

CHAPTER FIFTEEN

David replied to a series of questions. Most pertained to his personal opinion regarding ways in which people in the developed world could act to preserve endangered species after the forests were gone. He briefly responded to each suggesting to the shock of some and the delight of others that he personally disapproved of zoos from a humanitarian and philosophical perspective.

A reporter from the Jakarta Post who had been taking notes near his cameraman asked David for his opinion of forming protected nature reserves. David told him directly and pointedly that it wouldn't work. Encroachment by loggers and people burning wood for fuel would eventually clearcut the trees and destroy them. He told him that it would be more useful if threatened species were allowed to remain in the same forests nature had already provided for them. He added that it would be helpful if governments were prepared to use armed force to protect the animals rather than protecting the loggers. David also considered suggesting that pulp production should be banned, but instead told the reporter that if newspapers would stop using pulp and paper and move to digital only, millions of acres could be saved.

At precisely eight twenty-three he thanked the audience and left the podium to yet another round of loud standing applause. He again thanked the audience and walked away, saving the moderator the embarrassment of quieting the crowd.

He sat between Shannon and the colorfully attired Sumatrans who all smiled in unison at him like a posed lineup of Indonesian happy faces. One Nigerian from among the two rows of delegates from Africa and South America gripped David by the shoulder and spoke quietly. "Where were you twenty years ago?"

"We'll win this," David said with his hand clasping that of the tall, red robed man. "But it'll take a … it's going to require a fundamental change, a very different approach."

"I fully agree with you," the man said as he handed David a business card. "Let's keep in touch."

"I'll email you."

"You were wonderful," Shannon said while David pocketed the card. "I'll kiss you on the cheek later."

"Most excellent speech, Doctor," Gary said, and shook his hand while remaining seated. "That's the first standing ovation I've ever witnessed at one of these stodgy conventions."

"Thank you," David replied, then he turned to the Sumatran woman sitting alongside him. "I would like to speak with you and your friends for a few minutes after Doctor Zaqi finishes. Would that be okay?"

"Yes, absolutely. I loved your speech. My colleagues and friends did, too. It was right on the mark. We can visit a few moments right here as soon as our friend from Walhi finishes his presentation."

The moderator stood before the podium and introduced Doctor Zaqi, a short, slender man in his forties who peered at the audience nervously through thick spectacles. The podium was too tall for him to see over so he remained where he was, at the right side of the dark, laminated obstruction. His papers vibrated in his hands as he addressed the audience.

He spoke for forty minutes in general terms about what Walhi had done and was planning to do about preventing the ongoing deforestation. He spoke about organizing future protest marches, lobbying legislators, raising money and boycotting the companies responsible for the worst violations. However, his high-pitched voice was not only broken, it had the dead resonance of a defeated man.

By the time he ended his speech it had broken all the way. With his arms limp and his head hung low he spoke more, deviating from his prepared speech. "My tenure as the leader of Walhi has been a complete failure. It is for that reason I hereby resign my position as the executive director of my beloved nation's primary defender of our most precious asset: the rainforests." He ended there and walked away from his position beside the podium. He strode out the conference room door and out of the hotel without answering any questions.

When he became the executive director of Walhi he was in his late twenties, full of hope and optimism. At that time seventy percent of Sumatra was covered in rainforest. The few oil palm plantations scattered throughout the coastal regions were mostly colonial era oddities, producing cooking oil and food additives. Many of them were hundreds of years old and none of them were used as a wholesale source of biodiesel.

But during his administration a horrifying transformation occurred. It was as if someone walked into a dark room and flicked a wall switch, but instead of an illuminating light, the room was fast filled with dark demons. Overnight, green fuels, eco-friendly fuels and all manner of biofuels became popular. Renewable energy was widely embraced as the green energy rage swept the world. The EU took hold of the reins of this movement and led the destructive charge. As the last decade of the old millennium got underway Europe prepared to blast into a clean-burning, non-fossil-fuel future.

Environmentalists lobbied for it, climate change activists fought for it, and most importantly of all, multinational energy companies wanted the profits generated by it. The few weak voices speaking out against green energy such as Earth First!, Preserve the Rainforests and Walhi couldn't be heard over the thunderous cheerful shouts of approval from Big Green and their corporate and government allies. And when the concerns were heard, the messengers were attacked as radicals, troublemakers, even anti-environmentalists by the media, their peers among mainstream conservationists and by their governments. Their phones were tapped, their lives scrutinized, their reputations tarnished. Many lost their jobs for daring to speak out against the popular new paradigm. Government-sponsored rats appeared among their ranks. The infiltrators signed up posing as eager new recruits, as friends, and speaking the enthusiastic language of eager activists.

However, there would be a price to pay for this green energy love fest. The Sumatran rainforests would have to be sacrificed, much like tropical rain forests in Peninsular Malaysia, most of which had been cut down during the eighties and nineties. And there appeared to be nothing Walhi, Save the Rainforests, or any other environmentalist organization could do about it. Then Direct Action appeared on the scene offering a radical approach and with it, a striking ray of hope.

CHAPTER SIXTEEN

After David, Gary and Shannon had shared a few friendly moments with the African, South American and Sumatran delegations, including exchanging contact information, they went straight to their rooms. Shannon had changed her mind about dropping into the Blue Martini for a drink, which was a relief to David. He was concerned that Dani would be tending bar, didn't want to be distracted with warding off his endless advances.

To save donor money, Gary and David had shared one room while Shannon, whose trip was sponsored by her teachers union, had her own. It was across the hall, three doors down.

As soon as David opened the door to his room he saw that someone, most likely a member of the hotel staff, had placed a standard white letter envelope on the floor, just inside their door. It was unsealed, and there was a note inside. He picked it up and slid the note out.

"David," the note, written on a sheet of standard sized copy paper, read. "Your solar panel and batteries will be at the FedEx facility near the international airport in Pekanbaru when you arrive Monday. Below find the address. You requested a Xantrex PowerPack 1500 battery for your field power station but all I could find on such short notice was a weaker fifty-two pound Trojan Gel battery. Therefore, I've included two. I had one of my employees test one and it holds power fine. It's already charged so use it first. It has the white cross painted on it. I hope you find that both batteries meet your off-grid needs. They were shipped overnight airfreight from another one of my oil supply companies in the Bay Area. We regularly ship solar power gear to Indonesia because the drilling sites are often off grid and remote. And I hope your rainforest project goes well. When you're finished with the solar unit, or if it requires servicing, bring it to the Sumatran branch office of Simmons Hydrocarbon Supply, Inc., in Pekanbaru. It's only a few blocks from FedEx on the main road. Just pull up to the loading dock. They'll be expecting you. Regards, Cir Lynch."

"What's it say?" Gary asked.

"It's from Cir Lynch. He's an old friend of mine," David said. "He manages a company that ships materials and supplies to oil and gas projects in remote places." Then he shrugged and summarized the content of the note. Next time he was in the bathroom he'd rip it up and flush it.

"That's wonderful. I can't believe it'll arrive on time," Gary said while holding his phone in one hand and pointing at it with the forefinger of his other hand. "Where we'll be, basically in the middle of nowhere, there won't be any power. A high quality solar energy station will be needed to operate my testing equipment, that is, if we have time to do it in the field."

"I agree. Monday's journey to Sumatra should prove to be very productive."

"Let's hope so. Save the Rainforest is paying us nicely for our river water testing expedition."

"About eight grand," David said.

"Anyhow, I'm going to read awhile, then go to sleep," Gary said. "I'll see you in the morning. Wake me at the crack of nine, if you will, please."

"Count on it," David said while he folded the note and jammed it into a back pocket. "The first presentation is at nine. It's yours, which means I'll be pouring cold water on your face around six."

"Fine. What a bully. Imagine threatening the man who rescued you from the clutches of the cute bartender in the Blu Martini bar when you were in one of your moments of weakness."

"And I'll never forget that, Professor Jackman," David said as he opened the door and left the room, heading for the one three doors away.

Gary went after him, catching up near door number two and whispered to David. "We didn't order a portable solar energy station. Collecting dead fish and water samples in the Siak River and its tributaries for STR doesn't require a power station of that size. That three gallon freezer of mine is the latest design. It'll hold a charge for forty-eight hours. The equipment I brought along should be enough."

"I didn't order one either, but I think I know who did," David replied in a whispered voice. "I suspect the batteries contain some costly heavy metals. We'll know more tomorrow when we pick them up."

"Oh. A change in plans?"

"Maybe. But we have to be nimble in this line of work. When we get to the airport we may need to rent a truck, not a car."

"I was thinking a four-wheel drive truck might be even better. The roads can get rough in the eastern Barisan foothills."

"The people can get even rougher," David said.

"Good point. Let's get a truck," the tired professor said. "A really big one."

David knocked on Shannon's door. "Good night, Gary."

"Good night," Gary replied and shuffled back to his room.

Early Sunday morning Shannon took a solo taxi ride to the Jakarta Cathedral. The Neo-Gothic brick structure was built between 1891 and 1901. In 2002 renovation work started fourteen years earlier was finally completed.

She arrived in time for the seven thirty a.m. mass. The sanctuary was packed with Indonesians. In that crowd of worshippers there were about a dozen of European ancestry. After mass she spoke with one, a computer engineer from Spain. She asked him about the media reports regarding radical Muslim attacks against Catholics. He had lived in Jakarta for five years. He assured her that the discrimination directed at Catholics in Indonesia was limited to a few isolated incidents, most of which involved popular resistance to efforts to expand existing churches or construct new ones in predominately Muslim areas. The engineer explained to her that Catholics, with nearly four percent of the population, had a centuries-long tradition in Indonesia. Most citizens viewed them as part of their nation's cultural wealth. He pointed out to her that in East Nusa Tenggara, one of the nation's large central provinces, seventy percent of the population was Catholic.

Born and raised in the Catholic faith, Shannon had always maintained a soft spot in her heart for the church. Sitting and kneeling inside this tall holy structure lifted her spirits and energized her commitment to protect and save the forests. She had often called them God's most sacred creation.

And with the advent of the new Argentinian pope she was giving serious consideration to rejoining the worldwide flock. The joy she gained from this one hour mass put her one step closer to visiting with Father Kieran O'Brien at the Catholic church in Cahersiveen. Father O'Brien was the one who had decades ago baptized her. He knew Shannon and her family well and would be eager to engage with her in such a discussion. She would decide what to do when she returned home to Ireland.

She had shared this regained ecclesiastical interest with David and he was both intrigued and delighted. The only times he had been inside a Catholic church was for a handful of weddings. He always had walked out of the sanctuary feeling somehow rejuvenated, motivated to engage in altruistic activities.

At three in the afternoon Shannon gave her presentation. Afterward the three had an early dinner together in the executive dining room and for the first time, the flamboyant waiter, Dani, didn't make an appearance. Afterwards they decided to turn in early. They needed to get good and rested before Monday morning's flight to Pekanbaru.

CHAPTER SEVENTEEN

The ten-million-rupiah per month salary of a sergeant in the Indonesian Army was now fluctuating between the equivalent of five and six hundred US dollars. Two years ago it was more like a thousand dollars, but the recent worldwide economic downturn had hit their beleaguered national currency hard. The impact struck everywhere, particularly among the working class. However, the fact that the Indonesian economy was in shambles was most visible to a visitor by the two-hour-long gas lines snaking seemingly everywhere in cities and towns throughout the former OPEC nation.

Their national foreign currency reserves, which had once been well over a hundred billion US dollars, had been nearly depleted, spent mostly to finance their addiction to costly imported oil. It was now nearly impossible for an army enlistee to keep a home, own a small motorcycle or cheap car and live a somewhat normal life off base without somehow earning at least twice his salary. A working spouse could make up the difference, but those who didn't enjoy the benefit of a partner's extra income often moonlighted.

Most enlisted soldiers, particularly the lower ranking ones, lived in barracks where they could eat and sleep for free. Master Sergeant Ahmad Supraman was not one of them. The thirty-seven-year-old career soldier wanted to be as far away as he could get from the annoying teenage recruits when his shift ended.

As the chief clerk in charge of record keeping at the main arms depot in Riau province, he controlled the weapons as they moved in and out, seven days a week, twenty-four hours a day. The paperwork consisted of a dizzying and bewildering array of triplicate copies, quadruplicate data book entries and confusing computerized verifications few could possibly understand or decipher. Ahmad was one of those few and he played it to his personal financial advantage. His trusted circle of army clerks and truck drivers was small, secretive, and went back fifteen years.

The shipments of new M16s from the United States arrived monthly. Each day those and the Indonesian-made Pindad SS1 rifles were checked in and out by the thousands as soldiers went out on patrol throughout the province. Sometimes a rifle was reported lost or stolen. Ahmad personally took care of the paperwork in such cases. Other times they were accidentally crushed or dropped, some damaged beyond repair. One of Ahmad's many responsibilities was to record and then properly dispose of all non-functioning firearms. He carefully monitored the lost and damaged weapons statistics from the entire Indonesian military. He was careful the attrition rate from his base did not deviate significantly from the norm. It was the perfect scam.

The double-fenced and well-guarded supply base where he had been stationed for the past two decades was located four kilometers south of the airport. Long ago it was located downtown, right in the city center, three blocks from the Siak River. But back in the sixties it was attacked and raided by dozens of angry, pistol-waving police officers. They were seeking revenge after two of their own were shot and killed by a group of intoxicated army soldiers.

None of the police officers were killed or wounded during the evening raid, but four soldiers were killed. The arms they were guarding vanished and the depot was destroyed. Soon after tensions had subsided the base was rebuilt at a more distant, safer location outside the city limits, far removed from the center of town.

Twenty years ago when he joined the army the replacement facility was surrounded by orchards and rice fields. The base was enclosed by dual rows of barbed wire fencing. Guards walked the perimeter between the fences twenty-four hours each day. It was an exact square measuring two hundred meters on each side, which was small by military standards. It contained a few administrative buildings, a barracks, and a concrete structure containing the weaponry. The rest of the land within the fences was paved. The concrete was now severely cracked and narrow fissures laced everywhere allowing grass and weeds to absorb the hot sun as they probed skyward. Rows of heavy military vehicles were parked alongside the fence on all sides. This is where Ahmad had been counting the days until his retirement.

The orchards and rice fields were long gone. The base was surrounded by a light industrial district. The rough, under-engineered roads leading to the base were constantly pounded by the elements and hammered by the steady thunder of heavy trucks and military vehicles. They were either dusty or flooded. Today they were dusty, but the dust kicked up was nearly hidden in the thick haze caused by the fires.

"We need fifty rifles," the man whispered to Ahmad as he stood at a street vendor two blocks from the base. He was waiting for his order of rice and spicy vegetables and did not expect the intrusion. It was noon Sunday and the sidewalks were crowded. The food on the base was made by teenage recruits, most of whom hadn't yet learned to boil water when they joined the all-volunteer Indonesian army.

"Fifty? Are you planning a communist revolution?"

"It's to fight the forest burning, not arm an insurrection," the man replied. "The plantation owners are hiring armed guards and we need to level the playing field."

"For that noble cause I propose a deep discount. One thousand US dollars each and I'll toss in ten thousand rounds of ammunition."

"I was thinking seven hundred apiece, payable with ten one-ounce gold Krugerrands. I have them with me now."

"Deal," Ahmad quietly said as his lunch arrived. He paid the old woman vendor and stepped aside some as the man discreetly slipped the heavy roll of coins into his plastic food bag. They hit with a solid clap on the Styrofoam container holding his lunch. "Behind the same warehouse as last time. Be there Monday, at precisely ten a.m. Only you and one other man. I'll be watching but you won't see me. Here's how it will go. Plan on a five-minute load transfer. I want my driver back on the road fast. All my trucks now have GPS units and I don't want to disable the devices. The idiots from intel review them now and then and it can raise suspicions. Pulling over for a few minutes is normal. They need to stop if they make or receive phone calls and that's considered acceptable. As usual, my driver has no idea why part of his load of scrap metal is being off-loaded early. For a million rupiahs he won't care either. All he knows is he needs to pull over and stop as soon as his phone rings, remain in the cab, and stay parked for five minutes. You back behind him and work fast. No one will look twice at two military vehicles parked in that area. After you close the tailgate he moves out, straight to the metal recycler."

"We want a larger shipment next time," the man said. "We'll talk again soon and I'll tell you exactly what we need."

"I'll do what I can," Ahmad replied. "Whatever I come up with you won't be disappointed."

The man nodded in understanding then walked away without saying goodbye, disappearing fast into the lunch hour crowd of warehouse workers. The meeting had lasted ninety seconds. Ahmad peeked inside his lunch bag and smiled as a happy thought crossed his mind. "One step closer to retirement."

CHAPTER EIGHTEEN

As soon as their Monday morning flight from Jakarta to Pekanbaru's Sultan Syarif Kasim II International Airport arrived, David, Gary and Shannon located the hotel shuttle which would take them downtown to the Grand Jatra Hotel. They were well aware that the air in Riau Province was smoky and sooty, but it was still surreal to be in a city with nearly everyone wearing protective face masks. They had theirs ready and slipped them on when they boarded the shuttle. In the hazy air the sky was no longer blue, but brown. It was impossible to see more than a few blocks.

There was no security stopping guests as they went through the entrance and they walked right in through the wide glass doors unsearched. The absence of stone-faced police, swaggering soldiers and the pushy private security guards they dealt with in and around the Marriott was as refreshing as the cold air embracing them in the pristine, recently remodeled lobby.

David and Gary had reservations for a double room and Shannon, a single. They planned to stay for six nights. After checking in and dropping their bags off in their rooms David returned to the lobby and arranged to have a rental truck delivered to the hotel. It was eleven a.m. and already hot, but the thick humid haze, which even managed to sneak into the lobby, made it practically unbearable.

"I hope you enjoy your Tata Xenon," the talkative representative from the rental company said. He was in his mid thirties and spoke perfect English, as did many businessmen and women in cities worldwide. He wore black slacks, black dress shoes and a white, loose-fitting button-down shirt which was open from his flabby neck to just above the top curve of his sizable belly. He was covered in beads of sweat. His black hair was neatly tied in a short ponytail. With all the gold jewelry decorating his fingers, neck and wrists he obviously had another line of work.

He hurried through a summary of the rental agreement and suggested the fifty-dollar-a-day, zero-deductible insurance coverage. David took it. After writing down the information displayed on David's California driver license he told him where to sign. Then he pointed out the half-dozen places to initial. "Here are your keys."

"Thank you," David said. "How much gasoline is in the tank?"

"It's diesel, not petrol. And it's full," the man said as he fanned his gold-festooned fingers in front of his face. "The law requires it. However, please take my business card. My name is Rio. If you run low on fuel, I can help you. I have a friend who will fill your tank without the ordeal of waiting in line three or four hours."

David took the card and decided he would keep it close at hand. "Thank you. I just may do that. We'll be driving all around Riau province, even into the Bukit Barisan. We're scientists and we're here to collect soil and water samples from the Siak River and some of its mountain tributaries."

"I see. I presume you are environmentalists, most likely here trying to do something to preserve the rainforest."

"Yes, that's correct. We are that. There are three of us."

"Well, I have some bad news for you. It's too late. There is very little forest remaining. The way things are going, in a few years it'll all be gone. Poof," he said with a mournful expression while waving his shimmering rings high in the air.

"I understand about a fourth of the rainforest remains, at least on Sumatra. We'd like to do our part to save what's left."

"Yes, maybe a fourth. But it's mostly in the mountains, some in reserves. But the logging and burning will eventually get the trees there, too. In five years it will all be gone. Then we will breathe freely once again. But at what cost?"

"Saving what's left should be done no matter what the cost," David said.

"I believe you are performing the work of Allah. I strongly approve of what you're doing. So does He. I know this to be true."

"I'm happy to hear you say that."

"Don't get your hopes too high. When the forest dies so will our nation. Most people here will agree with me on that. They are protesting daily and their voices are getting louder. And it's all because we're slowly running out of oil. You see, David, not many years ago Indonesia produced so much oil we exported it. Some to Japan, some to Singapore, some to Europe. Our oil tankers shipped crude oil all over the world. However, those days are gone forever. So we needed something else to trade for the oil we now need. And that something is palm oil. Foreign companies came in. They began burning our forests to clear land for their plantations. At first few protested. But lately more and more are voicing their anger. Some are even fighting back."

"I read little about protests. Western news rarely covers Sumatra. There was one story recently about a protest at a mine west of here."

"It made the news because soldiers shot and killed eight protesters. People are protesting daily at the university. The army has established a presence there. The mines are often closed due to the unrest and soldiers have begun guarding the access roads to many sites."

"In front of our hotel there are several dozen people protesting against deforestation."

"This makes me happy." Rio then offered his hand and David gripped it warmly. A heavy gold bracelet appeared from under Rio's right cuff. It was obvious he had figured out a few clever ways to profit in the poor economy. "Allah is on your side. You will find many friends here. A few enemies, too, so be careful. Your accent tells me you are from the US. Americans are not very popular here. You might consider telling people you're from Canada. Avoid the protests and be wary when you drive into the Bukit Barisan. It's a lawless land."

"I was here last year without any problems."

"Mark my words. The situation is changing. The resistance to the forest clearing is finally taking root, growing faster than their newly planted oil palm trees. People are getting killed. The plantation owners now have spies everywhere. The army is patrolling, pretending to guard the forest, but they're really guarding the mines and plantations owned by the rich foreigners. If you encounter any problems remember to call me. My name is Rio," he repeated, then he flashed his gold-festooned fingers once more. "If you run into any kind of trouble while you're in Pekanbaru do not delay. I'm telling you to call me immediately. I have connections who can fix any problem."

"Thank you," David said. He climbed into the truck. A plastic half-liter bottle of cold water was on the passenger seat. A gift from Rio. He cracked it open, took a sip, set it upright in the drink tray and fired up the engine. He had to pick up Azka then drive to FedEx.

"Keep my number handy," Rio said through the closed driver's side window.

David lowered the window. He returned Rio's smile. "Thank you. I will."

CHAPTER NINETEEN

"Hey, Azka," David shouted. "Get in." The noise from a crowd of protesters filled the air. He pulled his Tata to a halt in front of the Universitas Riau. Azka was speaking with someone. He saw David and ended the conversation.

The university was located three minutes from the hotel. If David had remained inside the hotel he would have been unaware of the loud, several-hundred-strong crowd of mostly university age protesters. Many wore white face masks, not to hide their identity, but to offer some defense against the ever-present smoke particles discoloring the cloudless sky.

David decided he would save some inconvenience, and some time, and ask Azka if he wanted to come along. The FedEx facility was located near the airport, to the south of the surprisingly clean and tidy downtown. That cleanliness stood in stark contrast to the filthy smoke-filled air.

After the coming money hand-off he knew there was no way Azka would be comfortable carrying so much wealth by himself on a public bus. Furthermore, it would be risky for him to move it across town in a taxi. Plus he probably could use a safe place to open the package most likely containing more Krugerrands.

"Good to see you!" David said smiling at the first sight of his Indonesian buddy.

"You have a truck," Azka replied through David's open side window as he approached the truck. When he opened the door and climbed inside the chanting from a modest-sized crowd of protesters filled the cab.

"I'd suggest we join the protesters but we have a lot of driving to do this afternoon. First, I have something quite heavy to pick up near the airport. We can talk about it while I drive. After I tell you what it probably is, you may be happy we got a truck. Oh, I also brought you this memory card. Don't open it, especially not on your computer, laptop or phone. It has instructions on how to build a simple magnet bomb. Just pass it on to the appropriate party."

"Okay. That's definitely not my area of expertise. But I know someone who could put it to use. What do you have to get at FedEx?" Azka inquired.

David summarized the message he had received at his hotel in Jakarta the previous evening, but made no mention of Chuck. "The solar power gear is big and heavy. I'll need to take it somewhere safe to open it, but I have no idea where. Do you know of a place where we could do it?"

"I know just the place," Azka said.

"Great. Could you please navigate, show me the best roads to take to the freight facility? I should pick it up as soon as possible. It's not the sort of thing I want to leave in the FedEx warehouse too long. Plus I'd probably get lost if I simply aimed the truck south."

"There's always a chance the airport officials inspected the shipment," Azka said.

"A very remote chance," David said. "Half the oil Indonesia produces is pumped out of the ground on Sumatra. In this central part of the island oil drilling and support equipment is flown in daily and by the planeload. In fact, I wouldn't be surprised if most of the freight FedEx flies in here is related to the oil industry. Just to be prudently cautious, I'll drop you off a few blocks away. When I get to FedEx I'll take care of the paperwork, load the truck, then come get you. If there's a problem they'll most likely snatch me at the warehouse. Give me thirty minutes."

"It's risky shipping that much gold."

"It's a brilliant way to move it," David said. "It isn't drugs or explosives. It's gold. Easy to spend. Everyone loves gold. People will often reach for it instead of cash. And better yet, it's not very high on the list of what customs is searching for. Remember, everything we do from here on in is risky. But sitting back and allowing the rainforest to die is far riskier."

"I can't imagine letting that happen."

David dropped Azka off at a market, three blocks away. The pick up went without a glitch. The clerk asked for David's identification. He showed him his passport, but he didn't photocopy it or write anything down. He just glanced at David's passport and shouted at a worker in the back to fetch the shipment and help the customer load it into the truck. "A message was attached to the invoice," the clerk added. "It says this is the first of three deliveries. The second one will arrive tomorrow, the third, Wednesday."

"Perfect," David replied, and he folded the message and stuck it in a back pocket. He was shocked that more gold or cash was on the way so soon. "Thank you. I can't perform my research without this equipment. I'll be back tomorrow."

David pulled to the curb near the outdoor food market where he had earlier dropped Azka off and waited a minute. After two minutes of nervously drumming his fingers on the steering wheel, he saw Azka emerge from the crowd of shoppers with a transparent plastic bag containing assorted fruit. A newspaper protruded from the top.

"How did it go?"

"Fine," David said. He pulled into traffic and was nearly nailed by a speeding army truck. "That was close."

"They drive like that all the time. It's one of the reasons the police hate the army. The soldiers drive like maniacs."

"I've been meaning to ask you about the driving here. Most former European colonies require people to drive on the same side of the road as the colonizers. So if the Dutch drive on the right, why do Indonesians drive on the left?"

"We learned about that in school. It happened when the British occupied Java back in 1811. Stamford Raffles was in charge. He made everyone ride their horses and pull their wagons on the left side of the roads, just like they still do in the UK. No one bothered to switch it back after the Dutch returned four years later."

"Now I know. But what makes the army so arrogant?"

"Not sure. They think they can do anything they want. They've had quite a few shootouts with police over the years. In fact, the army weapons depot in Pekanbaru was once downtown. They had to move to the edge of the city after it was raided by police. It's less then a kilometer from here."

"Any army against police battles lately?"

"Some, but not like the big one. It was before I was born, but there's a long simmering feud between them. I think the root of the problem is that most of the soldiers are outsiders, from Java or the other islands."

"That could do it. What's in that bag, buddy?"

"Fruit. And a Jakarta Post," Azka said. He pulled out the newspaper. "Check it out. Three carloads of palm oil executives were shot and killed. Some reporters from Singapore were accompanying them. They were killed, too."

"When? Where?"

"Yesterday afternoon," Azka replied. "Maybe seventy-five kilometers west of here. It's a remote area. The bodies were discovered in a roadside ditch. According to the news, one had a note nailed to his head."

"I'm not very hungry," David replied.

"Don't be so squeamish. Here, have a mango."

CHAPTER TWENTY

After removing the screws securing the top of the marked battery and setting them aside on the hardwood table David spoke. "Here we go. The moment of truth."

"Look at all that gold," Azka said. "American Eagles this time. This is how you finance a revolution."

"Yes," David said. "This is the way it's generally done."

"They're beautiful," Azka said. "I've never seen anything like it before in my life."

David nodded and spoke as he held a few rolls in his hands. "Let's count them."

"Thirty rolls of twenty," Azka said. He helped David stack them on the table in his grandmother's tiny living room. It doubled as a dining room and constituted half of the two-room plywood shack she lived in with her aged sister. The small house was covered by a corrugated steel roof which had rusted brown after years in the wet humidity. The other room was the bedroom. It had no door. His grandmother was out running errands while her sister was sleeping soundly on the right side of their shared queen bed. When it rained heavily the racket up above would obliterate any snores like those now blasting from that room. "Six hundred coins. Two million US dollars' worth. It may take some time to distribute so much."

"Too much money. What a terrible problem," David said.

"That's not very funny. At an average salary of fifty thousand rupiah a day, many workers are nearly starving as it is," Azka said. He held up the bag from the market. "This bag of fruit and the newspaper cost me sixty thousand. There is no fundraising. It's impossible."

"Pardon my poor humor."

"No problem," Azka replied. "Pardon my sensitivity. I'll have this spread around Sumatra within forty-eight hours."

"There is something else. A man at the hotel mentioned there are daily protests in this city against the palm oil companies. I've heard nothing about it. Why hasn't the media reported this?"

"They begin to gather every morning at ten. They're protesting daily at the university and in front of the provincial government building. We're told to write an article only if government property is destroyed or someone's seriously injured or killed. Twenty-five protesters have chained themselves to the main gate to the Chevron Pacific Indonesia complex. Army soldiers arrived to cut the chains and Pekanbaru police officers chased the soldiers away. The cops are now protecting the protesters."

"Just like in Medan," David said.

"Yes," Azka said. "Like in Medan. There's also a hunger strike. It started out as one older man. He wanted to call attention to the damage caused by the paper industry. It's now grown. Ten hunger strikers are now sitting in front of the Riau Andalan Pulp and Paper company offices. They've sewn their lips together and have refused to eat until they close down operations."

"Ouch."

"Tell me about it. Last year seven protesters starved themselves to death by sewing their lips shut. They sat in front of the main entry gate to the Asia Pulp and Paper plant in south Sumatra until they died. That single pulp mill consumes two square kilometers of rain-forest each day. It's the largest of its kind in Indonesia. Its primary product is toilet paper, all of which is exported to China."

"You mean the South Sumatran rainforest is being clearcut so the people of China can have cheap toilet paper?"

"Yes."

"All the protesting in the world can't stop the destruction."

"I agree. But the protesters are getting more and more creative. It's always been like that. The people here are constantly protesting one thing or another. For the Post, it isn't considered news unless things get out of control. But this past year the focus has been on the deforestation. And with the recent wave of killings, my newspaper chose to fly me here to investigate."

"They couldn't have picked a better man," David said with a sly grin. "Is there any way this money could be used to make the protests larger? Maybe offer free lunches? Print posters or handbills for activists to distribute around town?"

"My friends are experts at this. A meeting is scheduled for tonight to distribute the funds and discuss everything. They'll have a plan and if Allah is willing it will bear fruit, not only here but in Medan, Dumai and on the other islands. In fact, I guarantee it."

"Excellent."

"David, the money you donated Saturday morning was spent quickly. It went to good use. However, fifty thousand is one thing, two million is something else. I just can't get over my immense responsibility over so much wealth."

"You and me both. Seriously, now. My money source wants results. I told you there could be vast sums of money heading your way and there is. I presume the Direct Action network is aware the money's coming. It must be distributed immediately to minimize the chances of it getting stolen or seized. Based on my experiences here the people are generally very receptive to taking a firm stand against the destruction. No one likes what's going on. I firmly believe the people of Indonesia have had it. They've let the forest destruction continue long enough."

"I couldn't agree more. Would two or three days be okay?"

"Make it one. We could have another shipment any time, maybe tomorrow. So don't wander off far," David said.

Azka's jaw dropped. "Another? So soon?"

"Yes. And it may be as big, or even bigger. I won't know until the last minute. I'll meet you at the same place as usual at six. We should be back from gathering samples by then. I'll explain everything. In the meanwhile, plan on distributing more gold. Lots more."

"I'll get moving."

"One more thing."

"What do you need?"

"Could you somehow get rid of this torn apart battery for me?"

CHAPTER TWENTY-ONE

The Riau Mining Company was in the business of extracting gold, silver and copper from open pit mines carved out of the Sumatran rainforest and refining it into various sized ingots. Most of the copper was shipped to China. Because there were no rail lines serving central Sumatra, the refined ingots left for the port of Pedang on heavy trucks and from there to various Chinese ports.

The gold and silver ore was a byproduct. Ingots, refined on-site to international purity standards, were flown all over the world. They left the refinery in helicopters which flew the precious cargo to Pedang, guarded the entire time by well-armed men. The open pit mines were notorious for depleting fast, so operations moved from one rainforest location to another. From the International Space Station the scarred landscapes they had scraped out of the jungle over the past century were visible as cruel brown gashes scattered across Sumatra.

With precious metal prices at record highs, their mining operations were running at full speed. That meant they needed explosives to free huge amounts of earth for their operations. Because of the recent unrest, soldiers were used to escort and guard the deliveries of truckloads of explosives.

"Selamat pagi, Ahmad," the man standing in line at the lunch counter said. He stood behind the sergeant. Both wore white respirators. It was four p.m., hot, muggy, and visibility was the worst in Pekanbaru history.

"Pagi," Ahmad said. "The air is terrible today."

"It's always terrible, especially this late in the afternoon. Two hundred rifles tomorrow at the same time and place," the man lifted his mask and said without further small talk. "Plus fifty thousand rounds of ammunition. I also need ten RPG launchers and plenty of rockets delivered as soon as possible."

Ahmad calmly paid the woman and picked up his lunch. He then turned and faced the man who's name was still unknown to him. The two stepped out of line and strolled a short distance down the sidewalk, away from the crowd at the stall. In a low voice Ahmad spoke through his mask. "RPGs? Are you insane?"

"There's more. We want to hijack the shipment of explosives heading to one of the Riau Mining Company's open pit mines tomorrow morning. The trucks leave your base at five a.m. I suspect you know which shipment I'm referring to."

"Yes," Ahmad said. "I do. The protesters are accusing the mine operators of polluting their river. There were a thousand of them blocking the gates yesterday. More are expected today. We dispatched two hundred soldiers to clear the entrance today and the same is planned for tomorrow."

"My sources tell me the mining company has requested a larger than usual army escort for the explosives. We intend to steal them. All of them. Unless, of course, you can arrange to sell them to us."

"I'm not in charge of the company's explosives. Only our weapons."

"Too bad. It would have been simpler, cleaner."

"What I do know is that one truck has the explosives, but it'll be surrounded by five other trucks, two carrying supplies and three more, each filled with ten or fifteen armed soldiers. Last week five tons of explosives were hijacked along that very highway. Attacking it would be suicide."

"Not at all. And we don't intend to seriously harm any of your soldiers."

"If your men kill any of my soldiers there will be no more arms."

"Understood. But if one of them screws up and shoots first we'll have no choice."

"Their rifles are unloaded. They are only a visual deterrent. My soldiers know better then to discharge firearms near the explosives."

"Good. Here's the plan. The truck with the explosives will have a flat tire a short distance before arriving at a certain one-lane river crossing. You are aware of which one. Most of the soldiers' trucks will have already crossed by then. You must arrange things so that only one truckload of troops remains behind the one carrying the explosives when they approach the bridge. We'll take care of the rest."

"I can manage that. However, two hundred rifles is a bit more than I can handle on such short notice," Ahmad said as they stood by a nearby fruit stand and whispered. "If we're lucky you'll get one hundred, but some may require minor repairs. And you'll get the fifty thousand rounds of ammunition. The RPGs will take a few days, but I'll try to have at least one and a case or two of rockets ready for you tomorrow."

The man dropped a roll of gold coins into Ahmad's lunch bag. Then he reached into his pocket, pulled out two more rolls and dropped them in with a double thunk. Before vanishing into the crowd he whispered to Ahmad once more a final instruction with a thinly veiled warning in case the soldier was unable to deliver. "This should cover everything. And make it nine a.m. Tell your driver to wait ten minutes this time. I'll see you again soon. Say hello to your wife for me. Selamat tinggal."

CHAPTER TWENTY-TWO

T wo years ago the decades-old two-lane steel bridge crossing the mountainous turbulent tributary of the Siak River had washed out. It was in a rough, heavily forested area, the steep jungle terrain useless for planting oil palm trees or it, too, would have been burned to the ground long ago.

A one-lane replacement bridge was soon installed, intended to be temporary, in place only a few months until the government could fund a permanent structure. Mine engineers had warned their truck drivers to cross the river one at a time and to drive slowly to keep vibrations to a minimum. The army had issued a similar warning to the drivers of their military vehicles. The caravan guarding the shipment of explosives was no exception.

"I believe the front tire is flat," the driver said as a truck in front of him quit kicking up dust and started across the bridge. In the purple pre-dawn light it was followed across by two trucks filled with soldiers. An older, nondescript white flatbed with wooden side rails stopped some distance behind, maybe fifty meters back of the caravan. It was a big truck, its headlights barely nosing through the dark foul air. The driver was not visible.

"It can't be flat," the guard next to the driver said.

"I need to pull over and stop right now before we reach the bridge."

"A flat? The heavy-duty tires on these Tata 407 flatbeds never go flat," the guard from the mining company seated next to him said. "That's part of the reason we use them."

When the truck stopped, the driver opened his door and jumped out, crunching in the gravel for a closer look. The guard did likewise, but on the left side. The driver barely had time to glance at his flat front tire and say the words, "An arrow's sticking out ..." before he was knocked to the ground, hard, by a metal bar to the back of his head swung by an unseen someone. When he hit the dirt a boot kicked him in the ribs while masked men bound his feet and hands. Before he was blindfolded he peered under the truck and saw that his guard was face down in the dirt, bleeding from the back of his head after receiving the same treatment.

As he curled up in pain, still struggling to catch his wind on the rough road, he further noticed that the troop carrier behind his truck had stopped at his truck's rear bumper. With his face against the gravel he observed that both vehicles were surrounded by a large band of armed men, their faces covered by red cloth, some aiming their rifles at the two trucks, others scampering here and there. They were otherwise dressed in the fashion of common laborers, filthy shorts and worn out shirts. Some wore shredded sandals. At least one was barefoot.

Then the cloth covered his eyes.

After the driver and guard in the truck carrying the explosives were securely bound and blindfolded they were dragged off the road and shoved down the steep ravine, but they didn't tumble far.

"Do not move," they were warned after they had rolled to a stop in the thick foliage. The two froze in fear.

"Leave your weapons, ammunition and all your clothing on the bed of your truck and get out," one of the large group of raiders meanwhile ordered. His voice carried far in the thick smoky jungle air, which had just been filled with the daily sunrise-inspired squawks, screams and whistles of assorted rainforest creatures. When the rebel shouted his command the symphony ceased and the forest turned quiet as night.

When the young soldiers hesitated he spoke again. "Get out and line up in the ditch. If you do as you're told no one will get hurt. Now move!"

After the soldiers had kicked off their military boots and climbed out of their gear they lined up behind their truck in their underwear as if for an unannounced three a.m. barracks inspection. Without a word men quickly bound them with twine, legs tight at the ankles, arms behind their backs. Canvas sacks were placed over their heads and they were shoved into a sitting position on the side of the rutted dirt road. Several other raiders climbed aboard the truck and salvaged the soldiers' clothing and boots. Fat drops of rain began smacking everyone on the head as thick clouds, unseen through the smoke, put the sunrise on hold for a few more minutes.

Others among the similarly masked men who had knocked them down went to work fast, shuffling the boxes out of the side of his truck and into a pile down the road a short ways. Two of the men untied and tossed aside the covering tan tarp. Another grabbed a crate of explosives. He ran toward his side of the narrow bridge with a companion. The other troop-carrying trucks had crossed the bridge and disappeared around a sharp bend, no longer visible through the gloomy pre-dawn darkness.

The nondescript heavy work truck that had paused a distance back had meanwhile pulled in closer, the man driving now visible, his nervous hands tight on the wheel, two dark eyes darting side to side above his white face mask. Indonesian words were crudely painted on the sides, most likely the name of a fictitious construction company. It made a U-turn. Then he backed right behind the last army truck. The young driver got out. As he and the other rebels began loading rifles, ammunition and crates of explosives into the low-railed truck a horrifying explosion ripped apart the bridge and the silence that had fallen upon their small corner of the hazy rainforest. Bits of wood and other debris rained down close. Thankfully no one had been killed in the operation. By the end of the day eleven more bridges in that part of the Bukit Barisan would be destroyed.

CHAPTER TWENTY-THREE

It was six thirty a.m. Tuesday morning. The sky was still dark, tinted with a slight orange-gray glow coloring a low slice of the hazy horizon to the east. The air was filthy. A terrible fog of forest fire soot seeped into their eyes and bored into every pore. They all wore white respirators, as did most others racing along the streets of Pekanbaru. Shannon sat on the passenger side while David drove. Gary found a narrow gap in back behind David. The center and left side of the bench back seat held their solar energy station. The aluminum case and the freezer containing the rest of the water and soil sampling equipment were beside the solar unit. The battery was on the floor behind Shannon's seat. The broad panels were on the bed in back.

The risk of catching malaria or dengue fever was always high once outside of urban areas. For that reason when they got to the first testing site they'd spray their clothing. A can of a powerful insect repellant containing diethylmethylbenzanide, also known as DEET, was waiting in the glove box and would be put to good use.

The emergency camping gear was squeezed in the back seat, too, wherever it could fit. They took the extra food and clothes in case they had to remain in the remote forest overnight. If their truck broke down they'd be glad they packed it. The temperature wouldn't get under seventy-two degrees at night so sleeping bags weren't needed on the trip. They hadn't planned an overnight stay so the only non-scientific gear they packed was a compact tent for shade, three folding chairs and a portable stove to boil water and cook.

The next FedEx pick up would occur late that afternoon. David had decided to not share the details of the smuggling operation with Gary and Shannon. All they knew was that he had to pick up solar power units. They didn't know that after stopping at FedEx he planned to meet Azka in front of the university. He would meet him at six. There was no time for sightseeing.

The sampling kit and all the rest of the scientific equipment belonged to Gary. It was mostly the same items the two men had used along the Columbia River, the same sampling equipment the old physicist had been using for years.

Officially Gary was in charge, with David and Shannon as his assistants. However, since the funding for this six-day Sumatra trip was provided by a grant from Save the Rainforests, and the true reason for their trip was to distribute funds or otherwise assist Direct Action, David set the itinerary.

Shannon would help as needed, but mostly she would enjoy her tour of Riau as a sightseer. She had been continuously taking pictures with her phone and planned to record every moment of her first trip to Indonesia.

They decided it would be a good idea for each to carry fully charged phones. In case anyone was interested in tracking their movements, all they would discover would be three environmentalists gathering routine water samples and, if they got lucky, a few fish from rivers in the Riau province. It also meant they had to refrain from discussing the true reason for their trip when their phones were near.

"Let's roll!" David said to Shannon and Gary as he pulled the rented Tata truck into a safe break in the pre-dawn thickening throng of cars, trucks and motorcycles. They all raced this way and that as if hurrying through the haze meant they breathed less of it.

Few honored the solid white traffic separation lines. All moved fast, as if fleeing from an outbreak of some new disease. Countless bicycles joined in, some on sidewalks, others mixed in with the traffic, somehow all safely zigging and zagging through the noisy scene of moving chaos.

David accelerated fast, barely enough to merge, speeding quicker than he liked, but just enough to fit in. As he drove west, heading out of downtown, the mass of vehicles sped away from each annoying traffic light as if it were the Indianapolis 500 starting line, blasting away full throttle. They honked at each other and burned precious fuel they'd waited hours in line to buy.

As they drove through the western suburbs the traffic thinned, but the smoke from the fires grew thicker. The red taillights of vehicles two hundred meters ahead were no longer visible. They were heading into what was starting out as the worst burning season Sumatra had ever faced.

"Slow down," Shannon said in her mask-muffled Gaelic accent.

"Huh?" Gary replied through his respirator.

"The underpass ahead. I want to get a picture of that graffiti."

"What's it say?" David said slowing the truck to a near crawl. "I can't read it and drive at the same time."

"It's in English," she replied taking a flurry of shots. "Got it. It says, 'Death to Tree Cutters-DA.' I presume the DA means Direct Action."

"It's picking up steam," David said.

CHAPTER TWENTY-FOUR

As soon as the explosives had been made ready, the three former Indonesian navy divers assembled and donned their underwater gear. Their first dive was about to begin. The three lightweight Diver Propulsion Vehicles, known as DPVs, bobbed gently in the dark ripples. They were fully charged and could operate for far longer than the six hours they would be needed.

They had already made one trip, shuttling the lift bags and cables which they had positioned on the murky, debris-strewn seabed alongside the heavily laden fertilizer ship. The targeted ship was docked close by, less than four hundred meters away from the dilapidated Port of Dumai warehouse. Transferring the watertight containers of explosives would take the three divers five additional round-trips, but they'd easily be done with the entire operation by noon, thirty minutes before the assembled explosives were scheduled to be detonated.

Over the past several years the three divers had become disgruntled with the direction their nation was headed and they weren't alone. More and more they and others in the military had come to believe that their beloved native land was being transformed into a farm benefitting a handful of wealthy foreigners.

Throughout Indonesia, including Sumatra, the rainforest was nearly gone. What remained were massive lowland plantations and in the foothills a ravaged moonscape where logging and mining operations had destroyed the land. None of Indonesia's widely disbursed islands had escaped the carnage, a fact readily apparent to members of the Indonesian navy who had the best opportunity to see it first hand when patrolling the nation's scattered territories.

The movement to stop the destruction of the Indonesian rainforest was gaining support from nearly all sectors of society. A few members of the powerful Indonesian armed forces had turned in support of the protesters. Sympathetic yet still quiet voices were heard among both officers and enlisted men. It was a new development. Voicing these concerns was risky and could potentially ruin their careers. Some among the military took it one more step by secretly providing logistical and intelligence information to the environmental radicals. A few went as far as to offer their highly skilled expertise, a bold move that could cost them their lives.

The three divers in the warehouse were among the latter, the ones willing to make the supreme sacrifice for their vision of a better nation, without compensation, even if their identities would forever remain unknown.

The abandoned dockside warehouse where they prepared the underwater charge was locked tight, unused for five years and falling apart fast. It was slated for dismantling as part of a major port renewal project, long delayed due to a lack of funding. White, faded, plastic-covered official notices pasted to each side confirmed its pending doom, now delayed indefinitely by the decaying Indonesian economy. Vines crept up the sides, a few nearly reached the rusting curled lip of the steeply angled corrugated steel roof. The north end faced the strait, the other a neglected gravel road. It was surrounded on the other two sides by fast-growing foliage.

It was at the end of a narrow, broken-up, potholed access road and about a kilometer west of the main entry gate. The road was slated for widening and paving, but only if the long-planned port reconstruction project on the west end of the port ever got underway.

The steel siding hanging off the decades-old, ten-meter-tall structure was badly rusted, as if it was aware of its fate and had long ago given up hope. A narrow finger of seawater from the Strait of Malacca bisected the dock alongside and found its way inside under the rusting wave-lapped wire fence guarding the open mouth. It remained forever open as if screaming endlessly toward the strait. It had once formed a man-made inlet for small boats to enter and offload cargos of coffee. Longshoremen and boat captains alike were nicely protected from the sun and rain. The dark, wet inlet was surrounded by an ancient wooden dock. The end of the inlet was large enough to park a truck, maybe two. That's where the men with their mountain of explosive packages had gathered in the spider web glistening gloom.

A barbed wire topped cyclone fence surrounded the former coffee bean warehouse. The swinging chain link gate was broken. That allowed anyone to access the wide sliding vehicle entry by simply shoving it open, which is where it generally remained. Bushes and tall weeds climbed alongside here and there, as if attempting to scale over the fence.

A string of faded red rectangular signs was affixed to the inside of the fence, maybe ten or fifteen meters apart. The signs featured a simple black drawing of a man with a rifle and another man lying prone alongside a fence. A red spot adorned the fallen man's chest. The crude artwork warned passersby in whatever language they spoke that any trespassers would be shot. It was safe inside, and the perfect place for the men from Direct Action to do their work without interference from anyone.

The smoke and haze outside had become so thick it was impossible to determine if it was cloudy or not. The air was warming and the sky was brightening, but the wrong color. Instead of blue to the west, a Venus-like rusty-orange had taken over. Nearly everyone was wearing face masks to intercept some of the larger particles of the burning rainforest. It also helped hide the identities of the faces captured by the security cameras aiming at the entry.

As the phony inspectors in their white van pulled near, the wide roll-up door, partially hidden by a small grove of thick trees, rose. It closed as soon as the van cleared the doorway. The two men jumped out and worked fast. They were eager to get safely back on the road where they could find a concealed place to change the van's license plates before returning to the repair garage where a quick coat of brown paint and new registration papers would give it a new identity.

The final load of plastic-wrapped explosives was neatly and gently stacked on the wood floor, precisely where the divers' stone-faced young female guard had instructed. Twenty minutes later, and without as much as a goodbye nod of heads, she peered through holes in the walls to ensure no one was nearby. When satisfied, she again raised the door and the two men and their van departed.

When the deadly mission was complete the divers would escape by sea, underwater, unseen. When the divers left the warehouse for the last time their guard would walk from the warehouse dressed like a common janitor which was, in fact, her occupation. A white respirator would cover her mouth and nose, a red hijab hid her hair and her semi-automatic handgun and six spare magazines would be safely holstered under her standard dark blue coveralls.

She wouldn't walk out the main gate. She wouldn't drive, either. She didn't even own a car, although one day she hoped to. Instead, she would use a popular shortcut leading up a well-worn footpath long ago cut through the tropical foliage leading to a hidden break in the perimeter fence. It was roughly a half kilometer west of the gate and not far east of the warehouse. The path led to the main port access road. The shortcut was often used by janitors, manual laborers and other low paid workers at the port. Patrolling soldiers and security guards would rarely pause to question or even wave at them as they drove by. It was as if they were practically invisible.

While on the narrow access road the van slowed and pulled far to one side, into a long meandering tire-carved mud puddle, as an army patrol approached. They waved at the bored roving soldiers who waved back from inside their olive green electric patrol cart. The men then continued driving on the long dock past the stacked containers, the overhead cranes, the administration buildings, and finally through the main gate where they exited the port for the last time. They waved at the stationary port guards standing at attention at the official entry gate, the same guards who had earlier let them pass through. The building inspector impostors had delivered everything the divers had requested and it had only taken them three trips. Their job was over and they had performed their roles perfectly.

The gate guards waved back courteously but their attention was focused elsewhere. The two in the van ignored the fifty, or so, sign-waving protesters who lined the sidewalks outside the gate. Some of them had arrived hours earlier at the crack of the hazy dawn to express vocally and by waved slogan-painted signs their displeasure with the arrival and loading of yet another palm oil ship. They did notice that none of the signs mentioned Direct Action.

The gate guards and army patrols were too busy photographing and observing the morning protesters to pay close attention to a van from the city building Inspection office. It was a typical official van they had allowed into the port area numerous times over the preceding months, including twice the previous afternoon.

Other soldiers and security guards were out on patrol, but they, too, were preoccupied. It was a typical boring Tuesday morning at the port so instead of watching the buildings rust or the weeds grow they were busily playing digital games or socializing with friends on their touch screen phones.

Luckily, they were far too occupied to bother poking their heads inside the dilapidated old warehouse. If they had stuck their faces inside they would have had them shot off by the woman from Direct Action. Her sole assignment was to guard the divers' piles of gear and explosives with her life.

She had been drawn into Direct Action through a friend of her late husband. His friend was also a soldier, one of the two who had dropped off the explosives and other equipment. She joined the radical group after the death of her husband, the father of her only son. He had been an enlisted member of the Indonesian army. He was beaten to death by army intelligence agents after he refused to open fire on a crowd of protesters who had gathered at the entrance to a silver mine. The people were expressing their anger at the pollution the mine was causing to a river that flowed through their village. Nine of them had been shot dead and twelve wounded.

The elite former navy divers she guarded were arguably the best trained in the world. Among them they had thirty-two years of experience both dismantling and detonating underwater explosives for the Indonesian navy. They had been assembling the gear and the stolen explosives for weeks and were eager to get the project underway. Although this was by far the largest explosion they had ever assembled, the principles involved were essentially the same.

They worked fast, with the care and efficiency of an astronaut on a critical emergency spacewalk. While they worked their guard stood by, ever alert to any approaching intruders. They knew that the offloading of the vessel was planned for midafternoon, right after the federal inspectors had finished their routine paperwork. There was no room or time for error.

The loads of explosives were finally ferried into place with the help of the fast-moving DPVs. The three tons of explosives were finally unified electronically and the timer was set for precisely twelve thirty. The process of situating the huge bomb had taken them just over four hours. Because the divers had never set an explosive device anywhere near this powerful they were not fully certain it would detonate. But if it properly detonated the ship's cargo as planned it would match the 1947 Texas City fertilizer ship explosion and register right up there with the most recent North Korean nuclear test.

The ten-meter-long, tubular explosive device was then raised into position and suspended above the seabed by a long string of light lift bags. The serpentine mass hung six meters above the seabed in the long dark triangular gap between the seabed, ship's hull and the dock. It remained suspended, positioned tight against a precise spot on the hull by six anchored cables. The cables not only prevented the huge deadly load from rising too high into the narrowing dark canyon between the ship and the dock but stopped it from meandering away from its intended location, across the steel hull from the dead center of its full load of volatile fossil-fuel based fertilizer.

This final phase took the divers another hour. After a quick inspection and without pausing further to admire their handiwork they decided it was ready. Immediately after setting the timer they silently drifted away on their electric craft. It was eleven forty-five. If the device detonated as planned they had no time to waste. They would arrive at their isolated pick-up point in twenty-one minutes. It was an escape route they knew well and had practiced twice before. It would take another six minutes to load the DPVs into a waiting truck and eighteen more to vanish into a secret corner of the old run-down port city.

CHAPTER TWENTY-FIVE

The two hundred kilometer morning bus ride from Pekanbaru to the port city of Dumai took Azka and his friend, Reza, a little over four hours. Because the passengers in the back smoked cigarettes non-stop they sat together up front, a couple of rows from the driver. He also smoked while driving but at least he blew most of his fumes out his window.

The oversized, high-back seats offered the two a chance to talk safely about the gold delivery and the plan, as long as they whispered. The four pounds of yellow coins at the bottom of his daypack felt like a lead brick when he picked it up. But when the pack was on his back it appeared no different from any of the other ubiquitous packs common among day travelers.

During the Tuesday morning ride, his daypack remained stowed on the floor, between his shiny black dress shoes. Both of their cell phones were turned off and stowed inside a pocket near the bullion. A snack of assorted local fruit and his notes filled the rest of the space. Each time Azka reached for another piece of fruit his fingers brushed against the few rolls, offering a moment of mixed comfort and anxiety.

Their return ride departed at one thirty so they had two hours to conduct business. If the haze was less severe, and the potholes fewer, the two could have enjoyed the scenery. However, all that surrounded the bus during the bumpy ride was thick smoke. The ever-whining air conditioner waged a relentless, somewhat successful war against the hot foul air. Azka still had to work on a Jakarta Post story. He'd write it on the bus ride back and email it to his boss after he got back to his low-cost hotel in Pekanbaru.

He knew he couldn't miss his six p.m. appointment with David, but all he could think of now was ensuring the successful delivery of what remained of the gold coins. It was going to a secretive Direct Action cell dominated by a vibrant brand of Islamist radicals he strived to avoid embracing too closely. However, the greater cause forced this unexpected alliance with the well-organized holy warriors. And to make the delivery alone would be irresponsible with so many coins involved. As long as his allies delivered a solid attack against the palm oil profiteers he didn't care who got them, although he would be cautious and do whatever was necessary to avoid getting caught.

His sole contact with this small yet influential group was his friend Reza, a student leader from Pekanbaru. He was an ardent and committed environmental activist who had been arrested three times for minor protest-related offenses. Azka had interviewed him numerous times, occasionally quoting him in articles published in the Jakarta Post. Reza was also a practical joker, constantly tossing friendly jabs into his speech, some of which were offensive to those who didn't know him well. But his credentials as an uncompromising defender of the rainforest were solid. His connections among those the Western media might call radical Muslims was just as solid.

In fact, Reza's connections with the secretive Indonesian branch of Islam, which had assumed a leadership role in the fledgling Direct Action movement, were more than mere rumor, according to whispers Azka heard from other contacts. But any questions the reporter had in that regard would remain unasked. The same radical connections could be suggested about many of the growing number of young Muslim activists recently energized into action by the upsurge in protests against the destruction of their nation's heritage. In this regard Reza didn't stand out, at least, hopefully, not in a manner noteworthy enough to warrant observation by law enforcement officials or the feared military. After all, nearly all of the environmental activists throughout Indonesia were Muslim.

Nevertheless, the two men moved cautiously once they disembarked from their bus upon their arrival at the run down Dumai terminal. It was located too far from the port to walk so they took a city bus. A few minutes later they got off the bus, about a kilometer from the port and began walking, ever mindful of anyone observing or following them.

While they were walking among the busy foot traffic on a short pedestrian overpass two old and tired-looking palm oil tankers were visible in the hazy distance. One was dockside at the longest of the port's six piers. The other anchored not far off.

The Port of Dumai stretched along two kilometers of waterfront, although the oil exporting facilities were at the east end and a dry dock was situated away from the containers far to the west. Each end was isolated from the main central dock and not visible to the two men due to the polluted air.

The name of the tied up ship, the Isola Corallo, was painted in large black letters, the words barely visible through the haze. Wide brown fingers of rust streaked its hull. It had just berthed that morning, not far from where they walked. A dozen men could be seen gathered alongside the dock preparing to perform their various assigned responsibilities.

Men in filthy orange coveralls scrambled about on deck performing docking duties repeated hundreds of times over the years on the ancient vessel. It would soon be filled with palm oil. A few hours after that it would sail to Rotterdam, according to its schedule. It was a regular visitor among the countless tankers that sailed into and out of the tropical port on the busy Strait of Malacca.

The other ship, with Victory Prima painted on its side, was waiting its turn to offload. The small container ship carried a miscellaneous cargo including consumer goods from China. It also held a variety of petrochemical products including pesticides, paint, as well as two standard-sized containers filled with the type of high explosives needed in the mining industry. That portion of the cargo had been loaded the day before in Singapore.

Another smaller ship had just berthed, too. Its bow nosed not more than twenty meters away from the rear of the rusty tanker. The name of the ship was printed too small to read through the haze at this distance. It was delivering a full load of highly explosive ammonium nitrate fertilizer, but Azka and Reza had no way of knowing this. The customs officials and crewmembers now onboard, as well as those accepting delivery of the cargo, knew what it contained but for them the volatile cargo was routine.

The longshoremen also knew what the ship carried as did six members of the small cell working for Direct Action. One of them was a dockhand now helping secure the Isola Corallo. He couldn't help notice bubbles rising to the water surface as he secured a cable. This was unexpected and very unusual. He glanced around and was confident no one else saw them, which was good. As soon as the ship was secured he would leave on a long lunch break away from the port. While walking down a busy city street near the Dumai Administrative building he would make a number of phone calls using a portable voice scrambler. He would speak quietly. No one on the sidewalk would hear him or think twice about a man from the port speaking into a hand-held device.

Dumai was the largest palm oil terminal in Indonesia. The number of ships loading and unloading cargo there made it one of the economically stressed nation's busiest ports. Security was tight, access limited to passport-carrying ships' crewmembers and badged port personnel.

The perimeter was surrounded by a tall barbed wire fence. Cameras recorded everything so the two didn't approach too close. The dock platforms were patrolled by roving army vehicles, clearly visible in the distance. The reason for the military presence was primarily to protect the lucrative palm oil shipments, a nice thick slice of revenue from which went directly into the pockets of the local army commanders in exchange for their protection. The supplemental docking fee assessed by the army was an insignificant cost of doing business in that unstable part of the world. Few complained, and even fewer complained twice.

"This is the port where most of Indonesia's palm oil is shipped out," Reza said as they continued walking without breaking their pace. Their phones were in their front pants pockets and turned on. As long as they spoke softly there was little chance an eavesdropper could monitor their conversation over the roar of traffic. "Eighty percent of the cargo shipped from Dumai is palm oil. Can you guess what the largest import is?"

"I'm not sure," Azka replied as a line of trucks stormed by. "Is it rice?"

"No," Reza replied, a bit louder than the screaming pack of motorcycles racing by. "That was number one. Now it's number two. Try fertilizer. It's used to grow the oil palm trees. You see, when the forests are cut down the rain washes away the soil and its nutrients. It has to be replaced."

"That's insane. It's also dangerous. It'll kill off the fish in the rivers. I should have all these facts memorized by now."

"One mind cannot carry every fact, Azka, especially one as filled with facts as yours."

"Hey, c'mon now."

"Only joking," Reza said. "I read this tidbit not long ago and will not forget it. Either way, one could say they're exporting the rainforest. All of it."

"The soil is nearly dead. After a few more years of insecticide spraying even the bugs will be extinct. Our entire island will be dead, soil included."

"God cannot be happy about this," Reza said. He thought back a moment to the time when he was a child. His father and only uncle were beaten to death while in army custody. They had been rounded up because they had been suspected of participating in an attack on a military convoy during the unrest in the nineties. The public had little sympathy toward the army. Whenever the military travelled on the island it was usually in large numbers, always well armed. His animosity toward the Indonesian Army was deep-rooted and shared by many of the Islands' inhabitants. "The people responsible for this terrible carnage will pay dearly."

"That is the truth," Azka replied. "We have a sacred duty to stop the carnage. The forest and all the life it holds will be dead in a few years unless we're successful."

"God will grant us success," Reza said as the two reached street level. "The people are backing us, more and more all the time. The number of protesters grows larger each day. Look! There's a gathering. Why don't we go check it out? You can report on an actual live protest at the Port of Dumai while we're here."

"No way. Not with what I'm carrying," Azka said.

"I don't mean right now," Reza said, while the two passed by a row of food vendors. "After the meeting."

"As long as we're at the bus depot by one-fifteen."

"Easily," Reza said as he glanced back at a beat-up white compact car. It approached slowly from behind with rap music thumping. Two young men sat in front, each wearing trendy oversized sunglasses atop standard-issue white respirators. It made them indistinguishable from many of the other younger drivers and pedestrians in the rough port city. "This town is a dump. I can't wait to get out of here. Look at those two scumbags staring at us."

Azka smiled. "I read once that the safest thing a tourist can do after arriving in Dumai is to get out as fast as possible."

The car moved closer. When it slowed to match their pace the passenger issued an order through his open window. "Get in." His words were precise, spoken fast through his mask, yet low in volume, barely audible over the annoying music blasting from the car stereo.

When Azka glanced at Reza for a fraction of a second his expression was clear. He didn't recognize the two. Neither did Reza, at first.

"Now," the man said. He reached back and popped open the back door. Thumping music common among certain youth all over the world splashed out into the street.

The two nervously climbed in. With the back door closed and the windows up most of the music was trapped inside. The car then pulled away from the curb and merged into the fast moving tangled mass of bicycles and other traffic.

"Hey, Reza. Enjoy your bus ride from Pekanbaru?" the driver asked with a grin.

"Huh?" Reza replied while fumbling with his seatbelt.

"Don't bother. The seat belts are broken," the front seat passenger said. "Like everything else in Dumai."

"He asked if you enjoyed the bus ride," Azka said to Reza in a very low voice.

"We did," Reza said. He leaned forward, his face close to the driver's right ear. The passenger placed a bony index finger to his lips to convey the universal sign to speak softly. "How did you know we took the bus? And who are you guys?"

The young driver smiled, raised his oversized, yellow-framed sunglasses above the top of his spiky, red-tinted hair and glanced back a moment while somehow avoiding a collision with a small passing motorcycle and dodging a slow-moving truck. "C'mon, Reza. It's me, your friend Denny from Medan."

Reza smiled, tapped Azka on the leg, and in a loud voice said, "You're not Denny. You're his queer cousin. My good friend Denny wouldn't listen to this American gangsta rap crap."

Denny playfully swung a fist across his seat back. Reza ducked to one side. The baggy sleeves of a loose-fitting white shirt brushed Reza's face.

"Easy now. I was just kidding. I honestly didn't recognize you. What the hell happened to your hair? Your boyfriend make you do that?"

Denny swung his fist back again. "Very funny. I cut the sides off yesterday. Shaved my beard, too. You like the red spikes? I colored it myself."

"Tell him it looks good or he'll get all upset," the front seat passenger said.

"Hey, mister stupid," Denny whispered with his face contorted into an exaggerated snarl, his finger aimed at the smaller passenger's skinny chin. He ignored traffic a moment and jabbed his finger into the man's ribs. "We were told to use a disguise when we picked these two guys up. So I have a disguise. Where's yours?"

"What do you think these orange sunglasses and respirator are for?"

"It looks great," Azka said leaning forward on the seat. "A fine disguise. Both of you. Very fashionable, too. How long are you going to keep your hair like that?"

"Until right after I drop you two off. I hate this shade of red. It makes me look like one of those talk show faggots from Singapore."

The passenger laughed, then turned serious. He faced Reza and spoke quietly. "We're dropping you two off at the next intersection. Leave it on the back seat, under the blue towel."

"Sorry, Reza," Denny said. "I would love nothing better than to hang out with you and your friend a while. But we're told to pick you up, then drop you off as soon as possible. Rolling around town four deep'll attract the wrong kind of attention. The less time we're together in this car, the safer it is."

"I understand. When this is all over we'll hook up, spend a few days in Pekanbaru, or even Medan," Reza said.

"We need results," Azka said to Denny. "The forest clearing must stop."

"Soon," Denny replied.

"Very soon," Azka said.

"Very soon," the nameless front seat passenger said. "Sooner than you could possibly imagine. Until then, Allahu Akbar."

"Allahu Akbar," Denny and Reza both said at the same time.

"Allahu Akbar," Azka also said. He dug through the bottom of his pack and pulled out the four rolls of gold coins. He covered them with the blue towel in the narrow space alongside Reza as the car slowed.

The car stopped at a busy downtown curb, the sidewalk jammed with fast-walking, mask-wearing pedestrians. Reza exited and jogged around the back of the car and onto the sidewalk.

"See you," Azka said as he opened his back door, the much lighter pack in his other hand. "Nice to meet you two."

Denny and his passenger nodded once and the car disappeared into the hazy city, the muffled thumping of rap trailing far behind.

"How about we take a taxi to the port," said Reza as they walked away. "We can check out the protest."

"Good idea," Azka said. "But maybe we shouldn't get too close."

"It might be suspicious if a popular reporter from Jakarta and a known environmental activist from Pekanbaru avoided a protest," Reza said. "I believe these guys have something truly spectacular in mind, and it probably involves a ship, or maybe something at the port. Either way the authorities will be all over it like white on rice, as the Americans say. Even though we paid cash for our bus fare, our faces have been recorded on the bus passenger videos, both onboard and at both of the terminals. We may as well get our cover developed by interviewing a few protesters."

"You're right," Azka said. "Maybe covering this port protest is the best idea. As long as we don't stay too long."

"Couldn't've asked for a better one. Right at the port itself," Reza said as the two passed a nondescript brick building. At face level, the street side wall had the words "Direct Action" brush painted in tall, fat black letters. Underneath the two words was the stencil-sprayed image of an automatic rifle.

He tapped Azka on the arm and said, "Your paper will want a picture of that."

While Azka snapped a few quick shots with his phone Reza excitedly spoke. "Hey! Taxi! Azka, his green light is on. Let's get him."

The taxi stopped for them. The three kilometer ride to the port meandered through the old colonial part of town. It was slated for a major renewal, but the foreign investors had recently acquired cold feet as the economy worsened. During the ten-minute ride Azka counted six similar Direct Action wall murals, four of which were in English, clearly intended as a warning for foreigners. He snapped pictures of them all, a few times asking the driver to slow down which resulted in an unfriendly concert of angry honking horns.

The protest at the main gate had been loud and lively, but the two hundred, or so, protesters they saw earlier from a distance had dwindled to far fewer, several dozen, at most. Men in army uniforms were flapping their arms and excitedly shouting at everyone to leave immediately. Some stragglers lingered, but they soon left, too.

Vehicles approaching the port were turned away. A queue of cars and trucks drove out, no longer delayed by the mass of picketers. The protesters were walking south in groups both large and small.

Shortly before noon a number of anonymous phone calls had been made warning everyone to vacate the port immediately. An analysis of cellular transmissions indicated the call was made from downtown, about a kilometer from the port. It was a congested area populated at that time of day by tens of thousands of residents and urban workers.

The voice of the caller had been electronically altered and impossible to trace. One call was made to the port administrative building's general information number, another to the office of the mayor of Dumai, Khairul Anwar, and yet another to the personal cell phone of the chief of security for the port. Every newspaper and television station in Dumai received the ten-second call, too. All of the calls were the same. The voice stated he was from Direct Action.

Each call emphasized that everyone had less than fifteen minutes to escape from the coming blast. The caller further warned that anyone involved in the destruction of the rainforest would be killed. Then the connection ended.

The phone used was a cheap disposable device sold in countless stores throughout Indonesia. When he had finished his last call he ditched into a filthy, litter-strewn alley. Using a common wrench he carried for work he smashed the phone into small pieces. Then he smashed the pieces into tinier bits. He then kicked the tiny bits of plastic until they vanished into the urban debris.

"Why are they all leaving?" Azka said.

"Let's ask someone," Reza said. He summoned a protester over. He carried a large sign attached to a length of white PVC pipe. The sign read, "My Rainforest is Not for Sale."

"Where's everyone going?" Reza asked. "It's only noon."

"The city administration building," the man said. "The army ordered us to leave. They claimed the port is being evacuated. One of the gate guards said something about a bomb threat. But I'm doubtful. We've heard that one before. I don't believe anything the authorities say."

Passengers, dockworkers, security guards, all of them were streaming out. Some went door to door along nearby streets warning everyone to flee immediately. Most did, but many stayed behind. They were doubtful and unsure if they should risk leaving their businesses unattended. Other than the handful of soldiers who stayed behind to man the gate, which had been left unattended when the port security guards had fled, the port was now vacated.

The protester spoke. "We are few in number. We can't argue with them. I asked one of the soldiers at the gate why we had to leave and he waved his rifle and shouted for me to get moving. I did. Instead we're going to Plan B. We're demanding that the city cut off water and electricity to the port until all forest products are no longer exported."

"How far away is the administration building?"

"Two kilometers," the man said. "Maybe a bit farther. A twenty or thirty minute walk. There will be a huge gathering there. It was just announced. Please join us."

"I think we will," Azka said, as he pulled out his notebook and began an interview with the random protester while walking away from the port gate.

When they were two blocks from the old colonial city administration building the rhythm of drums and chanting reached out to greet them. Three thousand protesters had gathered and more were flowing in from all directions.

The authorities and administrators of the passenger ferries that had been preparing to depart for the Malaysian port of Malacca and elsewhere had directed all passengers to disembark and to leave the port immediately. They had ordered the passengers to get as far away from the port as possible. The staff had, no doubt, added to the mix of people in the growing crowd. Crewmembers busily working on arriving or departing vessels watched the exodus without knowing the reason for the sudden evacuation. Azka took a flurry of digital images on his phone and emailed them to his boss in Jakarta along with a brief summary which he tapped out on his phone with a flurry of dancing fingers.

"You type messages on that phone of yours like a teenager. How you do that so fast?" Reza asked.

"Practice, buddy. Lots of practice. I know a twenty-three-year-old reporter who can type and send text messages while her phone is in her handbag."

"Voice activated, probably."

"No. They don't allow cell phones in court during trials. She practiced so she could send updates from court on her smuggled phone."

"We could use her on our side."

"She is, believe me. Many reporters are, but it's mostly unspoken. The authorities would demand we were fired if we were open about it."

"Oh, they'd do far worse than that."

A group of masked, identically dressed teenagers, boys and girls, scattered into the crowd. All wore blue denim pants and white, long sleeved shirts and red baseball hats. None of the girls wore black hijabs, but those with long hair had it under scarves or tucked under their shirts. With their white respirators the girls looked identical to one another. The boys did, too. Army and police officials who later scrutinized fuzzy CCTV images would be unable to identify any of them.

Their hands were filled with leaflets taken from a box that had somehow appeared on the sidewalk in front of the stately white government building. Within a few minutes the teenagers had vanished and everyone in the crowd had one of the leaflets in their hands. They announced a typewritten warning that anyone found delivering a forest product or assisting in the destruction of the rainforest would face the death penalty. Ominously, it also warned all foreigners to get out of Sumatra by the end of the week. Any foreigners found on the nation's third largest island after that would risk being killed on sight.

Azka took a picture of the threatening flier, emailed it to his boss in Jakarta, and began folding it. Just as he stuck it in his bag a flash of light lit the hazy sky, as if a million bolts of lightning had shot through the air at once. Two seconds later a shock wave struck. It was powerful enough to knock an adult to the ground and terrifying enough to get the growing crowd of protesters scrambling in all directions for cover, once they had regained their footing. Two seconds after that a hideous roar filled the air. It is impossible to accurately describe the explosion of three metric tons of explosives igniting a cargo ship filled with fossil fuel fertilizer. But the resultant mushroom cloud might have been visible across the Strait of Malacca and all the way to Kuala Lumpur if the fires from the rainforest burning hadn't reduced visibility to five hundred meters.

The force of the thunderous blast sent out a shock wave, smashing windows and ruining street vendors' displays in a three kilometer radius. It flattened every building within five hundred meters and was later compared to a small nuclear explosion. Shrapnel from the destroyed ship was found six kilometers away.

The palm oil carrier, the Isola Corallo, was shoved five hundred meters from her berth and had pierced another arriving palm oil carrier, the Victory Prima, amidships. What remained of both ships had capsized and sank, blocking the northern ship canal. Their sailing days were over. The port was devastated and would remain inoperational for more than a year.

CHAPTER TWENTY-SIX

The wet morning mist had mixed with the haze and covered the Tata's windshield in a brown, wet, sap-like smear. It was made worse by the fanning wiper blades. Window washer fluid helped, for a time. As the morning wore on the fog lifted leaving in its wake an ugly brown haze. The hidden tropical sun, which rose steadily over distant Pekanbaru, brought with it a sticky humidity causing a sheen of perspiration to begin dampening the clothing of the three visitors.

With the high price of fuel, traffic was fairly light. David's map from the hotel identified the road as paved, but washouts had reduced long sections to freshly bulldozed gravel, including the section they were now driving. Funding to repave was nonexistent. In fact, logging and mining companies had taken it upon themselves to maintain the highway, a transportation artery critical to their cash-generating operations.

Nearly getting clipped by the speeding and aggressively tailgating motorcycles, cars and trucks was part of the charm of driving on Sumatra. One white work truck had been the only truly frightening close call while driving along the narrow gravel road. The lone driver of that heavily loaded, canvas-covered flatbed was seemingly oblivious to the disaster he nearly caused when he blasted down the center of the rutted road forcing David into a ditch. "Goodness," Shannon had said in her soothing Gaelic accent. "I wonder why he's in such a hurry." Had she known that the truck was bouncing along carrying five tons of freshly stolen weapons and high explosives she would have understood the driver's motivation to get his delivery completed as quickly as possible.

David reversed the truck out of the ditch and drove it back onto the road. They continued climbing the looping switchbacks.

"Let's stop along here, somewhere," Gary said while tapping a few knuckles on the inside of the truck's windshield. It was a few kilometers up the road from the now-forgotten near miss.

"There's a good place to pull over," Shannon said. "Ahead on the left."

"The water in this tributary is an unusual shade of brown. I want to collect some samples," Gary said. He had brought seventy-two pre-labelled four-ounce hard plastic bottles with him on the trip. Half were with him now and the rest at the room. They were designed for the task, a standard size used by scientists all over the world. Their oversized tops would allow Gary to scoop mud or soil inside. The lids, once tightened, would remain airtight indefinitely. But ideally, they had to remain chilled or frozen. The freezer was on the back seat, by the battery, latched but unlocked. Both were covered by a large bent square of cardboard to keep away any direct sunlight and guard from the prying eyes of potential thieves. He would transfer the containers into the freezer when they returned to the truck. "It'll be interesting to find out exactly what's in the water."

"Calling it interesting is the understatement of the day," David said.

It was eight fifteen in the morning and the three had reached the rolling foothills of the Bukit Barisan. Cell phone reception had died many kilometers back. So many streams and rivers flowed from the hills and into the meandering Siak River it was tough to keep track of them all by name. It was also easy for a non-native to make a naming or spelling error. In order to avoid mistakes Gary simply labeled his sample containers by their numerical coordinates using Gary's hand-held GPS device. If it ran low on power it could easily be recharged off the solar generator they had in the back seat of the truck. The best part of the GPS device was that identifying the correct name of each mountain stream could be done at UC Berkeley's Campbell Hall by a graduate assistant. That would be needed before the samples were sent to the commercial testing lab in San Leandro, not far from the university.

David pulled over and stopped. All three got out and stretched. After everyone had been sprayed with mosquito repellant he and Shannon walked to the side of the road to survey a path to the river. Gary reached across the back seat and extracted his large aluminum case and joined them. When Gary closed his door David pushed a button on his key, locking the truck.

The fast-moving stream wasn't far from the road but getting there meant trudging through a field of mud. It also meant first hiking a short distance down a rocky embankment, then mushing through the mud. Both were tasks David and Shannon would find easy, but Gary, with a cane in one hand, wasn't eager to perform.

"David, could you steady me while I climb down that cliff?" Gary asked.

"It's not exactly a cliff," David said with a grin, which faded as a deep rumble grew louder by the second. "But I'll give you a hand."

"Why don't I help you, Gary, while David carries your gear?" Shannon said over the passing roar of a convoy of army vehicles each of which spit gravel against the side of their rental as they passed close. "Why's everyone in such a bloody hurry around here?"

The three paused to watch the six heavy trucks pass and when they had, David spoke. "That sounded like a locomotive. I bet that maniac in the white truck we saw blast down the road earlier pulled over for those soldiers."

"Plus those soldiers didn't appear to be in a very generous mood. If he didn't get out of their way," David said, "he's probably in the river."

"Hey!" Gary said. "What's that?"

"A helicopter," David said as a different kind of heavy rumble filled the sky. He flattened a small map on the hood of the truck.

"More like a bunch of helicopters," Gary said.

"They're above the haze, but heading the same direction as the convoy," David said.

"There must be some serious action in the mountains," Shannon said. "The wind's blowing east. They'll be able to get a clear view from above, long before the troops in the trucks arrive."

"I'm getting nervous out here," Gary said, clinging to Shannon's elbow while he cautiously made his first step down the rocky embankment. "Let's get those sample containers filled and get back on the road. The military is getting restless out here. I'm already eager to get back to the hotel."

"It's barely eight," David said while focusing on his map. "The day is still young. Remember, we're a group of environmentalists. No one'll screw with us. I say we drive into the hills. There's an unpaved road heading west out of Riau Province and into the edge of Western Sumatra. If we roll west on that road, no more than sixty or seventy kilometers, we'll cross lots of small mountain streams and rivers. With the assorted logging, mining, slash and burning and whatnot they'll each provide us with excellent samples. If you look west you can see smoke rising from mountain hotspots off in the distance from here. With the samples from here we can form a nice snapshot of the clearcutting activity all through this central portion of the eastern Bukit Barisan."

"It'll be more than enough for me to write a well-documented presentation," Gary said as Shannon took more pictures.

"Let's get it going, then," David said. He didn't want either of them to know about his relationship with Simmons Hydrocarbon Supply so he kept that to himself. "But we turn back no later than noon. I have to drop off this solar unit along the way to the FedEx office. Time'll be tight. I gotta be there before five thirty. That's when they close."

"Tomorrow," Gary said. "Let's take the Trans-Sumatran Highway north, like we had planned earlier."

"That'll work well. I have to pick up another solar power unit at FedEx tomorrow," David said as he folded up the map, stuck it in one of his oversized denim shirt pockets, and gripped Gary's case. "That'll give us plenty of time to get excellent water and soil samples throughout the central lowlands east of Dumai."

"It'll work out best if we leave the hotel early, before six in the morning," Gary said. He then took step two and slipped on a large boulder. He accidentally smacked David in the ankle with his cane. "Sorry."

"No problem."

"Then if we drive west four or five hours, we'll be back in plenty of time. As long as we don't have to descend very many more cliffs."

After collecting the water and mud samples they returned to the truck. Gary carefully packed them in the freezer along with two small dead fish he found floating in a shallow pool near the bank. They got in and continued west, up more winding gravel switchbacks. They entered what had recently been lush tropical rainforest. Not long ago it was a green and magical land, for eons filled with the various sounds of the many colorful birds and countless kinds of wild animals. Its broad canopy had recently reached high toward the sky, a home for countless forms of life found nowhere else. But it had been transformed into a wasteland. All gone.

It was now burned to the ground, awaiting its new role as a palm oil plantation, like the fingers of the ones creeping up through the many canyons below. As they gained elevation, pulling over now and then to take water and soil samples, the sun came out. The sky directly above became blue, a silvery shade similar to Shannon's eyes. The ever-present haze had finally cleared, at least along the stretch of bumpy road they now drove. For the first time since their arrival in Sumatra they removed their face masks outdoors. It allowed them to enjoy deep breaths of clean air but did little to alter their somber mood.

On the way back down the mountain they stopped at a viewpoint they had passed earlier and got out of their truck. The wind had picked up and as a result the expected buzz of mosquitos was thankfully missing. Their Tata was the only vehicle parked, but the wide space could have held a long caravan of buses and cars. The prominent gaily painted Indonesian Travel Bureau sign that greeted them was made for tourists. It had faded some, but had been there for fifteen years, according to the date printed in the lower right corner. The large sign claimed that on a clear day one could see nothing but tropical rainforest in all directions. It pointed out that on the clearest of days one could catch a sun-reflected glimpse of the Strait of Malacca two hundred kilometers to the east.

The remains of a weather-beaten wooden structure, possibly an old tourist accommodation, sat a short walk from the sign. The bullet riddled wall of the one-story building faced them. The sunlight poured through an opening in the partially missing roof. It was a reminder of a long forgotten battle, most likely between the army and past rebels.

What they could now see in the distance below was a fouled ocean of fire-fed haze nourished by flames raging in the remote foothills. More fires burned in the mountains to the north and south but none nearby. Smoke billowed high above the far off flaming treetops. Although the sky was surprisingly clear and the sun temporarily shined bright where they stood, thick thunderclouds filled the sky and floated east across and above the smoke and the lingering distant haze. The black rainclouds dumped heavily here and there, not as severely as during monsoon season, but typical for late spring.

The land on either side of the road nearby was a ruined and rutted wasteland featuring deep canyons gouged by several years of heavy rain falling hard on the clearcut denuded landscape. The ancient trees along this mountain valley had been cut down and the logs removed. What remained had been ignited, in typical fashion, probably two or three years earlier. Passing trucks overloaded with thick logs sped by, clear evidence that logging operations continued unabated in the distant hills. The Asian elephants, orangutans, gibbons, siamangs, Sumatran tigers, clouded leopards, macaques and the rest of the primates and other wildlife painted in a cartoonish fashion on the old sign had disappeared long ago from this devastated area.

Grasses and small shrubs attempted to reclaim the moonscape, but erosion halted their efforts. Soon the plantations would march through with their tidy monoculture rows of stubby oil palm trees or coffee shrubs. The foreign plantation owners didn't care if the topsoil eroded. Their crops would be fertilizer fed and artificially flourish the modern way on the newly created wastelands. It would be as if the crops were growing on an island-wide sterilized sponge. In fact, insecticides and herbicides would be generously applied to ensure that no other life was allowed to move in.

Animals were not allowed. Each year over a thousand orangutans were clubbed to death in order to remove them from their habitat and prevent them from encroaching into the tidy rows of oil palm trees. Other mammals that strayed onto the plantations were shot or trapped, some sold to zoos around the world.

It was apparent that the road they were on had been regularly repaired. It was an endless process now required each time it rained heavily. The large piles of gravel pyramiding on roadside turnouts were testament to the dire need for constant roadwork.

"Did you guys hear that?" Shannon asked.

"Hear what?" Gary said. Gary's hearing wasn't quite as reliable as it was back when he was in his teens, before the popularity of amplified rock music damaged them. It wasn't quite poor enough to require a hearing aid, or two, but not quite good enough to pick up on the distant rumble from Dumai.

"Maybe thunder. It came from the east," David said. "I heard it, too."

The haze obscured the view of the plains below. It was as if a brown fog covered it all, fed from the fires raging in the foothills not far from where they stood. The vista stretched east from their vantage point for about two hundred kilometers. In addition to the newer oil palm plantations a rich farmland was spread below growing rice, coffee, a wide variety of fruit and an assortment of vegetables, mostly consumed locally. It took eleven minutes for the thunder from the Dumai explosions to pass over the farmland and up the devastated foothills. It only took a few seconds for the mushroom cloud to push aside the haze and appear like a detonated atom bomb in the distance. Therefore, by the time the muted thunder reached their lookout, the dark cloud had expanded fully reaching its maximum size.

"Wow!" David said. "What's that?"

"I have no idea," Gary said. "My guess would be a very large explosion. Maybe even a nuclear blast. It's huge!"

"Where is it?" Shannon asked.

"I can't tell, other than it's to the east," Gary replied.

"Dumai is approximately that direction. A bit northeast. Most of Sumatra's fertilizer is shipped into that port. Most of the palm oil is exported from there, too. Unless a fertilizer ship exploded, which is doubtful, I'd say it was a small nuclear explosion, which is also doubtful."

"Ya got me," Gary said. "We'll read about it when we get back."

"I can get a cell signal in Bangkinang. We'll get the story when we pass through in a few hours."

"It's a very pretty town," Shannon said. "It's small, maybe twenty thousand people. When I retire that's the kind of place I'd like to live."

"If you don't mind wearing a hijab," Gary added.

"He's right," David said. "Some of these small Indonesian towns are old-school Muslim. They welcome visitors, but some don't take too kindly to outsiders moving in, especially infidels like us."

"I'm no infidel," Shannon said. "I was born and raised Roman Catholic, just like my mother and father, and their parents before them, and on and on back to the time of Jesus."

"You mean the Apostle Peter," Gary said.

"Yeah, all the way back to him," Shannon said with a grin. "Maybe I make a better biology teacher than a historian."

"Well, either way I'd suggest we schedule an extended visit to Bangkinang before buying a condo or a home there," David said. "The locals might misidentify you, an obvious European, for someone involved with palm oil, mining or deforestation."

"Wouldn't that be an interesting twist," Gary said. "Speaking of twist, check it out, down and away in the distance. The twisting road looks like it goes into a tunnel, but it's really heading into the haze."

"Weird," Shannon said. She took a few pictures of the illusion.

"Let's get moving," Gary added. "I'd really like to ship these containers back to the United States as soon as we get back to Pekanbaru. David, is there any way we can we stop at the FedEx office and ship them today?"

"I can do that," David said. "Less clutter in our hotel rooms. I'll bring them with me when I pick up today's delivery. Since there's no time for us to pack them properly, I'll ask the staff at FedEx if they could package them all up for us. The glass containers are in your case. I'll ask them to bubble wrap them and seal them tight. I'll drop you two off as soon as we get back to the hotel. If there're no traffic delays I might even have time for a very quick shower."

"That'd be a good idea," Shannon said with a playful smirk. "And it'll be one fewer thing to worry about in case there's a problem of any kind tomorrow."

"I agree," David said.

Then she pointed into the distance toward Dumai. "And by problem, I mean military roadblocks."

"Or in case something like the explosion in Dumai hits the airport in Pekanbaru or Jakarta," David said.

"That would be game over for us," Gary said. "We'd have to swim to Malaysia in order to get home."

"That would be terrible because I can't swim very well," David said.

"If Direct Action blew up the port of Dumai we may consider an early departure," Gary said.

"Good luck," David said. He had read once that during nearly all periods of mass civil unrest the civilian air transportation network is one of the public transportation modes that continues to operate. "There will certainly be flights out, but if things are heating up that much you and a million others will be thinking about getting off Sumatra, too."

CHAPTER TWENTY-SEVEN

"Run, Reza! Run!" Azka was on all fours and ready to get up and scramble. His friend was flat on his back, motionless, his arms spread wide across the paving blocks. Azka moved close. He grabbed his buddy by the shirt and shook hard. "You okay?"

"I'm fine. Give me a few seconds. I lost my wind."

Azka helped him up. "What was that?"

Azka whispered into his friend's ear. "They told me to expect an action soon. Very soon. I had no idea it would be anything like this."

"I need some pictures of whatever blew up for the paper. If I miss this opportunity I'll be in huge trouble."

"Huge trouble?" Reza said. "You and huge trouble go hand in hand. Okay. The port first. Then we need to go to the bus depot. It'll be jammed with people trying to get out of town."

"And others arriving fast. It'll be absolute chaos."

"Let's run straight to the bus depot now," Reza suggested.

"No. Well, yes," Azka said and he tugged on one of Reza's arms. "C'mon. Let's run fast and get as close as we can to the port. I'll skip interviewing anyone. But I do need pictures. We'll go to the bus depot from there."

"The buses will be jammed soon. If we're late we may have to hitch a ride to Pekanbaru."

"No problem. I've done that before," Azka said as he and Reza slowed to a fast walk. They decided that with the dust from the explosion and the thick haze it was impossible to draw enough air into their lungs for jogging.

"You can interview people fleeing," Reza suggested as they fast-walked toward the port.

"Good idea."

It was almost like a repeat of nine-eleven. Sidewalks were crowded with survivors, many covered in brown or white chalky powder, all streaming away from the port. Rescue workers, police, firefighters, soldiers and others, including reporters, were hurrying toward the site of the incredible explosion. Hospitals were placed on alert and told to be prepared for an unknown number of wounded. The Red Crescent Society was activated. Ambulances were streaming in with sirens blaring. All were eager to help in any way they could to perform their vital social responsibilities.

It was approaching quarter to one. Things were happening fast. Soldiers had already blocked access to the port. Twenty minutes after the blast a security zone would be established closing access to all streets within ten blocks of the port. Most people within that zone had either already fled or been killed in the initial blast. The dozens of fires still raging would burn all afternoon. All fire fighters could do was battle the flames from the rubble of nearby structures. It was like a nine point five earthquake had struck.

Anyone approaching the security zone was directed by soldiers to the street leading to the main entrance. Assorted officials and emergency response vehicles queued to gain entry. Now and then a shot rang out, probably directed at a looter.

At this point anyone leaving or entering was frisked. Their faces and ID cards were photographed. Azka and Reza were part of the small crowd of emergency workers that had gathered there but they had no intention of entering. The face images and pictures of each person's identification card were immediately emailed to the regional security office by authoritative smart phone wielding government officials dressed in civilian clothing. Reza took out his cell phone and snapped a few shots of them without their knowledge. Identifying them could come in handy later.

The number of rescue workers was swelling fast but even they couldn't get to the port. As much as they wanted to help, accessing the port was impossible due to the flames and heat. The two turned away and walked to the same pedestrian bridge they had crossed earlier. From that vantage point they snapped dozens of pictures as well as a one-minute long video of the carnage. While crossing the bridge it struck Azka that he may be the only reporter from the Jakarta Post in Dumai. After repeated failed attempts to call his boss in Jakarta Azka changed his mind about leaving Dumai. He decided it would be a good idea to stay behind and report on the events as they unfolded.

Azka dug through his wallet and extracted one of his business cards. He scribbled on it with a pen he pulled from his shirt pocket while Reza stood by in awe.

"Reza, take this. When you get to Pekanbaru give it to one of the desk clerks at the Grand Jatra Hotel. Ask them to deliver it to this man's room. He's an American scientist. I'm supposed to interview him this evening for a story. He needs to know I'll be late getting back to Pekanbaru. If the phones remain out of order here I won't be able to reach him. Could you do that?"

"Of course. But you can't stay here. We have our orders. And besides, the army will not allow reporters anywhere near the port. They'll arrest you if you try to interview anyone. And don't you have another delivery arriving soon?"

"Maybe," Azka replied, unsure if he should get more specific about his foreign contact, even with such a close friend. If for some reason the Indonesian State Intelligence Agency, commonly known as BIN, decided to talk to Reza it would be best if he knew nothing.

Azka was torn between his commitment to Direct Action and his responsibility as a reporter. He stood silently by his friend a minute, thinking.

"Well? We're running out of time."

"Give me a few seconds."

"You're deciding between your job and the revolution, buddy," Reza whispered. "You know as well as I do that you really have no choice. What am I supposed to tell my cell? Am I supposed to tell them you wanted to bump heads with the military and write a story without their approval? They're probably in every newsroom by now. Use your head, man. This is war. The story will be whatever the army wants it to be."

"You're right," Azka said. He tore the card into tiny pieces. "Let's go hop on the bus."

While the two walked south on chaotic Jendral Sudiman, a normally busy avenue which led directly away from the port, they got lucky and hitched a ride in a private car. The driver, a port mechanic fleeing from the blast zone, drove them all the way west on Jalan Hasanuddin which brought them to the bus station fifteen minutes before departure.

CHAPTER TWENTY-EIGHT

With their return tickets on the one thirty bus to Pekanbaru they managed to board without trouble. The bus station was jammed with people, some with tickets and others hoping to catch a bus to anywhere. Some were offering as much as five times the normal fare for a ticket out of Dumai. One man had offered Reza a gold ring. Others, many with panicked expressions, had offered cash. One offered fifty euros. Another pleaded with them to take a hundred United States dollars. They politely declined all offers.

By one twenty the two men were seated on their bus. Before it left, they observed police, military and plain clothed BIN agents milling about the bus depot comparing the faces of passengers to pictures staring back from iPads and similar devices. Others scanned the crowd via CCTV monitors. They flipped through the digital images while they surveyed the moving crowd of passengers. Occasionally they would discover a resemblance and pull someone aside. They would approach them, stare at the passenger's face, then stare at a picture on the screen. Occasionally they would stare again at the passenger. If still unsure whether or not they had a match they would escort the person into an office.

Once inside an interview would begin. Usually the chat would only last a minute or two and the subject would be released without an apology. Sometimes the interviews lasted longer. Other times they would be rough. Suspects got slammed around, some even pepper sprayed or punched. A few were led away bleeding to the Army's nearby 004 missile base for even rougher treatment in an effort to extract names, phone numbers and addresses. The officials needed information fast and nearly an hour after the initial explosion they still had nothing to go on.

They also had their orders: find out who was responsible for the attack and get it done fast. With hundreds killed and many more injured or missing it was the largest terrorist attack in the history of Indonesia. The port of Dumai was destroyed. All buildings within a half a kilometer of the Isola Corallo had been flattened. Structures as far away as four kilometers suffered varying degrees of damage. Windows were reported shattered as distant as six kilometers. A twisted one ton section of the demolished fertilizer-carrying ship was later found two kilometers away.

The force of the collision with the dislodged cargo ship triggered a fuel fire on the caved-in remains of the Victory Prima. More than two hours later firefighters had yet to approach it. The crew somehow had miraculously managed to escape by diving into the water and swimming to shore. Every ship in the Port of Dumai was either on the bottom of the sea or ablaze. The entire port and much of the port district would have to be rebuilt from scratch.

At precisely one thirty-five, as their bus was heading out of Dumai toward Pekanbaru, another explosion rocked the port. The bus trembled, but remained stable and continued. The burning fuel on the Victory Prima had ignited, detonating a shipping container filled with bags of fertilizer. This explosion was huge, too. If not for the initial blast an hour earlier it would have been the largest explosion in the history of the country. The ship split apart and sank within minutes as if it were a shattered child's toy.

The military had now been granted the green light to be as rough as they pleased. Throughout Indonesia basic civil liberties had been suspended following a two p.m. emergency presidential decree. The nation was now in a state of martial law. How officials went about extracting information that might help find those responsible was of little concern to the ruling government. The brutal arm of the military had been unleashed and mobilized throughout Sumatra.

The entire executive board of Walhi and hundreds of radical environmentalists and their supporters were being arrested and rounded up in an afternoon sweep. In response, mass protests had broken out in Padang, Pekanbaru, Palembang and in dozens of other cities, small towns and villages throughout Sumatra. Similar protests on Java and throughout Indonesia were just getting underway. The army was mobilizing to fight. The resistance was preparing to fight back.

CHAPTER TWENTY-NINE

In Medan, Indonesia's third largest city and the largest on Sumatra, an estimated five thousand protesters had gathered at the infamous Tanjung Gusta prison demanding the release of those incarcerated during the afternoon wave of warrantless arrests. It was a prison made famous by the 2013 inmate riot. That action had resulted in the mass escape of two hundred inmates. Protected by sympathetic civilians most of them remained at large to this day. This time, prison authorities and police were under orders to shoot to kill anyone entering or leaving the facility without authorization.

But that prison protest was a mere sideshow compared to the fifty thousand people gathered at the sprawling port facility in nearby Belawan, a ten-minute drive north of Medan. They had gathered for a protest planned days earlier to stop a crude palm oil tanker from berthing and picking up its load. Longshoremen had stopped work and joined in sympathy with the protesters who had massed a distance away by the main gate. Ship guards, port administrators and contractors were all ordered to leave until the army could clear the protesters away.

The acres of concrete alongside the docked ships were usually crawling with men dressed in an assortment of brightly colored coveralls, some on bicycles, others putting back and forth in small motorized carts. The overhead dock cranes that ceaselessly loaded and unloaded containers were silent and still. The heavy trucks that carried containers from the port had been parked and vacated.

A long queue of big rigs snaked for kilometers in an orderly line of diesel power. It started at the port gate and clogged the primary access road through the outskirts of town and half way to the Trans Sumatran Highway. It had caused a monumental traffic jam, which was worsening by the hour. The port itself was now strangely empty for the first time in anyone's memory.

A division of soldiers prevented access to the port. More soldiers were reportedly en route. Hundreds of troops had gathered at the main gate. Although the army was widely suspected of being involved with the notorious premans, the generic name for the violent criminal syndicates controlling commerce in and around Medan, few of the new recruits were active in the illegal activity.

Many of the mostly teenage soldiers were sympathetic to the protesters' cause. Few were from Sumatra, but simmering outrage against foreign exploitation of the nation's land had been spreading everywhere. It had become a unifying thread among the country's highly diverse population. Top ranking officers were concerned that their soldiers may be reluctant to obey an order to advance on the crowd of peaceful civilians. So they remained where they were and awaited further instructions from Jakarta.

Worried about the protesters' safety, hundreds of police officers from Belawan and Medan had gathered, too. More cops from Binjai and other surrounding cities had arrived as well, intending to protect the huge crowd. A historic, deep animosity between the army and the police had once again crystalized. The police had gathered a distance away from the soldiers, who had warned them to stay away from the gate.

At four a contingency of police from both Belawan and Medan moved out on foot. All had their handguns holstered, but many carried rifles at the ready. They passed through the military encirclement warning the army against attacking them or the protesters.

A tense standoff continued throughout the late afternoon. Army barriers went back up. Heavy military vehicles directed their intimidating guns above the crowd. Snipers from both sides were soon positioned on warehouses and rooftops. Agitators on both sides attempted to provoke a battle. They shouted insults at one another. A few rocks and other projectiles were thrown back and forth by agents provocateurs on both sides. The overwhelming majority wanted the protest to remain calm. Those attempting to instigate a battle were immediately stopped, some roughed-up by those nearby. But the line separating the two sides remained respected and somehow held. Most importantly, no shots had yet been fired.

As darkness fell the water supply to the port was turned off. Shortly after that the power to the port went out. Generators soon started humming and the dock area was once again illuminated, not as brightly as before, but enough to see. About that time a long convoy of civilian vehicles arrived, mostly light trucks, maybe fifty vehicles in all. They intended to bring food, water and other supplies to the protesters. Military officials initially refused to allow them to pass. They queued single file in front of the main gate as instructed. Soldiers stood by and watched while approximately fifty police officers armed with automatic weapons held low calmly walked a wedge through the army barriers, thereby allowing the convoy to enter the port.

Among the vehicles entering were five small flatbeds delivering neatly stacked boxes of fresh fruit, including one truck carrying a few dozen boxes of freshly picked bright yellow mangos. In front of the fruit on the flatbed was a two hundred kilo sample of the explosives hijacked earlier that morning. The driver of that vehicle, an elderly employee of a fruit wholesaler, had no knowledge he was carrying explosives. But his passenger did. He was a mine employee and an explosives expert. He was also a core member of Direct Action. It was his day off. He usually spent a portion of it lifting weights at his gym or jogging if the air wasn't too foul. His assignment today was to skip his fitness routine and instead detonate his cargo wherever it would cause the most damage, ideally alongside the port's towering fuel tanks. He was also ordered to escape. A man with his skills wouldn't be allowed to sacrifice himself.

"Stop the truck," he said to the elderly driver after they had slowly passed through the largest section of the crowd. The boxes of fruit had all been distributed by men who had scampered aboard and handed them to willing hands among the protesters. When the fruit was gone the hungry volunteers had jumped off and disappeared into the crowd. All that remained on the truck bed was a steel tool box positioned near the cab. The truck stopped.

"I'll park the truck and join you in a minute," the passenger known only to the driver as Suharto said.

The old man got out. Suharto drove past the crowd. He continued cruising east past the rows of neatly stacked containers and the dock-side open-air warehouses. He slowly moved along the quiet, darkened port until he saw what he was looking for, off in the distance: a white cylindrical storage tank, maybe ten meters tall and fifteen in diameter. When he drew closer he saw the rest of the tanks, all eight of them. He turned off his headlights and slowed. He was in a poorly lit remote area, hundreds of meters from the body of protesters. A small sign on the side of one tank read, "Petrol." He parked at the far side of that tank, close enough so the side of the truck bed grazed its wall. He got out.

The petrol storage tank was one of four located near the far western end of the waterfront. The others were used to store bunker fuel and were close by. The one he parked beside was also an easy stone's throw from a cargo ship that had been nearly filled with logs when the protesters closed the port. He climbed atop the truck bed and inserted a small flashlight into his mouth. He tinkered briefly with an electrical panel located inside the tool box.

When he was through he jumped off and walked back toward the crowd. It was dark so he was careful not to trip over strewn steel cables and thick ropes snaking about. It dawned on him that the haze had lifted, or maybe it was being blown to the south. Sea air filled his lungs instead. It made him smile, thinking of his childhood growing up in the port of Pedang, on the west side of the island. As a child three decades ago the thought that the rainforests would vanish in his lifetime was unthinkable, something few ever considered or mentioned. But today on Sumatra children grew up without ever casting their eyes on a forest. Deforestation had become the first topic of daily conversation.

He thought about how nice it was to breathe fresh sea air and be away from the mine. He continued walking along the waterfront until he reached the crowd. He had paused only once along the way to wave and shout a cordial greeting to a lone seaman standing idly at the stern of the looming log carrier. The seaman watched as the lone pedestrian melted into the distant crowd. He hoped the protest would end soon so he could get a shore pass and tour Medan's red light district, which was his favorite. That was his final thought as he vanished in a shockwave of heat and light.

CHAPTER THIRTY

I
t wasn't only those on the island of Sumatra who were experiencing the impact of a newly awakened population. Tired of watching their rainforests vanish under the relentless and recently accelerating assault of international corporate destruction those living on Java and the other islands had mobilized, too.

That evening protests had broken out in Jakarta. By the following morning graffiti with a stenciled image of a rifle under the words "Direct Action" appeared throughout the capital city.

The two p.m. suspension of civil rights Indonesian President Bambilo Yudhoyono had issued amounted to a formal declaration of war against the insurrection. This granted him the authority to suspend portions of the constitution related to the protection of otherwise constitutionally protected freedoms.

His first order was to direct the armed forces to activate all military reserve units. Recent recruits were pulled out of basic training and placed on alert. His next action was to place military intelligence officers in the newsroom of every newspaper, large or small. Publishers were ordered to allow the officers final authority over anything they posted online or published. In addition hundreds of websites voicing support for the environmental movement were blocked.

While collecting water and soil samples in the mountains David, Gary and Shannon were unaware of the changes. They experienced their first encounter with the new order while on their way back to Pekanbaru. It was close to three thirty. The sun was still high, hidden behind the haze and darkened further by a tower of dark clouds. A typical tropical downpour greeted them as they approached the city. The thunder that hit reminded them of the dozens of military vehicles that had been rumbling past them heading west, probably toward the mines in the Bukit Barisan.

The road sign they just passed advised all who drove by that Pekanbaru was ten kilometers away. But none of them noticed it. Through the fast-sloshing wiper blades and the hazy air all they saw was more rain and the blurry images of flashing lights in the distance. As they drove closer they saw the two red stop signs placed in the center of the road. A flash of lightning followed three seconds later by thunder reminded them that the center of the storm was right above them. In case anyone overlooked the signs, or was distracted by the storm, heavy army trucks were parked haphazardly, blocking the road in each direction, and adding to the surreal scene. Shannon counted seven rifle-carrying soldiers standing by while other soldiers searched every vehicle both coming and going.

"This reminds me of the stories of Ulster my father told me as a child," Shannon said. "Right down to the rain. In fact, the parents in the town where I grew up told their kids the stories of British troops searching cars whenever they wanted."

David slowed, then stopped. There were ten or fifteen cars queued in front of him. At the nose of the line a car was being carved apart by eager soldiers. It was parked off the road, askew. All four tires had been removed and ripped open. Its door panels had been torn off and tossed aside. A portion of the dashboard was on the roof. Bits of the shredded seats were soaked and scattered on the side of the road.

When they drew nearer they observed three skinny men sitting on the ground alongside one another, a few meters away from what had once been their car. They were in T-shirts and shorts, dripping wet, rear ends in the mud. One of them was handcuffed, his head hung low. He had blood streaking down his face and neck, his white T-shirt now mostly red. "Well, we can tell our kids about this one."

"Our kids?"

"Oh, Shannon," David said. "I'm sorry. That was an odd Freudian slip."

"Sure it was."

"Really," David said with a half smile. "I was wondering what these soldiers will think of us. Any ideas, Gary? Hey, Gary?"

They had been waiting in line fifteen minutes. Gary had fallen back asleep. But his slumber was shattered when a baton tapped gently against his window.

"Gary," Shannon said. "Wake up. Roll down your window."

"I'll get the window from here," David said. He pushed the button on his driver's side door which quickly dropped the passenger window. Gary's head flopped at an odd angle and he awakened with a start.

"What the hell?" Gary said.

The baton wielding soldier began speaking to them in Indonesian.

"I'm sorry," David said to the soldier. "We're Americans."

"I'm no American," Shannon interjected in a dismissive tone of voice directed at David. Then she faced the soldier. "I'm a citizen of Ireland."

"What I mean," David said, "is that we only speak English."

"I beg your pardon," Shannon said. "I speak Gaelic, too."

"Americans," the soldier said without losing his officious expression. He shouted something at the other soldiers. Two more came jogging through the downpour to join him.

"I speak English," one of the two newly arrived soldiers announced. He was in his late teens. He stood there a moment, uncertain about what to do with this truck carrying foreigners. It was as if he had spent the morning studying in high school, most likely where he had learned to speak English, then donned his army duds for the afternoon shift. When he had collected his thoughts he barked out an order in a surprisingly high, child-like tone of voice. "Drive to the side of the road and turn your engine off."

David did as he was ordered while the three soldiers followed the Tata at a slow walk. When he stopped the soldiers gathered at Gary's open side window."

"Why are you driving to Pekanbaru?"

"We're scientists," David said with a smile. "The three of us are studying the river water in Riau Province. We're done for the day. Now we're driving to our hotel."

"Please step out of the truck. All of you," he said. As they did he pointed the business end of his rifle toward the front of an army truck. "Stand over there, by the side of the road away from your truck."

The English speaking teenage soldier then jogged away and conferred with an older man, whose dark green uniform shirt was festooned with an assortment of medals and ribbons. He was at least a captain, maybe even a major. He held a black umbrella. It whipped back and forth in the gusting wind but somehow kept his starched shirt and the top of his creased pants dry. David considered that if he was a major there must be something truly spectacular underway on this road.

"Hey! We're getting soaked," Gary said to the soldiers over the rush of the falling rain. "Could we please wait inside our truck?"

The soldier and officer glanced at Gary. Then they resumed their discussion without replying. A moment later two soldiers started rummaging around inside the truck, searching for nothing in particular as they fished through their belongings. When they were finished inside they crawled underneath the truck. One shined a flashlight beam here and there a moment. Then they crawled back out, reported to the officer, and left the area.

"Relax," David suggested to Gary. "This'll pass. A little rain water won't hurt us."

A few minutes went by and finally the young soldier approached while the older officer stood by and stared. "The captain wants to know what you're doing with all that stuff in the truck."

A sense of relief swept over David upon hearing the officer's rank. "Scientific equipment, mostly. A small, battery powered freezer, a solar power unit and a change of clothing for each of us."

"Is that all?"

"Yes. Oh, wait. We do have some food in the ice chest. It's on the back seat. We have river water samples in it, too."

"What about all those gloves?"

"Each time we collect a sample we have to change plastic gloves to avoid contamination. The used ones are in a zip lock bag inside the aluminum case. And that gizmo in the back protects the panels of our solar power unit."

"If it's a freezer, why isn't it cold inside?"

"We partially charged it last night," David said. "Apparently in this heat we'll need it fully charged from now on."

"How many days have you been in the mountains?"

"Just today." David quickly summarized where they had been while keeping tomorrow's plans to himself.

The officer called the young soldier aside and conferred with him. After a few minutes the young soldier returned through the continuing downpour.

"As soon as I photograph the pages of your passports you may proceed."

The two men carefully dug inside their shirts and into their water-tight document bags while walking toward the protective awning behind the military truck. Thankfully, Shannon's documents were with David saving her the trouble of partially opening her shirt in front of the soldiers.

The young soldier took close-up photographs of the documents with a small camera. Then he took facial pictures of the three and a final picture of the front of the truck, presumably to get a shot of the license plate.

The older man spoke through the downpour from a few meters away. "Doctor Reseigh, you and your colleagues are free to leave as soon as you pay the toll."

"Toll?" David said.

"Five hundred thousand rupiah," the captain said. Then he smiled. "I do speak some English. I presume you understand me."

"I understand clearly."

"This is nothing but a highway robbery!" Gary said.

"Shut up," Shannon said. She shot Gary a hard glare David hoped he would never receive. She reached into a front pocket and extracted a wad of Indonesian money she had acquired days ago at the hotel in Jakarta. "It's only forty euros. Here, I'll be happy to pay the toll."

She handed the young soldier a pile of assorted colorful paper notes while the officer stood by smiling a short distance away.

The soldier walked over and handed the cash to the captain, who said, "You are now free to go. Thank you for your cooperation. And be careful."

The three climbed inside the truck. David started the engine and slowly zigzagged his way through the obstacle course of vehicles. The soldiers scurried through the rain and the maze of crookedly parked military trucks in a failed effort to avoid a soaking.

When they were a few truck lengths past the roadblock he noticed in his mirror that the captain was standing in the middle of the highway, staring at them as they drove away. One hand was holding his umbrella, the other gripping a cell phone, pressed tight against an ear as he spoke into it.

"I'm thirsty," Gary said and he opened up his cooler. "Sons of bitches! Those bastards stole our last two cans of ice tea."

"Forget about the cans of tea," David said.

"But I'm dying of thirst back here."

"Drink water instead. It's better for you anyhow. Hey, Shannon. Can you get a signal on my phone or yours? I'd like to know what all the action's about."

"Okay," she said and began fiddling with each phone. "No signal. Maybe it's the weather."

"Weather?" Gary said. "Maybe. But I doubt it. Mine worked fine when we drove by here this morning. Now it's jacked up. The government's probably messed with the cell signals in an effort to keep everyone in the dark about what's really going on."

CHAPTER THIRTY-ONE

After dropping off most of the gear and taking a quick shower, David left Shannon and Gary at the hotel and headed straight to Simmons Hydrocarbon Supply to drop off the solar power unit shipped the day before. The next stop was the FedEx warehouse where he would ship the soil and water samples.

Gary went straight to his room to nap. He was out cold when David left their room. Shannon went to hers to shower, rest and have a drink while watching the television news. It was a little after five.

He still had nearly an hour before it was time to meet Azka. While en route to FedEx he noticed he was down to under a quarter tank of gas. He decided that after meeting with Azka he would join the first gas line he saw and top off the tank for tomorrow.

On the way to Simmons Hydrocarbon Supply he passed two stations that were closed and another that was surrounded by a queue of military vehicles. A police car was parked by the entrance to that one. The officer was standing near the front of his car. A soldier was angrily shoving the lone police officer away with fists to the chest.

The police officer shouted back angrily. A few other soldiers stood by laughing. Then the shoving soldier smashed a fist into the cop's face and he fell to the ground. David slowed, stared, but wisely kept going.

While he fought his way through traffic on the way to his drop off the gas line made him think of his mother and father. When he was a young child they had occasionally told him wild tales of gas lines, the ones that had twice formed back in the seventies when the USA suffered a temporary reduction in oil supplies. He considered it odd the random things that could trigger thoughts of his parents. His mom never mentioned gas lines again, nor did his dad. But as a young child he distinctly recalled hearing them tell tales of gas line parties or gas line study sessions among college students. However, his parents weren't ever college students. Not even close.

His father's life had been cut short early one winter morning twenty-some years ago in a solo motorcycle accident. He dumped his Aprillia Tuono on an invisible sheet of ice coating a Nimitz Freeway overpass while commuting to his bike shop in Fremont. He was going the speed limit but even that was too fast. As a motorcycle mechanic by trade he should have known better and slowed some. But he blasted across at sixty-five. The slick ice slid his Italian motorcycle into a steel light post. Both the red Tuono and his dad were demolished by the devastating impact.

David's mother remarried soon after that but she didn't marry up. His stepfather was a bike mechanic, too, but he moonlighted. He had a nice home and plenty of money. But he didn't get it from wrenching on the side. He got it by selling dope. Lots of it.

One evening he lost an argument over the financial details of a large cocaine transaction. It happened in Oakland, which is where he generally bought the stuff. The two Columbian businessmen who had supplied the product won the argument in an out of court settlement. It was resolved the old fashioned way, with gunshots. The Columbians kept both the twenty-two pounds of cocaine and the previously agreed upon two hundred thousand dollars in cash. The killers had successfully argued that the pile of cash was ten grand short due to a last-minute price hike.

His mother panicked when she saw the report of the murder on the ten o'clock news. Her new husband had always kept large amounts of cash in the home. She suspected the Columbians wanted it and she was right. They were on their way to their Daly City house when she fled with David and the cash. She dumped David off nearby with a cousin and disappeared with a healthy pile of emergency money. She was never heard from again.

By the time David was fifteen he had already met a few of his late stepfather's underworld contacts. When he was sixteen he made his first delivery for them. They were happy to test a trusted minor to move their drugs across town. After that the easy money was too attractive to resist. They showed him the ropes and David caught on quickly. He soon had his own drug operation up and running.

As a teenager he had heard rumors, traced down leads, and followed countless dead ends in an effort to track down his mother.

When he was sixteen he heard from a friend of a friend that his mother had hooked up with a group of Armenian extortionists near LA. The rumor, which he was able to partially verify after a week of detective work, was that the gang was collecting envelopes filled with cash from famous Hollywood actors in exchange for not sharing their unlawful romantic activities with the media. Her responsibility was to photograph the activity, which generally occurred in cars parked in alleys or other secluded places. The gang would then sell the photos and negatives to the celebrities. She took excellent photographs but played no role in assisting the gang with collecting the cash.

David immediately cut school, stole a car, and drove to Glendale to investigate. It was not only another dead end, but to make matters worse, while on his way home, his stolen car was stolen out from under him by what a witness had described as three heavily tattooed Mexican men.

It happened at a gas station and market south of the Grapevine after he had just filled the gas tank with his last remaining hot credit card. The car was a beautiful, black, three-year-old BMW. He had hot-wired it from a dark corner of the parking garage adjacent to the Century 20 Daly City movie theater.

The car was then boosted from him while he was inside shopping for some cold drinks and packaged snacks for the long drive home.

He had, of course, charged the snacks and fuel on the stolen credit card. The theft of the BMW forced him to hitch a ride to his new home in Daly City with his lunch, a liter of water, and little else to offer him comfort other than his ever-present calculus textbook. In the May heat the water didn't last long. Neither did his childhood dream of tracking down his mother. While standing on the hot onramp with his thumb out he decided it was her turn to come and find him.

He was pondering the childish logic of that youth-driven decision, as he had a thousand times before, when he saw the blue FedEx sign. He drove past it two blocks and the dark blue Simmons Hydrocarbon Supply sign appeared before him on the same side of the road.

The warehouse was exactly where he thought it would be. He drove around the building and straight to the back loading dock as instructed. The workers were expecting him. One saw him drive up and he yelled inside for another worker.

The two warehousemen jumped off the platform and quickly unloaded the equipment from the Tata in a minute flat. They left the battery on the floor by the back seat.

"How about the battery?" David said.

"Keep it," one said. "You may need it."

"Thank you," David said. He waved goodbye to the two men and they waved back. The stop had taken under three minutes. He would easily make it to FedEx before they closed.

He then pulled away and drove there. He turned into the lot and parked by the door immediately focusing on the task at hand and forgetting about the thoughts of his mother and father.

He got out, opened the back door to the truck and grabbed the portable freezer. First he placed it on the asphalt. He then stacked Gary's aluminum case on top of it. With a grunt he picked up both, remembering to use his legs like the cartoon man in the diagram posted to the door to his university lab always instructed him to do. He closed the truck door with a modest toe kick and walked to the front door.

He opened the steel push release with one hip and rotated his way inside happily winning the race with the fast closing glass door. He walked inside and set the ice chest and case on the floor by the counter.

"Hello," David said to the exhausted looking clerk in the friendliest tone of voice he could summon. "I'm Doctor David Reseigh and I'm here to pick up a package. It should be another solar power unit, just like the one from yesterday."

"Good afternoon, Doctor Reseigh," the clerk said without so much as a hint of joy. "I'll have it brought out here for you."

The clerk pushed his way through a scarred, waist-high wooden door and shouted something out loud in Indonesian. All David understood were the words "solar power" and "batteries."

When he returned he spoke again, in English this time. "You have another package delivery scheduled to arrive tomorrow. You're getting to be a regular customer," he said.

"That's field work," David feebly replied. "You never know what'll be needed."

"Yes, I understand. But be aware of something. As you probably know, Indonesia may soon be under martial law. The president announced an emergency decree several hours ago. All flights into and out of the country could be disrupted. They're subject to fuel availability and other unimaginable variables. We were just informed that if we have martial law the TNI may borrow any plane on Indonesian soil for temporary use in any manner they see fit."

"I've been in the mountains all day. I hadn't heard about any of this."

"It's been on the news. An explosion sank three ships at the port of Dumai this afternoon."

"I'll check the news when I get to my hotel. And what's the TNI?" David asked.

"The army."

The thoughts in his mind were flashing around like an August sheet lightning storm over Arizona. What happened in Dumai? And had the rebellion spread? Was it something more than just the plantation attacks which had been occurring on Sumatra? Martial law meant the army would be running the country. But that was impossible. The newly elected president was the one who made the declaration. That meant the TNI was likely pulling his strings. If he wanted to remain in office much longer he had to watch every step.

None of the three had used their cell phones all day, other than occasionally using them as cameras while out collecting samples. They hadn't heard any news at all other than a brief remark from a hotel clerk who had mentioned something about the military taking control.

"I also have a shipment to send," David said to the clerk. "Most of it's in this ice chest. Some containers are in this aluminum case, too. This ice chest, well, actually it's a freezer, is battery powered. I need to bring it with me to keep my samples chilled, and in case I catch any fish. I'll have to keep everything cold so they can be tested later. Would it be possible for you or your staff to package the bottles in a suitable container such as a small ice chest? I'll be happy to pay any fee."

"Sure. We keep styrofoam ice chests for shipping food and medical supplies on hand. We close to the public in a few minutes. However, we can easily have it wrapped and packaged in dry ice before the nine p.m. departure flight."

David spent a moment transferring all the sample containers from the freezer to the floor near the counter. There was no water in the freezer, but even empty it was heavy. He had poured the water out in the parking lot of the hotel but he still needed two hands to pick it up and carry it.

He handed the clerk a piece of paper with a Berkeley, California, address on it. "This is the address." He then patted the ice chest like it was a pet dog. "That's all I need shipped."

The clerk tallied up the bill and told him the cost.

David handed him a stack of rupiahs. "Thank you for everything."

"No problem. I'll see you tomorrow afternoon," the clerk said. "Remember, the plane isn't scheduled to arrive until three in the afternoon. But it takes a few hours for packages to clear customs and arrive in this warehouse. Generally packages from the daily flight can be picked up before we close for the day. You might want to call before you drive here in case there's been a delay of some kind. Our phone number is on the receipt."

"I will. Thanks."

It was five forty when the two young warehousemen loaded the solar power unit and four new batteries into the back seat of the truck. It was a tight fit alongside the aluminum case and freezer.

Time was running fast. He was cutting it close. They had stayed ten minutes after closing time to help him. That left him twenty minutes to meet Azka. No problem, he thought. As he was backing out he glanced at the row of batteries on the back seat. Five of them. He realized that all four of the new heavy batteries had white crosses drawn on them. His mind raced and he could feel his pulse thumping through the palms of his hands as they gripped the steering wheel. It raced even more when he checked his side mirror and caught a glimpse of one of the warehousemen aiming his cell phone at him and snapping a picture of his truck as he pulled into traffic.

CHAPTER THIRTY-TWO

At precisely six David drove slowly past the university. All he could think about was that he had another shipment coming. It was probably another solar power unit, too. It was most likely packed with cash and gold. That meant he had to think of an explanation why they needed three solar power units when they hadn't touched the first one. Two could easily be explained. He could claim one malfunctioned or got stolen. But three? That wouldn't be credible. He decided to worry about that when the time came.

There was no time to stop at the hotel and retrieve his cell phone. That left him feeling vulnerable, unable to contact Gary or Shannon in an emergency. Worse, the gas tank was well under a quarter tank and he had yet to pass a filling station that was open. Deal with that later, he decided. First things first.

The usual bench where he had in the past met Azka was filled by a row of four young women, three chatting to one another, the fourth tapping on her phone. All wore dark blue scarves. Probably college students, he thought, most likely not interested in joining the loud crowd of protesters assembled by the old, stone administration building. Trees blocked his view but there appeared to be hundreds of them chanting some catchy slogan in Indonesian.

Where was Azka? He slowed even more, edging closer to the curb but there wasn't enough room to park. A horn from someone a few cars back blasted angrily and the car behind him followed suit with a few toots of its own. Rather than block traffic by stopping and waiting he decided to drive around the block and make another pass by the campus.

At six oh six he drove by again. An army truck was now parked near the bench and the girls had vanished. About a dozen soldiers had disgorged through the open back canvas flap and were standing by, seemingly unsure of what to do next. Two additional army trucks, the same type as the first, were pulling over. A few young male faces peered out from under the canvas which shaded the back. A bottle tossed by a distant someone smashed against the hood of the parked army truck spraying bits across the street in front of him. David swerved around the debris and hit the gas.

Just then, he saw a man jogging along the sidewalk, on the opposite side of the street from the action. It was Azka. With an arm waving and his head turned toward the truck he nearly bonked into a street sign planted in the center of the walk. Still waving he dodged left, sprinted around the steel pole and ran into the street. David pulled into the middle lane and slowed, then stopped, smack dab in the center of the three-lane road. A motorcyclist's fist banged on the side of his truck followed by an angry unintelligible shout. A car's horn honked and more angry beeping followed. David ignored it all, and with all the other horn honking and miscellaneous street noise so did everyone else. He popped open the passenger door from the inside. Azka hopped in and David hit the gas once more.

"Far out," David said with a grin. "You're here."

"Huh?" Azka replied, oblivious to the meaning of the anachronistic Americanism. "Far what?"

"Never mind. Are we going to your grandmother's house?"

"No. I've just been informed that someone important wants to meet you. I have to take you to him."

"No thanks. I already know you. That's plenty."

"They're adamant," Azka said. "I just got off the bus from Dumai twenty minutes ago. A contact met me at the city bus stop after I arrived. He gave me a lift here. Well, he dropped me off a couple of blocks back."

"Have you read the news?"

"No. I've been sitting on the bus for nearly five hours. I haven't heard any news the whole time. Fill me in on the latest."

"All I know for sure is that the military is calling the shots."

"I presumed that would occur soon."

"A clerk at the hotel said the army has seized power."

"Exactly. The contact told me that with martial law it's too dangerous to have the money pass through so many hands. So they've decided to snip me out of the loop. It makes sense."

"It's not martial law unless the military actually takes power," David said.

"But they either will soon or they already have," Azka replied. "No matter what President Yudhoyono says to the media, they're the power in my country now."

"Azka," David said. "I don't want to meet anyone. I've known you a long time. I only trust you."

"It's too late. I'm sorry, David. The army is following our moves."

"How do you know?"

"I didn't take the bus alone. I went with a friend of mine. He's from Direct Action. The army arrested him when he got off the bus. They ignored me and went straight to him. I kept walking out of the station as if I didn't know him. I hated to leave him but I had no choice."

"Screw this. If they come after us I'll lose them in traffic."

Azka smiled and spoke. "I think you're overreacting. My contacts are good and decent people, deeply committed to our cause. You'll like them. I'll tell you when to turn."

Azka directed David to execute a series of lefts and rights. After a few kilometers the streets of the poor residential neighborhood narrowed. The pothole filled two-lane asphalt roads soon became meandering muddy two-tracks. Traffic thinned, the vegetation thickened and a blue Proton which he hadn't noticed before now hung close. They turned down a dark side street and bumped along, dodging a few stray pedestrians and the worst of the deep potholes. A white robed young man with a cell phone pressed to his ear stared at David as he passed. A terrified calico cat with a missing tail crossed the street and scampered into some dark foliage.

"Pull over here," Azka said.

David pulled off the road and onto a bumpy stretch of mud alongside a strip of grass bordering a modest, two-story wood home. Narrow puddled paths bordered the cratered lane on each side. He stopped, barely off the left side of the road. Large leafy trees lined the road offering shade to the yards in front and to those walking by. It was a residential neighborhood, but in this shabby part of town the homes weren't built close to one another. It was like those in a typical poverty-stricken part of any American city or town.

The haze had cleared, some. The lights from taller buildings several kilometers away were visible in the distance; he wondered why. Did the wind change direction? Were the fires dying down? Had David glanced at the sky he would have witnessed an unusual sight for a late May evening in Pekanbaru. The brightest stars, and Jupiter, too, were actually visible. It was the first time they'd popped into view in weeks.

The home they parked by was similar to the others along each side of the street. It was constructed from some kind of tropical wood, built on four rows of thick wooden legs which raised the bottom of the first floor of the structure about head high. It was elevated to protect against flooding, as were the other homes in this flood-prone neighborhood.

170

It was nearly seven and the sky had grown dark. A dim porch light struggled to illuminate the deck and tried to shine on the stone footpath bisecting the lush garden growing in front. Less than a meter from the two parked vehicles a variety of different flowers bloomed. Although he was knowledgeable about tropical flora it was too dark to determine exactly what they were. All he could tell was that they were beautiful. Two large curtain-covered windows guarded each side of the green door. David saw the dark curtain covering the large window on the right move slightly. A slice of a man's face briefly appeared through the gap. A second later the face vanished and the curtain went still, matching the one covering the window on the left of the door.

As soon as David parked he saw that the beat-up Proton sedan which had been following them had nosed close behind his truck, stopping in the muddy tire ruts alongside the same plot of grass. Its headlights went dark and its engine went silent. Through his side mirrors David watched a young man climb out the driver's door and a much older man with a long, wispy white beard get out the front passenger door. Both doors quietly closed.

David turned his headlights off and shut down the engine, but left the key in the ignition. Two husky men he hadn't noticed before appeared out of nowhere and filled the narrow dark space between the two vehicles. Both stood as solid and still as large boulders. The two from the car joined them and the four conversed a moment. Before opening his door David leaned to the side and spoke quietly to his passenger. "I don't like this one bit."

"Relax," Azka softly said. "He's an imam. Not mine, but a very good friend's. However, I know him well and he knows me. He's a good and trustworthy man, well respected among his friends and followers."

David got out of the truck and remained by his door. Azka got out, too, and walked around, past the front of the truck to the driver's door. He stood by David with a nervous smile directed nowhere in particular as the old man in the robe approached.

CHAPTER THIRTY-THREE

In the chaos that followed the fuel tank explosion in Belawan the protesters panicked and instinctively fled toward the main exit gate. The faster fleeing protesters pushed and shoved their way past the slower ones. Some fell and were trampled in the scrambling throng. They ran in a mass toward and through the main body of soldiers who had assembled there earlier.

They squeezed through the narrow gaps between the parked military vehicles, a few at a time, but only a small number of them made it past before a second fuel tank exploded, then a third. Soon all of the rest of the tanks buckled in the heat and collapsed, adding fuel to the growing maelstrom of flowing flame.

The burning fuel poured off the dock and into the surrounding sea, igniting a berthed ship, then another. In a matter of minutes both exploded. Then the fire grew, reaching out and touching a third ship, this one anchored hundreds of meters out. It, too, caught fire but by then the crew had safely abandoned ship. The sky was illuminated in brilliant hellish blazes and although the protesters were far enough away it heightened their sense of terror.

As the trapped mass of protesters became bottled up at the gate, someone tossed a large stone over the parked troop carriers. It struck a soldier in the face. He fell to his knees where he screamed through bloody hands. When the other soldiers saw him they fired in the direction of the attack, killing many, wounding many more. The police returned fire and a fierce shootout began.

Word of the port battle soon spread to nearby Medan where an enraged citizenry took to the streets. On the western edge of Medan an army vehicle en route to the port was stopped by a burning barricade. The six soldiers inside were set upon by the gathered mob. Two were beaten to death. The other four fled for their lives leaving a path of strewn army clothing trailing behind them like Hansel's bread crumbs.

With most of the police protecting the protesters the rioters soon owned the city, at least for the time being. They delivered punishing blows to anyone and everything they deemed foreign. Members of Direct Action and their sympathizers quickly steered the crowd's anger toward those profiting from the deforestation. Warehouses and offices related to lumber and wood pulp exporters, coffee wholesalers, palm oil traders and mining companies were hit the hardest. Chinese-owned businesses were set ablaze. Workers at American fast food restaurants fled when their diners were set upon and destroyed. The offices of foreign oil companies were ransacked and torched.

The roads leading to Soewondo Air Force Base were blocked. It was located near downtown, close to the center of the unrest. It was largely left unprotected when half of the security force guarding the base was deployed to the port. It was quickly overrun. Only vehicles leaving were allowed through the gate. To slow the arrival of military reinforcements the air traffic controllers were pulled from their stations and sent home. The lights were cut, and mask-wearing rebels with RPGs were photographed by the runways, the images emailed to the media. The message was clear.

At eight p.m. Kuala Namu International Airport, located on the far eastern edge of the city closed. Thirty minutes earlier the electric power had gone out for ten minutes. Then it came back on. A weary public long accustomed to occasional power outages thought nothing of it. There were only two more scheduled arrivals at the small airport. One was cancelled and the other diverted to Pekanbaru. Airport authorities made no move to use emergency generators. They decided to resolve the issue overnight, as usual, and have the seemingly routine power glitch fixed by morning.

During that brief power outage a three-member Direct Action unit secretly scaled the perimeter fence. The airport police officers could have used their highly effective night vision goggles to spot them but the costly Russian-made devices were stolen so frequently the few in their possession remained locked safely in the weapons arsenal.

Under the cover of darkness they moved fast, set their explosives and fled. One of the devices they planted tore through the underbelly of a parked Japan Airlines A320 passenger jet. It caught fire and was soon engulfed in flames. The additional devices detonated a minute later. They ruptured two massive fuel storage tanks which sent flaming aviation fuel flowing across the north end of the runway. There were no injuries reported from any of the explosions.

An anonymous phone call later determined to have been made from a cellular device located within the passenger terminal warned of the existence of ten additional explosive devices. The caller claimed each had been hidden throughout the passenger terminal. They would go off at ten-minute intervals. Under normal circumstances it would take several days to perform a thorough search. The caller identified himself as a member of Direct Action. There were no additional explosives, but the terminal was vacated while a search was performed. With the damage to the fuel storage tanks the airport remained closed for a month.

Rioting and mass unrest had also broken out in the west coast port city Pedang, and in Palembang to the south. In each case propagandists from Direct Action spread leaflets and cash to ensure the popular anger was focussed on those ruining the rainforests. The flames from burning cities had replaced the waning forest fires. They had also ignited the spirits of a long defeated population. They believed that the ugly epoch of economic neocolonialism was coming to a close. No Sumatran wanted the forest clearing to continue. Yet until now they believed they had little choice but to stand by and watch their forests disappear. The foreign dominated decimators of their homeland arrogantly believed Sumatra would remain their wholly-owned plantation forever. However, for the first time a popular-backed resistance, led by Direct Action, had made them consider otherwise. And it wasn't only on Sumatra.

The CEO of the WWF, who had been in Jakarta for the environmental conference, was found dead in an alley not far from his room at the Marriott. As an avid jogger he rarely missed an opportunity to run. The quiet, cool, pre-dawn hours were the best time for jogging in Jakarta. Police theorized that someone knew this and followed him, fatally striking when the opportunity arose. The note nailed to his face was the same as the others. It was well known that he had made few friends during the conference after he had shocked attendees by proclaiming, "Palm oil isn't the problem. Non-sustainable palm oil is what we must fight against."

In Jakarta a small motorcycle pulled alongside the Mercedes carrying the Minister of Justice, Abdul Asad. With motorcycles constantly filling any gaps in the hurried traffic neither he nor his three bodyguards nor his long-time chauffeur batted an eye as they regularly zipped past his black luxury car. The heavy slap he heard when one of them passed wasn't the first time a passing bike had bumped them.

He was well aware of the rioting that had broken out in Sumatra. In fact, that was the reason the minister was leaving work so late. The hacking attacks on government websites had become more than a nuisance. Defending against these digital invasions was beginning to drain tech-savvy intelligence officers and resources away from more useful activities, primarily domestic spying. He had to curtail cell phone eavesdropping activity. In fact, when the Dumai explosions were reported he decided to simply disrupt all cellular traffic on Sumatra and blame it on the private phone networks.

The idea that Direct Action would attack him while driving home from work in the very heart of Jakarta on that beautiful Tuesday evening hadn't crossed his mind. As he fanned through a binder marked "Top Secret" the idea that he would need a bomb resistant vehicle hadn't crossed his mind either. An instant after the magnet bomb detonated, the minister and the other occupants of his car were killed. The motorcyclist and his passenger felt the shock wave. It rocked their small 250cc Yamaha but not enough to knock it down or hinder its escape.

Early the following morning seven additional magnet bombs hit their targets. One took out the Chinese Indonesian owner of Royal Golden Eagle International, which owned Riau Andalan Pulp and Paper. It was the largest pulp and paper company in Indonesia. Another took out the regional operations manager of Chevron. The CEO of Asia Pulp and Paper and his driver lost their lives in another attack.

The other blasts hit a host of highly paid palm oil executives. This wave of carnage occurred over a ten minute period during the peak of the morning commute. With the exception of an army general, who survived when the device intended for him instead detonated on his bodyguard's car, the targets were all top-level executives and their staff. None of them survived. This time anonymous phone calls were not made. It was obvious who had struck.

A forensic analysis of debris fragments by specialists from Interpol and the British intelligence agency, MI5, would reveal a striking similarity between these explosive devices and three magnet bombs used in Belfast the previous April.

CHAPTER THIRTY-FOUR

The old robed man walked slowly toward the truck. He had a decided limp. The two boulders remained where they were while the younger driver walked directly toward the elevated home. He climbed the stairs two at a time and quickly crossed the wide, covered, wrap-around porch. Upon reaching the door he kicked off his shoes, opened the door without knocking, and disappeared inside without fully closing the door behind him.

David glanced down at an unusual flowering plant. With the additional light he noticed that one of the flowers in front was a pink lotus. He moved in and squatted low for a closer look.

"Doctor Reseigh, I presume," the older man said, interrupting his flower inspection. The two big men remained in the shadow behind his truck. The fact that the robed man knew his name made David's interest in the flower vanish and his heartbeat race fast.

The man approached with short, clumsy strides and an outstretched right hand. A wide grin had appeared. David noticed several of his front teeth were missing. The ones remaining were yellow and crooked. But he had a difficult-to-describe aura of peace and tranquility about him. It was enhanced by his white taqiyah; the short rounded white cap on his head. The white robe reaching down to his brown sandals matched his beard and served to further soothe David's rattled nerves.

David shook hands with him, realizing right away that the thin bony fingers he clasped would snap apart if he squeezed too hard. He was skinny, short, and weighed no more than fifty kilograms, maybe as few as forty-five. The imam looked David straight in the eyes. He spoke perfect English, his voice high pitched, but clear and commanding. "My name is Imam Hasbullah Ali. I've heard nothing but good things about you and your work. I'm happy we finally get to meet one another. I believe we must have a talk. Would you and our good friend, Azka, please come inside?"

David shot a glance at Azka, who nodded back.

"Sure," David said. Then he followed the imam as he began walking down the muddy path toward the door. "Imam Hasbullah Ali, I'm very pleased to meet you, too. But I must admit I haven't heard your name before."

The imam spoke without facing David. "Without even meeting we've recently become very good friends, let me assure you."

David hadn't met an imam before in his life. It wasn't quite the same as meeting the Pope, who he hadn't met, either. He had no idea how he should address him so he stuck to the full name, just to be safe. "Since we're such good friends, Imam Hasbullah Ali, please call me David."

"Thank you, David," he said with a saintly smile. "And you may address me as Imam Hasbullah."

"Imam Hasbullah, I have some valuables in the truck, things I shouldn't leave unattended," David said as they began climbing the stairs. As soon as he spoke a light flashed across the muddy path and onto the weedy front yard. He froze momentarily when he realized someone had just opened the back passenger side door of his truck which activated the overhead light.

"It's okay. Come. Let my men carry your things. I've asked them to bring your batteries in the house. Then we'll all sit and enjoy some tea. Would that be agreeable to you?"

"Yes, of course," Batteries? My men? David knew full well he had no other choice but to follow along. When they reached the open door everyone removed their shoes and went inside, all except the two who removed the batteries from the truck. When they each had two in their arms, one of them gently toed the back door of the truck closed, extinguishing the light. After glancing up and down the street they, too, walked across the yard, up the stairs, and onto the porch. With their shoes on they entered the house and placed the batteries on the floor near a short table. Then they stood there and waited for further instructions.

"Have a seat on the couch," the imam said.

David surveyed the room. The long leather couch sat on the left side of the main floor, against the wall opposite from the steep stairway leading to the upper floor. He stood on stained dark hardwood which went wall to wall and through the central opening leading to a kitchen. He noticed two women there. One was boiling water, most likely for the tea, the other busily chopping something with a kitchen knife.

The white ceiling was so high a ladder would be required to change the three bright light bulbs beaming from the exotic bronze fixture attached at the center. A wide wood table was in front of the couch, close enough so David knew his knees would bump against it when he sat. It was covered with newspaper, the words printed in Indonesian. An assortment of mechanics' tools were spread on one side atop a pile of folded canvas sacks. The wall above the couch featured three large framed pictures of bearded men and smaller pictures of what were likely members of the family that lived in the home. The hands of a simple wall clock pointed at seven and ten.

The living room had been empty when they walked in, but David was aware of footsteps coming from the floor above. More than one set. Possibly three or more.

He sat on the couch, then Azka sat beside him. A woman came out of the kitchen with a metal folding chair and positioned it so Imam Hasbullah could sit across from the two. She then scooted back into the kitchen.

"I can no longer sit on a low couch," Imam Hasbullah said as the two strong men silently moved two of the four batteries from the floor to the table. "It's my tired old back."

The imam made a facial gesture at the two men who then went back outside without a word. They walked down the steps to somewhere unseen. David noticed a fat bulge under the back of the loose-fitting black shirt worn by the last one out. A handgun. The two men were armed. Those upstairs most likely were, too.

"I'm not much of a mechanic, David. So while you two open the batteries, I'll tell you why I know so much about you. Then I'll explain our situation so you can better understand our tactics."

The tea arrived at the same time as the two began disassembling the batteries. "Enjoy your tea. It's locally grown."

David and Azka thanked him.

The imam took a sip and began speaking. "For obvious reasons I'll not go into deep detail about our operations. But I'll summarize by saying we have supporters throughout Indonesia. In Pekanbaru, Medan, and in every major city on Sumatra we have alert eyes and ears reporting to us. It wasn't hard for us to suspect that the mysterious American money and gold was being brought to us by, well, an American."

"It could have been anyone," David said. "It could have been a Saudi prince or a disgruntled Chinese man from Singapore."

"Have you heard of Occam's razor, David?"

"Yes," David said. "It means the answer with the fewest assumptions is generally the correct one."

The imam grinned. "The next question we asked was, 'How many Americans are in Pekanbaru right now?' The answer is, as you know, not very many. So finding the solution to our little puzzle was surprisingly simple. We asked ourselves, 'Which American in this city fit the proper timing and had access to our organization?' A friend of ours working at the airport provided the final link a few hours ago. It was the batteries. There can only be one person. You. Things moved fast at that point."

"I haven't even been on the island for much more than a day."

"Once we began our investigation, finding out it was you took fewer than twenty-four hours."

"I'm very favorably impressed with your organization," David said. He thought of the picture-taking warehouseman a moment, then tossed a glance at Azka, who shrugged.

"Besides the guy driving the car you're the only person I spoke with since arriving in Pekanbaru," Azka said. "That's not counting the few I've interviewed." Then he realized it didn't matter. He had no doubt been under surveillance since the moment he delivered the imam his first share of David's seed money weeks ago. The imam was trying to save him, a fellow Muslim, from embarrassment.

"Oh, we were able to make our conclusions without the help of your friend, Azka. We would have asked him but we knew he was out of town today. If asked, he certainly would have been honest with us. However, I'm happy we didn't have to tarnish the friendship and trust the two of you obviously hold for one another. But the larger struggle may at times supersede mere personal relationships. You should understand this."

"I do. Why do you mention this?"

"From now on you will deal entirely with us."

David tried to speak but the imam held up a hand.

"Let me explain. We are called by many names, depending on the country," Imam Hasbullah said. "Some call us terrorists, others call us freedom fighters. We think of ourselves as the House of Islam, the base from which actions supporting our people emanate. The term we use for this is Darul Islam. We've been active on Sumatra for more than seventy-five years. Recently we've been gaining thousands of new members each week. The fog of hopelessness which has hung over our people since the foreign economic domination intensified is finally dissipating. But with that said, you and I are bound as one in our struggle to save Sumatra and the few remaining square kilometers of rainforest scattered throughout Indonesia. Therefore, if we have differences, let's put them aside."

"No problem. I was well aware that the funding I delivered went to a host of both Islamist and secular organizations. I've been advised by Azka that the leftist Democratic People's Party as well as Wahdi and a wide range of other organizations have been receiving a slice of the pie."

"The disbursements to our secular supporters will continue," the imam said. "Let me further explain our position. Then, hopefully, you'll understand."

A landline phone inside the kitchen rang. A short time later one of the women from the kitchen entered the room and filled all the teacups. She then whispered briefly to the Imam in Indonesian. He smiled and rubbed his bony hands together like a delighted teenager.

When she left the room he continued. "Let me tell you a story. Several years ago the Indonesian government invited five thousand imams to go forth throughout Indonesia and educate people regarding the horror of deforestation. I joined them out of my duty to my people and for our country. Many of my associates joined as well. After several months trying to help the government in this noble effort it became quite clear that we had been duped by the military and their paymasters, the transnational corporations that owned the growing plantations. We observed that the clearcutting and forest burning hadn't slowed one bit. We could plainly see that the people supported our efforts to stop the forest clearing, yet the cutting of the rainforests had accelerated, not only on Sumatra but throughout Indonesia.

"It was obvious that the army was more interested in protecting the plantation owners, loggers and miners than in slowing the destruction. We, the imams, were suspicious from the start and weren't one bit surprised when foreigners, protected by the army, increased the forest burning and expanded the plantations right before our eyes. For that reason the effort failed. My fellow imams and I quit. The recruitment of other imams came to a halt when none responded to further government requests."

"Can't the civilian sector of the government do anything?"

"Don't forget for a minute who holds political power in this so-called democracy. It's the army. And the army does whatever the foreign interests tell them to do. It may sound fantastic, but it's true. However, social and religious authority in Indonesia are held by us, the imams. On Sumatra the people often turn to us for counsel and guidance. It's a delicate balance. But the army is now angry and the scales are at risk of tipping, one way or the other. That is partly why you and I are meeting tonight. There is another reason, but I'll get to that in a few minutes. Please bear with me."

"It makes sense," David said. He now better understood the respect and power the imams held among the common people. One question remained unanswered. "Why not attack the army?"

"We're very cautious about that. It's a den of snakes we try not to agitate. We walk around them, if possible. Even when we conduct operations we try our best to never injure or kill soldiers. Although we sometimes buy or take arms and other supplies from them, we don't want to unnecessarily inflame the armed forces."

"I bet they're spread thin," David said thinking a moment about the vast size of the island. Sumatra is the sixth largest island on Earth. It's larger than Iraq or California, still heavily forested in the mountainous west, perfect for scattered guerrilla armies to vanish unseen. In fact among the six largest islands in the world, three of them, New Guinea, Borneo and Sumatra, are part of Indonesia.

"More so with the news delivered to me just moments ago," the imam added.

"What happened?" Azka asked.

"The seaport of Belawan has been destroyed."

"The entire port?" David asked.

"Details are slim. A large fuel storage tank exploded there less than an hour ago. From what little news we hear it appears two ships have been destroyed and a third is ablaze. Soldiers may have opened fire on protesters. Police protecting the protesters have fired back. A riot has started in Medan. Chinese businesses are being attacked. It's chaos. The army is asking foreigners to leave the city for their own safety."

David listened while prying on a panel that wasn't coming apart properly. Azka stared at the imam with his hands on his taqiyah and his eyes wide open.

The imam continued. "If this is true our goal is one step closer. Our primary target has long been foreigners and their stooges. We have no qualms about delivering them to their darkness."

David thought of the nails hammered into the heads of dozens of common laborers, most likely all of them Indonesians and Muslim. Then he thought of the macaques and orangutans and the thousands of unique forms of life fast screaming into extinction. He was also well aware he was a foreigner, an infidel, to many. His hands began perspiring and he dropped a large flathead screwdriver which put a nick in the floor. He picked it up and resumed work on the battery.

"When they're driven out of my country the destruction of the forest will stop. Plus Sumatra will no longer be considered their fiefdom, their plantation, and our people will no longer be treated like slaves by the infidels, as we have for the past four hundred years. But this takes money. You have been most generous offering it to us with no strings attached."

"There is only one string," David said. "Results. The destruction of the rainforests must stop."

Imam Hasbullah spoke. "Yes, of course. I believe the exact phrase you used was 'tangible results.' That's the word your friend originally passed on to us, through channels. I remember it clearly from early last month."

"That's right."

"We intended to do precisely that and we have. It's long been our goal. Our primary hurdle has been a lack of funding. Imagine the motivation it can bring. As we speak our men are in the plantations spreading the word. Last night seven thousand oil palm trees were cut down on Borneo. It's a drop in the bucket, yet they were thirty-year-old trees; worth a fortune to the foreign growers. Soon, on Sumatra, the fires will go out and the forest clearing will stop."

David wondered where the sudden trust had come from. The imam was speaking to him as if he were a trusted revolutionary fighter, yet they'd met less than an hour ago. They hadn't even searched him. Plus he was a foreigner. The trust was clearly in the general commitment David had demonstrated over the years. More importantly it was in the funding he had provided. "One of my concerns was that your organization might be suspicious of me. I thought that maybe you suspected the money I offered was intended to frighten away the oil palm growers in order to increase demand for conventional oil and natural gas. The Saudis and other oil exporters would profit nicely from that."

"We discussed that possibility," Imam Hasbullah said. "Please understand something. We have been approached by representatives of several governments over the past many years. I'll not name them, but they've offered us aid in exchange for our efforts at disrupting the palm oil trade. I can't speak for the imams on the other islands, but here on Sumatra we declined their offers, which were purely profit motivated. It is clear to me that your generous gifts come from the heart, with pure altruistic intentions. I trust you, David, as much as I trust my bodyguards."

"Thank you," David said.

"And thank you, Azka, for introducing our new friend to the base of operations."

Azka smiled but said nothing.

The imam continued. "Interestingly, the offers to pay us to disrupt the plantations ended some years back when they discovered that oil palm plantations consume about as much energy as they provide. If it wasn't for European subsidies and the green energy craze there would be little demand for palm oil. The plantations are what the oil industry calls a 'net neutral on energy.' With that in mind consider the following. Although Sumatra produces over half the oil and natural gas in my country, the terminal decline is well underway. Each year we produce less and less. In Indonesia there hasn't been a new major oil field discovered in decades. So where will we be several decades from now when oil production has slowed to a trickle? What will we do when the rainforest is all gone and no one's buying palm oil?"

"Mass starvation," Azka interjected.

"That's a real possibility," David said.

"It'll be worse than any horror imaginable. That's why time is of the essence. Recently the offers of aid have arrived again, not on Sumatra, but elsewhere. Some of our Persian Gulf benefactors have come to understand the severity of the damage they've caused throughout our rainforests. They believe there is a real opportunity to remove the foreign investors and forge a true Islamic republic in Indonesia. I happen to agree."

David pondered the imam's words while they each quietly sipped some tea. The woman from the kitchen appeared and again filled all three cups. David realized he really didn't care who ran the show as long as the forests were saved. "If they're providing as much money as I am, well, I don't see the tangible results on the other islands, the clear returns on their investment."

"There is much more to Indonesia than Sumatra and much more happening across our nation than one reads in the news. This island may produce most of the nation's energy, but on Sumatra we're only a small percentage of the population. Be assured, people are waking up elsewhere and they're organizing, fighting back, cutting oil palm trees and such. The people are no longer sitting back idly, doing nothing while their nation is bled dry by outsiders. The days of meekly getting run over by foreigners are almost over. In the coming days and weeks their efforts on the other islands will accelerate. Any oil palm grower who resists will have the life expectancy of a lit firecracker."

"I'm happy to hear this, Imam Hasbullah," David said.

The imam waggled a finger toward David. "You, Doctor Reseigh, are the one making an unprecedented difference right where it'll hurt them the most. By that I mean in the wallet. Their costs are skyrocketing. At some point it'll be too costly for them to clear the land whether it's for their coffee beans, palm oil or anything else. The army will demand more money to guard their operations and insurance rates will double and triple."

"Direct Action has been unleashed," David said. "I'll be watching the news more closely."

"It was a young girl, a sixteen-year-old secondary school student in Dumai, who came up with the name, Direct Action. Teenagers there are among our most effective supporters. They knew that if deforestation continues they'll have no future. The army is reluctant to arrest or torture school children, too."

"I saw them leafleting at the protest in Dumai, right before the first explosion," Azka said.

"It's the simple, humble people who do the little things that lead to great events," the imam said. "You two haven't heard any news all day, have you?"

"No," David relied. "We couldn't get a cell signal. And I've been driving all day, since before sunup."

"The cell phones aren't working very well today," Azka added.

"So you aren't aware of what happened in Dumai?"

"I only told him what I saw," Azka said. "I was knocked to the ground by the blast. But all I know is there was a huge explosion. What little I heard while fleeing to the bus station didn't offer any real information."

"I haven't read or seen the news today," David said. "But I did hear from someone that three ships were sunk at Dumai. While out collecting samples we saw the cloud of smoke from an explosion at around twelve thirty."

"It's now four ships destroyed," the imam said. "Another one sank late this afternoon."

"Were they palm oil ships?"

"One was a fertilizer ship, another was a container ship. But all four served the plantations. We are delighted, of course."

"Yes. Of course," David said while nodding his head in agreement.

When the imam stopped speaking David removed the last screw securing the top of the first battery he was dismantling. He then glanced at the wall clock. Seven thirty-five, it read. He was late for dinner and annoyed that he had no way of contacting Shannon and Gary. He and the imam had been speaking for a long time. Plus the batteries were a different, larger style and were taking longer to dismantle. It dawned on him that his friends at the hotel must be worried. "How about that," he said with a grin as he gripped and fanned a fat stack of colorful currency notes. "It's finally open. I'm holding euros. Two hundred euro notes, to be exact. One hundred of them to each packet."

As David said that he began stacking the yellow packets on the table. When he had extracted twenty-five packets he saw eight rolls of US gold coins at the bottom and pulled them out, too. Then he went to work on the next battery while the imam sat and watched.

Meanwhile Azka had finished opening his. He removed the top and extracted the contents, making a separate pile. He added it all up. "Twenty-five packets of American hundreds. A quarter million US dollars. And another eight rolls of Eagles."

The contents of the last two batteries they opened were the same as the one Azka had first opened. The imam sat quietly while David did some quick math. He was momentarily distracted by footsteps from above and ignored them. "Six and a half, maybe seven million US, depending on the price of gold. That's after converting the euros to US dollars."

David heard two car doors close and the imam spoke. "We must leave now. My transportation is here."

"This isn't your house?" David asked.

"No. I stay in a home alongside my mosque. It's on Jalan Lobak, quite close to the big hospital. I hope you have time to pay a visit while you're in Pekanbaru. This home belongs to someone I know, but I promised him I'd only need it for one hour. An hour has nearly passed so we must now go."

"What should I do about these batteries?" David asked.

"My men will dispose of them. We divide this money into four equal parts to support four operations," Imam Hasbullah said and he inserted roughly equal parts of the wealth into each of the sacks. When he was done he said, "No revolution can be successful without financial support. Your contribution is very much appreciated."

"I take that to mean others are contributing, too."

"As I mentioned, we have contributions arriving from all over the world," he said. "But none on this scale, at least not on Sumatra."

"Make sure Wahdi receives a share," Azka said, breaking a long silence.

"I will set aside some coins for them. But for now Wahdi no longer exists," Imam Hasbullah said. Then he spoke to Azka. "Everyone involved with them has been arrested. Sympathetic reporters are being arrested, too. We'll do what we can to free them. That's why we must conduct business directly through David from now on. You may socialize with one another but from this moment on you shall not mention me or David's role in supporting Direct Action."

"I understand. They can do whatever they want with me. I'll never say a word," Azka said. At that moment he realized that Muslim radicals had taken full control of David's funding.

"People will say or do anything to avoid torture," the imam said. "I'm sorry, Azka. You wouldn't last five seconds if a dentist from the intelligence division told you to open wide."

Azka cringed. "Who would?"

David ignored that remark.

So did the imam.

"I have another load due to arrive tomorrow. How will I contact you?"

"Pick it up in the afternoon, exactly as you've been doing. Someone will be in touch with you either before or after you stop at FedEx. That person will say, 'The stars will be bright tonight.' Then you reply, 'Fewer fires.' That person will take you to me. I'll be at another safe house."

CHAPTER THIRTY-FIVE

"Is David here?"

"He said he'd be back no later than seven thirty," Gary said through an exaggerated yawn. He had just been awakened after a long nap by the sound of Shannon rapping her knuckles on the door to his hotel room.

"It's only twenty to eight," Shannon said. She had spent the last two hours glued to the television in her room, occasionally flicking through the channels. At seven thirty-five she decided it was time to meet David and Gary so they could go out for dinner. She turned off the TV and walked down the hallway to the other room.

"I thought he'd be here by now."

"He probably stopped somewhere for gas."

"Maybe he's in jail," Gary offered in a whispered voice. "Or in some al Qaeda hideout getting his teeth pulled."

"That's not funny."

"It's not supposed to be. This whole thing makes me very nervous. And now he's late for dinner. Well, I'm hungry. Let's grab dinner downstairs in the hotel restaurant. We can leave him a note for when he arrives."

"Good idea. No sense starving while we wait."

"Maybe he'll call us," Gary said.

Shannon reached into her pocket and extracted David's iPhone. "Only if he finds a pay phone. He left his iPhone with me."

"Good luck finding a pay phone these days," Gary said.

"No point in bringing our phones with us. No cell signal. There's WiFi for my laptop, but the television news was more interesting."

"The hotel WiFi's fine, thank goodness," Gary said. "But we might as well leave the laptops here and enjoy a peaceful dinner."

"Good idea. Let me have your phone and I'll put all three in your room's safe. By the way, have you watched any news since we've been back?"

"I rarely watch TV. It's only there to brainwash the public and make the wealthy even wealthier."

"I couldn't agree more," Shannon replied as she stuck all three phones in the safe. "However, Bloomberg had news from Sumatra and it was interesting. Have you set a combination for this safe yet?"

"No. I've been so busy napping I didn't even realize the room had one."

"I'll set one."

After she figured out how the safe worked she closed the tiny door and locked it.

"There've been two major explosions today, right here on Sumatra," Shannon told Gary. "One in Dumai and another in Belawan. It's the port by Medan."

"I know where Belawan is."

"Fine, mister wake-up-grouchy. Well anyhow, it's no longer there."

"Belawan's been destroyed?"

"No. Just the port. Well, maybe not the entire port. An explosion tore through it a half hour ago. The Indonesian TV stations haven't covered it yet, probably because of the martial law."

"Martial law?"

"Oh, you've really been sleeping. Apparently there's something in the constitution that allows the president to declare martial law in a national emergency and that's exactly what he's done. The Indonesian news stations are covering it, but I can't understand what they're saying. It was also mentioned on CNN. However, they're now running a show about the trial of some dope dealer in Miami."

"CNN sucks," Gary responded. "How about Bloomberg?"

"Bloomberg's running a live interview with some oil tycoon who lives in San Francisco. Some guy I've never heard of named Chuck something or another. It's the only English language show on. We could watch that awhile. Maybe David'll show up in a few minutes."

"Who wants to listen to some billionaire oil tycoon?" Gary said. "If David's going to be late for dinner, tough. He can starve. But no sense us going hungry. I suggest he can find us in the hotel restaurant."

CHAPTER THIRTY-SIX

I t was eight forty-five when David dropped Azka off near his hotel. The night was cloudless, the air decidedly clearer. He hadn't worn his respirator since stopping at FedEx. He was overdue for a long run, but the air was still somewhat smoky, like approaching a campfire. In his opinion the air was too foul for jogging. It was impossible to see any stars other than the brightest few.

The fuel warning light on the dashboard lit up. He had passed four gas stations along the way. All were closed. Traffic was thinning considerably. There were fewer bicycles, but people pedaling by did so hurriedly and with purpose. The usual number of small motor-cycles zipped past and with fewer cars out they now dominated the roads.

Military vehicles, once few in number, now moved threateningly fast, back and forth as if they owned the streets of the city. They were making their presence known as if they were the only ones allowed on the road.

He parked the Tata in the hotel parking lot, clicked the key fob and headed inside. Unless he found fuel soon tomorrow's trip to the flatlands west of Dumai would have to be cancelled. The door to the diner was near the check in counter. Shannon stepped through it.

"David!" Her voice was a bit too loud for the quiet lobby. Heads turned, including David's.

"Shannon," he said. He couldn't believe how beautiful she looked in her dark blue chinos and light denim shirt. The new black Danner Acadia boots she had worn while collecting samples were somehow spotless. He walked fast to her.

Gary tapped the carpet with his cane and hobbled away from the restaurant's entry and toward his smiling colleague. They had just finished dinner. He wore tomorrow's clean tan pants and a wrinkled white shirt without a tie. If he had worn a silk tie the spatter of red sauce would have ruined it. Instead it left a thin streak connecting his top three buttons. His old brown work boots had been cleared of most of the day's mud but what remained matched his sour expression nicely. They contrasted severely with Shannon's as well as her toothy smile. Her grin was lost when she rose to her toes and gave her lover a peck on his neck.

"Hey, Gary," David said.

"Where the hell have you been?" Gary asked.

"I've been trying to find gas," he said as he broke free of Shannon's arms. The doorman was clearly eavesdropping. The two at the front counter were peering suspiciously at the three foreigners. "The truck's on empty. There aren't any stations open."

"What'll we do about tomorrow?" Gary asked.

"Let's get a drink in the bar," David suggested. "And discuss it."

"You must be starving," Shannon said.

"Now that you mention it, I could use something to eat. I'll ask the bartender. I bet they could arrange something. But first, I gotta take a leak something terrible. I'll be right back."

"That's our David," Gary said to Shannon after David hurried to the mens room. "A real classy guy. I'll bet you five dollars the bartender kicks him out. His clothes are stinkin' filthy and his boots are caked with it. I should've had his clothes shipped to Berkeley along with the mud samples."

"He's had a very busy evening, no doubt," Shannon said.

When David returned the three went straight to the bar. It was packed. The conversations among the small clusters of European businessmen and women were in Dutch, Finnish and other continental languages besides English. Thankfully the thumping dance music wasn't as loud and annoying as it was in the Blue Martini.

They found the only little round table left and sat on the skinny steel stools surrounding it. David ordered an American style hamburger and fries from the bar host, which to his happy surprise arrived in ten minutes, about the same time as their drinks. Gary and Shannon each had green tea, David an oversized can of ice cold Australian beer which he popped open a split second after it landed.

"If we can't find fuel for the truck we might as well take the hotel shuttle to the airport," Gary suggested. "I can't wait to leave. This city scares the hell out of me."

"Relax," David said then chomped a huge bite out of his burger. He gulped it down and took too deep swigs off his can. "I have an idea."

"You're ordering another beer and hamburger?" Gary asked.

"Good idea." David then got up and ordered another burger and fries from the busy bartender. To go.

"I think I know someone who might be able to get us some gas," David said. He took another bite of his burger. When he pulled out his wallet from a front pocket Gary stole a few fries off his plate. The wallet was still damp from the earlier downpour. He fished through a stack of business cards and pulled one of them aside, studying it a moment. He then took another large bite.

Shannon moved close and whispered. "You mean the people you met with?"

"Damn it. I should've asked," David said. He bit off another section of the burger and chased it down with about a third of the huge can. "I'll explain later, but we were busy. I didn't even think of it at the time. No, it's someone else. A businessman. The guy who delivered the truck. His name is Rio. I almost forgot about him. He said if we run into any difficulty while we're in Pekanbaru to call him and he'd fix it. He struck me as a slick shyster, but I'm out of ideas. It's worth a try."

"Hey, what's that?" Gary said. He pointed at the door.

When Shannon and David looked Gary stole another handful of fries off David's plate. "Oh, it was nothing."

"Quit stealing my fries or I'll post a picture on Facebook of you wearing that stained shirt," David said.

Gary was unaware so he tucked down to inspect the stain. "It's not that bad."

"It's embarrassing," David said and Gary fast snatched the last two fries off his plate. "Knock it off or I'll hide your walking stick."

"Would you two quit acting like children."

"I'll go call this guy," David said. "But I'll use the phone in the lobby, if there is one."

"There isn't one. And cell phones aren't working," Shannon said. "Is there an address?"

"Yes. But I have no idea where it is. I'll ask at the desk."

Gary spoke. "Here's a pen. Write it on the napkin and stick the card back in your wallet. No sense letting the desk clerk in on our personal shyster."

"I'm sure they're well aware of the guy," David said.

"You two can play spy. I'm going back to bed."

As David stood the host handed him a paper bag. "Your dinner, sir."

"Thank you. Charge it to his room."

CHAPTER THIRTY-SEVEN

David showed the napkin with the address scribbled on it to the desk clerk. She told him it was an apartment building only six blocks from the hotel. The clerk further advised David that the pay phones were removed many years ago. He went back to the bar and told Gary and Shannon he was walking there immediately.

"You're going alone?" Shannon asked.

"I thought it might be best."

"Good idea," Gary said. "My leg's acting up. I think I'll watch some news on television and get some rest."

"Well I'm not going to let you walk around town alone. I'm going with you and that's final."

"Fine. Let's get moving, then. Gary, we'll be back as soon as we can."

David and Shannon left while Gary limped to his room to catch up on whatever television news there was.

Pekanbaru is known as the cleanest big city in Indonesia. If not for Singapore it would probably be called the cleanest city in Asia. With gasoline and diesel growing scarcer fuel-sipping motorcycles dominated the urban streets. Most packed a passenger, or two. Few trucks and even fewer cars raced by. Even with the haze fading, the streetlights were orange and dim. They put out barely enough light to avoid tripping over a curb. A cluster of teenage boys on skateboards blasted at them and raced past, somehow avoiding a collision with the nearly invisible street signs and the rest of the pedestrians out and about. The rumbling of their tiny wheels made just enough racket to momentarily drown out the endless, buzz-like drone of small displacement motorcycle engines zipping up and down the street.

"That was close," Shannon said while the pack of skateboarders disappeared around a dark concrete building.

"It's like every one of my long bike rides in the Berkeley hills," David said. He had just finished eating his second hamburger and dipped into the bag for a few of the fries. "I damn near always come home with a few close calls, and sometimes a few very close calls. But only one crash, so far."

"Speaking of crash," Shannon said. "There's something I wanted to ask you. It's this whole save the rainforest thing. Is it possible we're jousting at windmills?"

"What do you mean?"

"I mean this whole thing about saving forests. Could it simply be that humans are predestined to destroy all of them, even devour everything in our path? Even Ireland was covered in a thick forest until people cut it down. In fact, all of Europe was once a great forest. What remains are isolated fragments."

"Most of the world was forested, too."

"It's like the Easter Island disaster everywhere we turn," Shannon said. "In my country the only forests remaining are tiny, carefully managed, and artificial. They're found in, maybe, a dozen parks. In fact, Ireland's largest, true, so-called indigenous forest is a manmade oddity in Killarney National Park. It's only a few acres and encircled by a tourist footpath. A wire fence designed to keep humans out guards the whole thing."

"Are you suggesting humans will, in time, no matter what we do, cut down every last forest on Earth?"

"I'm not only suggesting that. I'm telling you it's quite possibly a forgone conclusion. Even worse, I'm taking the idea one step further. I'm suggesting there may be nothing we or anyone else can do to stop the process."

"You mean the entire matter of providing seed money to the radicals may be a wasted effort?"

"Maybe. Oh, I don't know. It's just that the devastation is everywhere. Look at Laos and Cambodia, for example. Fifty years ago those countries were covered in lush tropical rainforest. Then came the war and the American defoliant spraying operations. Now they're practically stripped bare, converted into farms growing food for export to China. And Vietnam, Thailand, Burma, all of them aren't far behind. Malaysia is basically a corporate oil palm plantation. And forget about the Amazon. It's nearly flattened."

"So what do you suggest we do?" David asked. He reached into the bag for the final french fry. It was hiding at the bottom of his bag so he had to dig for it. "We can't sit back and do nothing. Someone has to take a stand. We have a golden opportunity to do what's right."

"I wouldn't be here if I felt we were on the wrong path, David. It's just that, well, maybe we're up against a natural force of some kind. It's possible that the worldwide destruction delivered by humans is, you know, inevitable."

"I refuse to believe that the process is unstoppable," David said as a convoy of military vehicles roared past followed closely by two police cars with sirens on and emergency lights flashing. "On the other hand, maybe I'm an idealist who's spent too much time listening to the rants of radical Berkeley professors like Gary."

"Something has to give. About the time Gary was born the population of Sumatra was ten million. That was an unsustainable number, too high to live in balance with the forest life. Now there are fifty-three million people on this island. All of them are struggling to achieve a First World lifestyle. This simply can't continue much longer. It'll reach a certain point, then bam, like tadpoles in a drying pond. I definitely don't want to be around when the die off hits. Something's got to be done to get the population under control or it'll be hopeless."

"You have any ideas?"

"It won't be popular but for starters how about cash payments for vasectomies and sterilizations? Or maybe a one child policy?"

"This is the building," David said, interrupting Shannon. "It's room 624."

Shannon tilted her head back to count floors. "A six story building. Rio has the penthouse apartment."

David peered up, too. "No surprise. Wait'll you get a load of my good buddy, Rio. His role model must be a Hollywood pimp from the seventies."

"Can't wait. David, are those stars?"

David laughed. "It's nearly June in Pekanbaru. No one'll see stars until August or September, not until the fires die down."

"I'm serious. That's Jupiter, straight overhead. And even with the streetlights the stars are peeking through the haze."

"I'll be damned."

The two each opened one of the two glass doors and went inside. David saw the elevator, considered the sporadic power failures, and headed up the hardwood stairs. Shannon followed him.

"Room 624," David said. He tossed the now crumpled paper bag into a trash can with one hand and knocked twice with the other.

"Yeah?"

"I'm looking for Rio," David said through the closed door.

"Who's this?"

"I'm David, the American from the hotel."

The door opened as far as the short brass chain allowed. A blast of cold air escaped and a pudgy face appeared.

"I remember you. You're the guy who rented the Tata truck a few days ago. What can I do for you?"

"You invited me to contact you if I needed anything."

"What do you need?"

"Some diesel fuel. Maybe sixty liters."

The brass security chain fell. Rio opened the door all the way. His hair was slicked back into a tight ponytail. He was dressed the same as before: black slacks, partially unbuttoned white shirt and about twenty thousand dollars' worth of gold chains hanging from his fingers, wrists and neck. He stepped aside revealing his living room. "Good to see you again," he said to David with a toothy, car salesman's smile. He then turned to Shannon with an outstretched hand while exposing even more white teeth. "I'm Rio."

"I'm Shannon."

They shook hands. "Good to meet you. Please, both of you come in. Shoes outside please."

"Thank you," David said and he crouched low to untie and remove his mud splattered lace-up boots.

Shannon kicked off her green athletic shoes and toed them into a tidy formation alongside David's boots by the outer wall. Both entered.

"Nice apartment," Shannon said.

Rio smiled at the comment. He closed and latched the door as soon as they were inside. "Have a seat on the couch."

They walked across the glistening green tiles and sat side by side. It was a black leather couch positioned in the center of the spacious room. Its four intricately carved wood legs danced out from each corner. It faced across a modern glass and chrome table at two black leather chairs. The sliding glass balcony door past the table offered a sparkling city view. Framed photographs featuring scenes of Sumatran wildlife adorned the white walls.

"Would you like a drink? Water or something stronger, maybe?"

"Nothing for me, thank you," Shannon said.

"No thanks," David said. "We're in a bit of a time crunch. We would like to be on the road by six tomorrow morning. But we're nearly out of fuel."

Rio laughed. "Let me understand this. You want me to find you sixty liters of diesel fuel, like, right now?"

"Yes. Tonight, if possible. All the stations I passed today were either closed or the lines were too long.

"This will be tough."

"If you can't do it, we'll start out earlier and find a queue somewhere."

"No need for that," Rio said with a smile. He picked up a landline phone positioned on the living room table. "I'll make a call."

CHAPTER THIRTY-EIGHT

"What took you guys so long?" Gary asked as David and Shannon entered his hotel room. It was nearly eleven and he was still watching television.

"Where's my cell phone?"

"The phones are all in our room's safe," Gary said. "The signal was weak earlier so we decided to leave them there."

"Mine's there, too," Shannon added.

"Plus we can speak freely with those damn things locked up," Gary said. "Unless the room's bugged."

David laughed. "If it is, we're in big trouble."

A BBC news report on the Sumatran port explosions was the top story. An Indonesian reporter was interviewing an army officer. The officer was explaining why martial law was needed to quickly find those responsible and to keep the population safe from further strikes. "We have determined that these were terrorist attacks. Suspects are in custody. More arrests are expected soon. They're being questioned and we should have more information tomorrow. That's all I have to say for now."

"David's good friend found us some diesel," Shannon said with her attention primarily focused on the television.

"Six bucks a liter," David added.

"He walked back to the hotel with us and had us drive him to a gas station next to a military base," Shannon said."

"It wasn't too far from FedEx," David said. "The fill up, sixty-six liters, cost me four hundred bucks in US money."

"That's double what it costs me in Ireland."

"The funny thing was a soldier manned the pump. He was apparently a friend of Rio's. It was a gas station the army had taken over. Military vehicles were in the short line with the truck. The three soldiers on duty weren't shy about taking bribes. One stuffed my cash in his pocket. All of it, except for whatever he peeled off and gave to Rio. Our truck wasn't the only civilian vehicle filling up either."

"We can talk about that all day tomorrow. Right now, I'm turning in," David said and gave Shannon's sleeve a tug toward the door. "That second beer made me sleepy."

"You mean the one you drank while driving to the gas station?" Shannon said.

"That one."

"You drank a beer while driving the truck?" Gary asked.

"Only one."

"What a knucklehead. What will he do next?"

"Nothing's next," Shannon said. "Except sleep."

"Good night, Gary."

"See you two."

CHAPTER THIRTY-NINE

The two low-ranking young men from the army's intelligence division sat inside a vacant hotel room on the second floor, next to the stairs leading to the lobby. They were in civilian clothes, but their short haircuts and stern demeanor were a dead giveaway that they were either police officers or with the military. Three laptops sat between them on the living room table, positioned so they could both watch the three screens at the same time. Empty paper takeout containers and plastic wrappers littered the floor under the table. Two tan paper cups of tea kept warm by white plastic tops were on the table. The logo on each read "Recycle Plastic and Protect the Environment" in English.

There were few assignments more boring than this one. They had been eavesdropping on hotel rooms eight hours a day, seven days a week for a month. It started when the wave of attacks by Direct Action began. This particular job held little promise of helping apprehend those responsible for the attacks. One glance at these three westerners as they entered the hotel that afternoon made it clear they couldn't possibly be associated with the Direct Action terrorists. However, they had their orders. The intelligence division in Jakarta suspected those financing the terrorists would be staying in an expensive hotel.

Their advance notes provided by the hotel management indicated that the two American scientists shared a room. One of them, Professor Gary Jackman, was a physicist in his seventies. He napped continuously, said little and couldn't walk without his cane. The other, Doctor David Reseigh, was an executive from Concerned Earth Scientists, an environmental group outside the mainstream, yet their focus was primarily on studying and publicizing the adverse impacts of deforestation. An Irish schoolteacher was the third member of the small study group. They were funded by a second group, Save the Rainforests. She was apparently the lover of the younger American scientist. He stayed in her room while Jackman stayed alone in the other.

The two men had one responsibility and that was to record conversations and if possible capture images. If they believed criminal activity was involved their responsibility was to contact their superiors immediately but take no aggressive action on their own.

This evening they were spying on the occupants of twenty-six rooms. Bugging them and unbugging the rooms of those who left had been routine and simple. As usual, none of their targets had made an effort to scan their rooms for cameras or inspect them for recording devices. The likelihood of gaining valuable intelligence from the guests in these rooms was so low they chose to drink tea and read Facebook on their own laptops rather than gaze endlessly at the boring images on the screens of the military's computers.

The two rooms rented by the small group from STR were both bugged late in the afternoon shortly after the Dumai explosions. There were fifteen known foreign environmental activists in Pekanbaru and all were targeted as possible suspects. The five staying in this hotel were considered low risk but their orders were to eliminate all of them as possible suspects. Three were in the group from STR, the other two were performing solo research. All of them had been under surveillance since midafternoon.

Their attention was now on the group of three. Two of them had just returned from an interesting outing. Their observations were entered into the daily report and revealed the following: At five p.m. Reseigh had taken a four hour drive in their rented Tata truck. The GPS monitor they had attached underneath the vehicle indicated it had first been driven on a direct route to FedEx. After fifteen minutes parked there it had returned near the hotel, only to pass the university, two blocks away. Then it moved away from the university on a zig zagging route to a private home in a poor western suburb. It remained there for well over an hour. The address was located and noted in case it was needed later. The truck then left the house, stopping one minute next to a cheap hotel not far from the Grand Jatra. Then it returned to this hotel. One of the agents left the room when it arrived and walked past the lot. He observed Reseigh heading toward the lobby alone.

While Reseigh was out driving, the old man and the woman had been observed and monitored in their rooms for over two hours, from shortly after five p.m. until seven thirty-five. The older man had arrived alone, around five, and slept until seven thirty. He woke up when O'Connell knocked on his door. They both went to dinner in the hotel's restaurant at seven forty. What they discussed while eating is unknown. At nine twenty Jackman returned to his room and immediately went back to sleep. At no time was anything spoken inside either of their rooms to arouse any suspicion that they were engaged in illegal activity.

At about nine Reseigh returned and joined the other two in the hotel bar. After fifteen minutes he and O'Connell took a walk. At around ten they departed in their truck and drove south of the city. The fact that they drove to a gas station now used by the army was interesting, but of little intelligence value to them. There was no point staring at the screen and watching Professor Jackman sleep so they paid no attention to him. The image of him covered by blankets appeared on the screen of the second laptop only briefly as they mindlessly flipped through the images sent by cameras secreted in the other two dozen hotel rooms. The three cell phones of the Save the Rainforests group had been placed in Jackman's room safe by O'Connell. With the military disrupting cell transmissions, and theft a concern, it wasn't all that peculiar for a guest to store costly phones.

At eleven thirty-six one of them spoke into a microphone using their code names. "Charlie Two, Foxtrot One."

"Charlie Two. Go."

"Reseigh and O'Connell have returned in their truck. Recording entry into the hotel lobby at twenty-three ten. We have confirmation and clear audio signal of them knocking on Reseigh's door. I can hear them talking with Jackman. We are monitoring. Our laptop's recording clear images. We have one adult woman and one man. Both appear to be in their early thirties. They are identified as Doctor David Reseigh and Shannon O'Connell. Both are now entering Reseigh's room. Visual is of the entire hotel room, minus the bathroom. Jackman is awake on the bed. He's grumbling at the two for waking him up. They're discussing the price they paid some soldier and a guy named Rio for black market diesel fuel. Jackman made a comment about the rooms being bugged. It was an obvious joke referring to the phones in the safe. Now Reseigh and O'Connell are leaving the room and heading to the woman's room."

"The two love birds aren't in Jackman's?" the voice said through Charlie Two's hand held device.

"No, sir," one of the two young men said. "O'Connell and Reseigh are now inside her room, the one where she and Reseigh sleep. They're sitting on the edge of the bed, face to face, whispering. The microphone isn't picking up their words. But they don't look very dangerous to me. Now he's running his fingers through her hair. Want me to tell you what happens next?"

"No. I get the picture. Record them anyhow. Focus your attention on the other targets in the hotel, especially the tourists. One of the others might be involved in these terror attacks."

"Copy. Charlie Two out," he said. He glanced at his wristwatch. Eleven forty. Only twenty minutes left on the shift. Then the midnight crew shows up and those guys get to spend eight hours staring at live videos of people sleeping. Then more live feed of them getting ready for breakfast.

CHAPTER FORTY

"David. Get up," Shannon said. "It's important."

"What's the hurry? It's only ten after five."

"I've got the television on. The news has a report from Sumatra. It's on BBC. It says the Indonesian Minister of Justice was assassinated last night. His car was blown apart by a bomb attached to the side of his car by the passenger on a passing motorcycle. Five killed."

"Don't change channels. I wanna see it."

David got up and stretched. Still in his boxer shorts he walked around and sat on the crumpled covers at the end of the bed, close to the television.

The British reporter spoke while images of flames from burning ships filled the screen. "Five cargo ships have been destroyed in two Indonesian seaports after explosions ripped through the ports of Dumai and Belawan yesterday. Experts are calling the one at the port of Dumai the largest non-nuclear manmade explosion in history. In messages emailed to media outlets all over the world, including the BBC, a little known group calling itself Direct Action has claimed responsibility for both attacks. The messages warn that unless the destruction of the rainforests stops and the cultivation of oil palm trees is ended further attacks will occur. They have also claimed responsibility for yesterday evening's magnet bomb attack on a vehicle carrying the Indonesian Minister of Justice, which destroyed the car and killed him as well as four others. We are awaiting a message from the Minister of Trade who is expected to announce this morning that there has been a suspension of all palm oil shipments pending resumption of insurance policies which have been cancelled for all ships coming into or out of Indonesia."

An arm handed the reporter a sheet of paper. He paused a moment to read it fast. Then he began speaking again. "This just in. There has been another attack. A tanker from Singapore and bound for Rotterdam has run aground into a rocky cliff near the Malaysian coastal town of Langkawi. It was carrying a full load of processed palm oil. Sources tell us it is taking on water. Details are few, but initial and unverified reports indicate someone or some group may have managed to hack their way into the ship's GPS guidance system and steer the ship off course. We expect more information soon."

After a short commercial he spoke again. "In other news from Sumatra the growing wave of attacks against oil palm tree growing operations has apparently escalated. Rioting which had broken out in cities throughout Indonesia are described as among the worst in the nation's history. In the northern coastal city of Medan over two hundred ethnic Chinese were herded at gunpoint onto a ferry bound for Malaysia and summarily deported. Also, the Medan airport remains closed after a series of explosions detonated alongside fuel storage tanks and inside the terminal."

"Wow," David said.

"Shush," Shannon said. "Let's listen."

"Rioters directed their anger at anything associated with the huge palm oil trade. Businesses owned by foreigners were targeted, as mobs smashed windows and set cars in fire. Entire blocks were ablaze, according to reports. Police officers siding with the protesters have been waging battle with army units in this incredible story of popular unrest."

Another talking head appeared on the screen. "Elsewhere in Indonesia eighteen workers at an oil palm tree plantation in Borneo were found shot and killed near their labor camp early this morning. A security guard made the grizzly discovery during a routine patrol. Local authorities will not confirm or deny a report that says one of them had a message nailed into his face, a note which allegedly included the words 'Direct Action.' Stay tuned for further information on this developing story."

"It's a revolution," David said as he stared at a commercial advertising a popular food market.

Shannon whispered in his ear. "We better watch what we say from now on. Foreigners like us will be under suspicion. This room could be bugged."

"How romantic would that be? Just like in the movies," David said. "I love you, Shannon."

"I love you, too."

"What time does the lobby diner open?" David asked.

"Six."

"Let's spend forty-five minutes in the gym and be at the door when it opens," David suggested. "Gary knows we're leaving early so he'll pop in about then, too."

"A gym session. That's the second best idea you've had all day."

"What was the very best?"

Shannon simply smiled at him.

"Crank up that laptop of yours," David said. "I want to spend five minutes on my email before we go to the gym."

She flipped her laptop open and pushed a button. In seconds it was awake, ready to perform as commanded. "Hurry," she said.

"Okay." David accessed his account. Like most everyone, he had a gmail account. But that's not the account he checked. The one he accessed had been provided by Chuck. It was through an obscure

Cayman Islands-based Internet company that promised a high degree of security. David knew there was no such thing as true Internet security, but at least it would be tough for an eavesdropper to break in.

There was one message. It read, "Thank you for returning that portable solar power unit. We really needed it for a project. I have a few packages for you to pick up at my company warehouse in Pekanbaru. I would like you to stop by there this afternoon around five thirty. With the unrest in your neck of the woods we're having trouble keeping the rigs supplied. Could you deliver it to the site for us? Don't tell anyone about it. It's filled with specially machined copper piping. The stuff's expensive. Thanks, Cir Lynch."

Cir Lynch was a trusted buddy of David's from the old days. He had cleaned up, as people say, and the two had stayed in touch over the years. Cir had been raised in a drug infested, predominately black Tenderloin tenement apartment and was now working for Simmons Hydrocarbon Supply. David had once provided Cir with a personal recommendation. That was good enough for Mister Charles Henry Simmons, who made a phone call to the personnel manager and that was that.

David suspected the note was really from Chuck. He decided not to tell Gary and Shannon about it, but he would drop by after FedEx and do as Chuck asked. Plus it would be interesting to visit a live Sumatran oil-drilling site.

CHAPTER FORTY-ONE

At six forty-five, right after breakfast, the three wound their way through the city and headed north on the Trans-Sumatran Highway. It would be their only day collecting samples on rivers and streams north of Pekanbaru. It was Wednesday, the last day in May. It would be a fast run up and back the historic highway.

Tomorrow would be June first. They planned to complete their sampling operation with a one-day drive south, all the way to Bukit Tiga Puluh National Park. There they intended to stay overnight and after possibly taking additional samples from rivers and streams they crossed along the highway, return to Pekanbaru by dark.

Today they had to return to the hotel by five in order for David to make his FedEx pick up. That left them with only ten hours to gather as many decent samples as needed.

The freezer was fully charged this time so there would be no need to ship the samples that day, as they had done the day before. Any samples they had could be kept cold two days in the hotel rooms' refrigerators. Shipping them could easily wait until some time Saturday morning, before turning in the rented Tata, and well before their scheduled early evening departure flight to San Francisco via Kuala Lumpur and Hong Kong.

While driving north they encountered two army roadblocks, both of which were near the turnoff to Dumai. One was to the south of the highway intersection, the other to the north. At each their truck was stopped and quickly searched. A small fine was paid each time for some unknown infraction and they were on their way. There were no photos taken at either stop. The soldiers had become more efficient since the day before. Maybe it was from practice. However, as soon as they pulled into the first checkpoint, and before any samples had been collected, David had the strange feeling their arrival had been known to the soldiers long in advance.

One soldier searching their truck even went so far as to ask Gary, "Is this the freezer where you store the water samples?" Gary told him it was. The young soldier had either made an accidental slip or he had been trying to tell the travelers that their passing through had been anticipated. Either way this odd question was asked too soon, before they had been quizzed about their reason for passing through. Either way it told the threesome they were being watched. They discussed it after driving off and concluded that the army was most likely grasping at straws, gathering intelligence shotgun style in their search for the bombers and that foreigners were high on the suspect list.

Later, while they were gathering samples in the Rokan River, it began to rain hard. Really hard. Gary and David were caught unaware. The sturdy boots they wore were soon gripped tight by the red-brown mud, which spread out in two wide avenues of runoff sludge bordering the dirty stream. With their shirts glued tight to their backs the two raised their arms high at the sky and laughed like schoolboys. Shannon observed them from a safe distance. She had busied herself by taking notes and snapping pictures. When the heavy rain hit she fled into the truck and began to label containers. She found plenty to do without coming into physical contact with the polluted muddy mess.

When the two men began playfully tossing mud at each other she opened the door to the Tata and shouted sternly at them to knock it off. When they didn't respond she got out, moved closer, and yelled louder. "Stop it, you idiots! That mud is poisonous!" she shouted. They quit tossing mud and went back to work. Thankfully, few of the toxic fistfuls hit their targets. Those that did washed off fast in the tropical deluge.

They stopped again at a small former fishing village which was located near a bridge. Local residents took a break from their daily routines to visit with the foreigners. They told the crew of Caucasian visitors that there hadn't been any fish in their particular Rokan River tributary for two years, at least not near their village where the stream crossed the Sumatran Highway.

Their earlier issues with skin rashes, hair loss, headaches and assorted intestinal problems had mostly disappeared once they avoided contact with the stream. With their wells contaminated and the water in their small village reservoir unsafe for human consumption, water for drinking, cooking and cleaning had to be brought in from Medan by truck.

With the chemical fertilizer runoff from oil palm tree plantations and the metallic effluent from mining operations the severity of the pollution was not entirely unexpected. Countless streams flowed through the plains north of the north Bukit Barisan. The small tributaries eventually gathered into several main rivers. One, the Rokan River, meandered north through the eastern flatlands, finally reaching the Strait of Malacca at the small town of Bagansiapiapi.

Interestingly, that town was founded by Chinese fishermen in the late eighteen hundreds. They had been attracted to the unspoiled tropical paradise primarily by the bountiful fish harvests which were plentiful, ready for the taking. Now, as a result of the negative impact from mining and deforestation, most of the fish throughout the Riau river system had died out. Some species had become extinct, others could be soon.

On the road back to Pekanbaru traffic was lighter than they expected and the air much clearer. They had brought along respirators but hadn't used them. Most of the people they passed, both on foot and in passing vehicles, weren't wearing them either. It was apparent that there hadn't been any new fires set for many days. What was fouling the air was the smoke from the last of the previously set fires.

Gary mentioned that on the television news he'd been watching early that morning, a BBC commentator had calculated that as many as four thousand plantation workers had been killed throughout the nation over the past six weeks. The true number was actually about two thousand, but the deteriorating political situation in Indonesia had captured the world's attention.

But when they arrived back in Pekanbaru what had gripped the attention of the three was their desperate craving for a shower, a change of clothes and a nice dinner in the hotel restaurant. David had to leave right after they returned, but a bit of catching up from BBC's televised news carried into their rooms on the hotel's satellite link was next on Gary and Shannon's list.

David and Gary were filthy, in very bad need of a change of clothes. A ripe odor embraced each of them. Shannon wasn't shy about reminding both men that they needed a shower, something she made sure to do about once every ten minutes.

For David, routine cleanliness would have to wait. He would need to drop them off and go immediately in order to make it to FedEx before they closed. The strange email from Simmons Hydrocarbon Supply said they'd stay open until he arrived. The fact that stopping at FedEx was becoming a daily ritual concerned him some, but he had no other choice. Hopefully, he wasn't the only absentminded scientist who required a daily shipment of forgotten, yet badly needed supplies.

CHAPTER FORTY-TWO

The portable radio buzzed. The senior of the two agents in the second floor room of the Grand Jatra Hotel picked it up and pushed the button on the side. "Foxtrot One."

Foxtrot One was the code name of one of the two day shift agents monitoring the feed from the bugs planted earlier in some of the hotel's rooms. Using the assigned code names was an old routine formality, not needed when speaking on their secure radios. But out of tradition they were nevertheless generally used by officers in the intelligence division. As the senior agent in the hotel room it was his duty to handle the agents' communications. It was one p.m. The two had been watching the activity, or, lack of activity, in the twenty-five targeted rooms since six a.m. They had one hour left to go on their eight-hour shift. They were ready to call it a day and hand it over to the agents on the afternoon and early evening shift.

"Foxtrot One this is Bravo Three. I have a job for you."

"I get off in an hour, boss. Make it a quick one."

"I don't care when you get off. I'm short handed. We have information about a guest in one of the rooms you're monitoring. Professor David Reseigh."

"We have his room and an associate's room under surveillance. Three in the group, but they don't always travel together."

"I read the preliminary field reports and I'm well aware of all that. Listen. We sent an agent to FedEx to find out why Reseigh was there yesterday afternoon," the regional intelligence supervisors said. His voice continued at low volume through the speaker of Foxtrot One's handheld portable radio. "It gets interesting. I'll give you the short version. His truck was wired at a roadblock yesterday afternoon by an alert army officer. We've followed up on his stops since then. One was FedEx. Their records show Professor David Reseigh picked up a solar power unit there yesterday and another similar one the day before."

"I reviewed his path," Foxtrot One said. "He didn't make any stops along the way."

"Well, maybe he did. The tracking shows he overshot FedEx his second time there. He went two blocks past, paused a few minutes, then he turned around by the back dock of an oil company supply warehouse and went straight to FedEx. If he was only turning around there were easier opportunities."

"The clerk said he told him he was using the solar power units to power his field testing equipment. However, yesterday afternoon he shipped a package containing water and soil samples back to the USA for testing. So the question is, why would he need a portable solar power station for testing if he isn't testing?"

"I agree," the field agent said. "Something's not adding up."

"It gets better," the intelligence supervisor said. "He has another shipment due to arrive on the three p.m. FedEx flight from Narita. The manifest says it's a freezer of some kind. Here's where you come in. We're running thin on agents, as you know. That means overtime. I need you to be at FedEx before three to greet the plane. We'll have two of our agents there with tools. They're both solid mechanics.

I want every cubic millimeter of his shipment searched and afterwards returned the way it was when he picks it up. That means by five. Record everything on your phone camera. Just pictures, not the whole movie. We don't want Reseigh to know we searched it. We want him to get it and go to his contact, just like he did yesterday, and the day before that. Our target isn't Reseigh. If he's dirty he's most likely a patsy, a simple delivery boy, disposable to us and to them. It's his contact we want. Agents will be standing by to follow him wherever he goes."

"I'll be there," Foxtrot One said. "What do we do if the freezer turns out to be just a freezer?"

"Then he's legit and we forget about him. Let me know immediately either way. If he's clean we stand down and move on to other targets. If he's dirty we let him take the freezer and drop it off. Then we hit the place hard. And I do mean very hard."

"Will the three of us be needed if it comes to that?"

"No. Our special projects team is on standby. If that freezer shipment contains contraband we'll want David alive so we can question him. After that interview we'll bury his body somewhere. Whoever else is still alive after we hit the place will be transported to the usual location where the army will press them for information. Then they'll get rough. Really rough. The team has a free pass to do whatever we want with all of them. They will not be serving them a candle light dinner, if you know what I mean."

"What about the KPK?"

"The Corruption Eradication Commission has been eradicated," Bravo Three said. "I found out the happy news this morning. We don't have to worry about them breathing down our necks again."

CHAPTER FORTY-THREE

The FedEx plane touched down at two fifty-two and blocked at three, exactly on schedule. The cargo was offloaded and delivered to the shaded, but not air conditioned, warehouse where four uniformed customs agents stood by waiting to perform their inspections.

Joining them were three plainclothes agents from the army intelligence. Two, including Echo Four, had arrived only moments earlier. The third had arranged for a quiet corner with a large empty table on which they could carefully search the package, or packages, addressed to Doctor David Reseigh.

It took the four agents fifteen minutes to locate the target cardboard box. It was nearly a cube, about a half meter on each side. It wasn't very heavy, only seventeen kilos. After passing it through the X-ray they found nothing unusual with the contents. They then placed it on the wide table, which was covered with a white sheet. They carefully opened the box so it could be resealed without suspicion. Inside was a portable battery powered freezer. It was expensive, capable of keeping anything inside frozen for twenty-four hours, less in tropical heat. A scientist using one in Sumatra would need a solar power unit to recharge it if he planned to be in the forest more than a day.

They put the cardboard container aside and moved fast, quickly removing the door, the back, and the side panels. A camera on a tripod recorded the whole thirty-minute operation in a series of still images.

"Out of luck, men," the officer said. He turned off the camera. "It's just a freezer. A clean one. There's nothing inside. Let's put it all back together exactly the way it was and move on to the other packages."

"What about that oil service supply place he drove by yesterday?" one asked. "The GPS says he stopped there for about two minutes, a hundred fifty-four seconds, to be exact. That's a lot longer than it takes to turn his truck around."

"You guys know the standing orders. We've all been instructed over and over again to leave the foreign oil industry companies and their employees alone. If headquarters found out any of us was screwing with a foreign energy company our heads would roll. And I do mean it would be the end of the road for all of us. So drop that thought."

"Yes, sir."

CHAPTER FORTY-FOUR

After dropping off Gary and Shannon at the hotel David began the drive to the FedEx warehouse. His stomach growled, letting him know it was nearly time for dinner. His pants were muddy and he stank like hell. A shower and a change of clothes would've been nice, but there simply wasn't time. It was already after five. No one representing the imam had contacted him. But since they had arrived at the hotel only moments earlier it was not a surprise.

As he made the first turn not far from the hotel he saw the massive protest. Then a roadblock appeared. Three army flatbed trucks were parked in the middle of the street. Dozens of soldiers stood near them, rifles at low ready, as if awaiting orders to attack. In the center of the street in front of the university a long line of police cars separated the protesters from the soldiers. Officers stood alongside the opposite side of their cars, their backs to the protesters, their eyes on the soldiers. They, too, carried rifles.

Several thousand people were milling about, many flooding off the sidewalk and into the street. He wondered if Azka was among them, notebook in hand. He felt vulnerable without his friend, the only person in Pekanbaru he really trusted.

Although the air quality had improved, nearly all of them wore face masks. It was not only due to the still somewhat foul air, but more importantly to keep their identities hidden. Most of the enthusiastic protesters appeared to be following the lead of a masked man with a bullhorn who was shouting slogans in Indonesian. Others held signs or wide banners, some in English. Many simply featured an enlarged image of an orangutan. One large banner held high by two women read, 'No More Burning!' Another prominent white banner held high on metal poles by two masked men proclaimed in large black letters, 'Direct Action!' It must have been four meters wide and two meters tall.

A long wooden barricade prevented vehicles from passing through the broad avenue. An emergency siren grew louder breaking through the incessant whine of countless passing motorcycles. Just as the siren grew loudest it suddenly quieted. The ambulance rolled up to the barricade. A police officer moved the yellow horizontal wooden beam just enough to allow the ambulance to pass through. Then he placed it back. Another police officer was in the street waving cars to an alternate route.

To better listen to the crowd David downed his window with the push of the button. After he followed the officer's direction and made the turn the chanting grew quieter. It was too late to hear much. The raucous scene grew smaller in his rear view mirror, then it vanished as traffic blocked his view. He decided to leave his window down and the four doors unlocked in case someone approached his truck while en route.

He made another series of turns toward the road leading south to FedEx. At the last light a young woman jogged toward his truck. While he waited for the light to change she excitedly tapped on his passenger side window then opened the door and climbed in. She glanced around outside a moment. During the pause David wondered a moment if she was his contact or a common hooker. He considered the fact that she wasn't too bad looking and his pulse jumped, and not just a little. He thought of the cash in his wallet then forced his mind away from that crazy idea just as she faced him without expression.

"The stars will be bright tonight," she said in perfect English. It shattered his brief fantasy.

"Fewer fires," David replied and busted out a toothy grin at the timely pun.

"What's so funny?" she asked.

"It's nothing. Well, I wasn't expecting a woman. Certainly not such a pretty woman."

She muttered something in Indonesian then switched to English. "Neither will our enemy. I'll be riding with you to FedEx. Then I'll direct you to the imam."

She sat upright, like a nun might. She wore a light blue headscarf, a matching blouse buttoned to her neck and loose-legged black slacks, a bit snug across her hips. Her running shoes bore the Nike symbol. They were white, like her gloves; one of which gripped a folded bright red umbrella. Since it hadn't rained it was most likely to protect her skin from the sun.

"What's your name?" David asked.

"Listen closely," she said. Her button nose twitched a bit as she ignored his question. Her stern expression remained. "An informant has told us that the military authorities suspect you're assisting us. An operative has by now been to your hotel and advised your two companions, Shannon and Gary, to leave for the airport immediately. They're taking the seven thirty flight to Kuala Lumpur. Seats for them have been arranged. I've been advised that your friend, Gary, fell ill."

David was in shock. "What are you saying? Is he okay?"

"He's fine. It's the story we're using to get the two of them out of the country. I understand this is a surprise to you. Late tonight they'll be safe and sound at a nice hotel in Hong Kong. Gary will be fast asleep and Shannon will be planning her downtown shopping with the cash we've provided her."

"Probably the same cash that I provided the imam."

"Definitely. The shopping story must appear legitimate."

"When will I see her? And Gary, too?"

"You'll join them tomorrow or Friday."

"Jesus," David said. "I just thought about something. We can't drive to visit the imam. The army probably has this truck bugged."

"You mean this bug?" She reached under her seat and pulled out a small black plastic object about a third of the size of a pack of cigarettes. The small opening on one side suggested it was operated by two AA batteries. The other side had a magnet affixed to it.

"On, no. If they know about me then they know about the other FedEx deliveries. They know it all. I'll be going to jail."

She smiled. "One of our people found this attached to the frame of your truck last night. They opened your door and placed it under your front passenger seat instead. So relax."

"Relax? I'm going to be caned."

"Are all Americans as nervous as you?"

"No. I'm the only one."

"And do all Americans smell like you, Doctor Reseigh? If I may be blunt, you smell horrible. I hope that stink is insect repellant."

"It's mostly mosquito spray. I've been working outside all day. I had no time to change clothes or shower."

"I'll accept that," she said with the same stoic expression. "Now back to the business at hand. Today's delivery is a small electric freezer, similar to the one you have now. You were placed under surveillance late yesterday afternoon. They know nothing about the batteries. As for the freezer, they know all about it, but it's clean. Our informant at FedEx told us Army intelligence agents have taken it apart and put it back together again. They found nothing inside. All you have to do is ask if your portable freezer has arrived."

"So let me get this straight. I drive straight to FedEx, not to the other place?" David said. Not mentioning Simmons by name was a last-minute attempt to protect his friend in San Francisco. They may not know about his relationship with Chuck.

"Correct," she replied, then aimed her right thumb over her shoulder, toward the gear scattered across the back seat and the solar panels on the bed. "There's no need for you to drop off that solar unit at Simmons Hydrocarbon Supply today like you did yesterday."

"Then why guide me to the imam?"

"After we leave FedEx you'll find out why."

"Why should I trust you?"

"You don't have to," she answered. "But it would be in your best interests. More importantly it would be in the best interests of your money smuggling operation to do as we ask. And that is very much my business."

David stared at her a moment as he dodged a truck parked in his lane. "You people know everything, don't you?"

While he drove she faced the windshield. Her eyes occasionally moved from side to side scanning in all directions. After a minute she spoke. "We have powerful friends throughout Pekanbaru including many among the police."

"Do you think the police know about me?"

"It's doubtful. The army and police hate each other. It's always been that way. The army shares nothing with the police, and the police share nothing with the army."

"What if the cops find out about me?"

"They'll probably give you a medal. They want the burning and clearcutting to stop as much as you and I do. I know how they think because my oldest brother is a Pekanbaru police officer."

"What about the TNI?"

"The army? In my country they are brutal, serving only foreign masters. They're greedy pigs, tools of the imperialists and infidels.

They serve as security guards protecting those who are destroying my country. But thankfully they are very weak on Sumatra. That's why they travel in large packs on this island. They behave like hyenas. We have little to fear from them because they have no evidence against you. And you're a foreigner. If the TNI detains us, which is very unlikely, I'll say I'm a prostitute. You'll agree that you picked me up on a street corner on the way to FedEx. They'll ask you to pay a fine and then free you. And I'll pay a small bribe and be done with it."

"Do you have friends in the energy industry?"

She smiled. "There's FedEx."

"They're not exactly the energy industry."

"Almost everything they ship is related to the energy industry," she said. "There it is. Pull in and park by the door."

He parked in the same spot as the day before. A dark nondescript older sedan was in the next space and he made sure to avoid bumping into it.

"I'll wait in the truck," the woman said. "Remember. Ask only for your freezer."

David glanced at his watch as he went inside. It was five fifteen.

The same clerk was there and he greeted David with the same sour expression he wore the day before. It was probably the same expression he had worn for the past four decades. He rose from the stool behind his counter and spoke. "Hello, Mister Reseigh."

"Doctor Reseigh," David corrected him with a friendly smile.

"My apologies to you, Doctor Reseigh."

"No problem. It happens all the time. Did my portable freezer arrive?"

"Why yes, it did. It's in the back. I'll have it brought here." He turned and parted the door to the warehouse.

He shouted loud and rapidly into the dark void in Indonesian. The only word David recognized among the roughly hundred shouted syllables was "freezer."

The clerk switched back to English. "It'll be here in one minute."

It was light enough for a healthy man to carry but it was wheeled through the door on a bent and ancient hand truck by an equally bent and ancient man.

"That looks like it," David said. "I'll take it to my truck. Where do I sign?"

While the clerk reached under his counter for a form the old man went back through the door to the warehouse. David heard a loud engine outside and glanced over his shoulder toward the double glass entry doors. The sedan he had parked next to was backing out of its parking space. As it stopped David noticed it was being driven by a young woman wearing a yellow headscarf.

"Sign here, and here," he said while pointing with his pen.

David did as instructed.

He picked up the cardboard box and carried it to the door. He paused momentarily, hooked a baby finger around the stainless steel door handle and pulled a few inches. He toed the door the rest of the way open and said goodbye to the clerk just as an orange blast of setting sun hit him in the face. The clerk was no longer in the entry when he said goodbye over his shoulder, but the woman in the blue scarf was still in his passenger seat, right where she had been four minutes earlier. He squinted and headed for the truck.

David hoisted the box over the sidewall and onto the truck's bed. When he opened up the truck door he saw that same sedan parked not ten meters away, close to the road as if waiting for a gap to form in the river of motorcycles and trucks passing each direction.

"When you leave go right," the blue scarfed woman ordered. "Then pull behind the Simmons warehouse."

When he pulled into traffic the battered sedan followed and moved close behind his truck and remained there for several blocks. David's heart was racing. How did she know about the Simmons shipment?

CHAPTER FORTY-FIVE

The newspaper Gary gripped used odd and distinctive oversized sheets of paper. The Singapore Straits Times was much larger than other newspapers, yet still eighty percent ads. He was having trouble turning the wide sheets of the Wednesday morning edition. They tended to wave around in an annoying manner with each flip of the page.

He had picked up a cold and constantly coughed and sniffled. Although they were seated near the gate most of the other hundred and fifty passengers waiting to board the flight to Kuala Lumpur were nowhere close.

"How the hell am I supposed to keep my sanity and act like a rich western shopper in Hong Kong with David trapped in Pekanbaru?" Shannon said.

"You have the looks and the cash for it," Gary said.

"That's not funny. You and David both have the same sick sense of humor. Did you know that?"

"So I've been told," Gary said. His face pinched some as a few fingernails on his left hand attacked a bothersome itch on his scalp. The released half of his newspaper settled on a raised knee.

"I'd smack you for that comment but I'm afraid I'd get contaminated. You really should tidy up."

Gary ignored her remark. He sat in the seat to her left, one of the many hard black plastic seats lined up next to the boarding gate. A young man in business attire sat two seats away from them and began staring at the screen of his tablet. The man glanced at Gary and moved to a distant seat.

Gary held the newspaper opened up wide, covering his upper body and face. His reading glasses hung from the oily tip of his long and pointed European nose. His greasy hair was aimed all over the place. He hadn't shaved. His pants were soiled after a day taking water and soil samples. Moments after they had arrived at the airport he had cleaned his boots in one of the international terminal's men's rooms. They were no longer caked with dried mud but were in bad need of a shine. The body odors he'd gathered during a day in the tropical heat hadn't been showered away. His blue denim shirt was soiled. He looked like a common American street bum. If not for Shannon he would have been sitting alone, fouling the air in a remote corner of the international terminal.

A thirty-something woman from the public health department approached him shortly after they sat down. It was about the same time that the passengers who had been seated near him scattered. She had been informed by an airline customer service representative that Gary was flying home on short notice because he had fallen ill.

She was dressed in white, head to toe, leather shoes, scarf and all. She smiled in a kind, compassionate manner and asked Gary if she could take his temperature. He grumbled yet agreed. His temperature was normal, thirty-seven degrees.

"Are you well enough to fly?" she asked.

"Yes," he replied through his tired red eyes. "All I have is a bad headache."

She carefully inspected those eyes with a penlight, first one, then the other. She took his blood pressure. It was one forty over eighty. After tapping some notes into an iPad she offered Gary an aspirin. He declined. She finally wished Gary well on his flight home and moved away in search of other potentially sick or diseased passengers.

"Gary," Shannon said. "Go into the men's room and clean up. You must have a fresh shirt in your carry-on bag."

"Fine," he replied.

He opened his pack and pulled out a disposable razor and his other blue denim shirt. Then, cane in hand, he tapped a path to the nearest men's room. Passengers in his path cleared aside as he hobbled by.

He stood by one of the sinks, removed his dirty shirt, and rolled it into a tight ball. With a wad of paper towels he sopped up most of the muddy stains and splatters soiling his pants. After shaving, then washing his chest and armpits, he slipped into a clean shirt. He felt nicely refreshed. He stood before the tall mirror and inspected his effort. His hair needed taming so he ran wet fingers through the tangled white mass. "Lookin' good," he said to his reflection.

He returned to his seat, stuffed the soiled shirt into his pack and went back to his paper. Shannon, who had managed to shower and change before the knock on the door came, smacked the back of the paper with the palm of her hand. The other passengers remained far enough away that none noticed her. "Hey."

"What?"

"You look absolutely dashing."

"Thank you."

"I still can't believe this is happening," Shannon said. "We're being deported by al Qaida."

"They're not al Qaida," Gary said. "You know their name is Darul Islam."

"I don't care what they're called. You heard what those men told us. It's the six fifty p.m. flight to KL or else."

"Listen, Shannon. This country is falling into chaos. They had no choice. And we have no choice. In my opinion we're lucky to be getting out." He gently shook the paper while eying the print. "You should read the stories. The only good news is that the air quality is finally improving. The Pollutant Standards Index for Pekanbaru is under eighty for the first time in weeks. In Singapore it's thirty."

"Right now it's David I'm concerned about. I'm terrified for him."

"David'll be fine," Gary said as the voice of a Malaysia Airlines customer service representative filled the air announcing that first class boarding had started. "Those men told us he'll join us in Hong Kong late tomorrow evening or the next day at the latest."

"And you believe them?"

"Yes. They seemed to me like fine, honest young chaps," Gary said. "I truly believe they have our best interests in mind."

"Theirs, too. Especially if the army found out about us," she said. "With us in town the operation could easily get, you know, complicated."

"That could be painful. At least they got us first class seats and plenty of shopping money."

"Seven thousand euros each," she said. "And David's still stuck here. That's some incentive. And I'm not going shopping. I'll save the money instead."

"Those two men who came to our rooms right after David drove away were more than just a little intimidating," Gary said. "It was their eyes. They were so damn serious. There was no way I was going to argue with them. In fact, they scared the living crap out of me. How did they know so much about us?"

"I have no idea, Gary. And I don't like this any more than you do. On the other hand sometimes one has to accept things like that and simply do as one's told, like good soldiers. This is definitely one of those times. We can't possibly be in the loop on every decision."

"I hear that. Anyhow, it's boarding time," Gary replied as four soldiers walked by with their rifles held close and aimed low. They were about three meters apart, faces forward, eyes searching everywhere. They passed by and continued their rounds.

"Then let's get on the plane, kick off our boots, and enjoy a nice cold drink."

CHAPTER FORTY-SIX

"Park in back by the loading dock," she told David. "Back right up to the edge of it."

He drove around the warehouse and backed up until his tailgate gently bumped the lip of the dock. The sedan parked a ways off, yet in plain sight. The same two warehousemen approached the truck, this time pushing a heavy four-wheeled wagon to the edge of the elevated dock. It held two small wooden shipping crates. They clearly expected David.

"These are for you, Mister Reseigh," the shorter one said. He was apparently the one who spoke English the best.

David corrected the man. "That's Doctor Reseigh."

"Okay, boss," the man said with a smile as he and his partner began muscling the heavy wooden containers into the back of the truck. "Your shipment arrived two days ago. We just today got the call from California that it would be you, not the drillers, picking them up this afternoon. You are here right on time. We close soon."

David smiled back at the man knowingly. The first one landed in back with a thud. Then the next one was placed behind it on the bed.

David was well aware that his pulse was racing, his palms sweaty. But he forced himself to act cool, like he did as a teenager with a newly delivered load of illegal drugs. Questions swirled around in his mind. Two days ago? Was Chuck testing the waters with the first two shipments before he trusted the big money shipment? The nervous manner in which his passenger glanced every which way didn't help calm his frazzled nerves. He hadn't been this rattled since he made his first four-ounce heroin buy as a seventeen-year-old. At least back then he had his crazy high school friend, Robert Martinez, along with that Glock nine of his under his coat. It was unthinkable to buy narcotics in Oakland without bringing along an armed guard. This situation, however, took "frightened" to a much higher level. But as nerve-rattling as it was, he had to play along.

"Have a nice day," the warehouseman said with a grin.

"Do I need to sign anything?"

The man only laughed and walked back into the warehouse with his work partner. The tall door closed and so did the warehouse.

"Go," she said. When you get to the road turn right. Then make the second left."

David did as he was told, the sedan clinging close behind. When he made the second left the sedan took off fast around him and made another left and disappeared around a bend into the darkening twilight.

"Keep going straight," she instructed. It was a tree shaded side street full of potholes running parallel to the main road. It clearly hadn't seen a rupiah in repair money in years. "From now on you must follow all traffic laws. That car now has your little black GPS box, the bug, as you Americans call it. It will fool anyone monitoring it into believing you're heading back downtown. But in a moment it won't be her car carrying it. She'll soon be passing it to another car heading out of the city, then it'll be passed to yet another heading back in. Then around eight this evening it'll be destroyed."

"Okay. I get the picture. You people are really well organized."

"Thank you. And turn on your headlights. It'll be dark soon."

After dodging countless suspension-rattling holes, then making a series of rights and lefts, David found himself in a quiet, well-manicured residential neighborhood, an upscale part of Pekanbaru populated by the wealthy. What at first appeared to be two motorcycle policemen parked by the unmarked entrance turned out to be a mere sampling of the community's private security force.

A shiny black American SUV soon appeared in his rear view mirror and drew close at times. As it passed under a streetlight he could tell it had four men inside. They continued winding through the neighborhood for another kilometer.

"Make a right into that open gate," she said. When he punched down his window and pulled in he saw a man standing by the mechanism, his hand near a lever. He parked in front of the large white home. With the broad wrap-around porch and red tiled hip roof the one-story home was impressive, although not out of place in that part of the city. It took no more than a fast glance to tell the house had been immaculately restored, as if it had been built recently rather than many decades earlier.

The black SUV pulled in right behind him, nearly touching bumpers. "Pull in more, all the way inside so others can squeeze in, too." David did and the tailgating SUV drew even closer. Then it stopped. Then another SUV just like the one tailing him, but quite a bit older, pulled into the driveway. The solid black metal gate then silently closed behind everyone.

Two young men in loose fitting tan business suits immediately exited from the second SUV. They were obviously bodyguards. It was a typical scene in this neighborhood and none of the neighbors gave it a second thought.

David shut off the engine and took in his surroundings. Tall trees lined the property in front. Flowering shrubs of different kinds bordered each side of the front yard. It was more than an acre, maybe two, depending on how far it went in back. A well-manicured lawn filled the unpaved space in front between the trees and shrubs. An ornately carved white fountain cut out a sizable portion of the center of the freshly mowed green grass. The asphalt circular driveway was unlit, but the home's entryway had one light on right above the dark stained double door. In that low light two large men stood on each side of the wide entry like stone lions, possibly the same men from the night before.

Out of the corner of his eye David saw four other men exit the first SUV. They paused a moment to confer with the two security men in tan suits. When all six approached his truck together, David's bladder loosened slightly. In the poor light he couldn't get a decent description of the ones who had followed him on the drive over. He did, however, notice the four sported white taqiyahs and each had long wispy beards. They also carried holstered side arms, the bulges barely visible under their loosely flowing oversized white shirts.

He thought back to old movies he had watched while growing up. He remembered that kidnappers rarely revealed their faces to their victims. Whenever they did it spelled bad news, often painfully bad news. A nasty chill went up his spine when he realized none of the people around him wore facemasks. Questions jumped out at him as he nervously sat in his truck. From what little he knew few disliked foreigners as much as Muslim radicals. Yet they appeared to trust him. Why? Did they know about Chuck? After what happened at Simmons Hydrocarbon Supply they must. Did they now trust this American scientist serving as the representative of a dying wealthy philanthropist? If not, did they plan to bury him somewhere?

His female companion opened her door. "This is the end of the road, Doctor. Now you visit with the imam," she said with a cheerful smile. She hopped out and closed the door. David got out, too, just as the four bearded men began muscling the two heavy crates out of the truck's back gate. They left the cardboard box containing the freezer alone.

"Now?"

"Yes. Then we'll be through with you," she said and walked toward the entry.

The men carried the heavy wood containers toward the side of the house where the garage was, but off to the right side some and part way behind the home. One of the men grew exhausted and had to rest not far from the corner of the house. He placed his end of the crate on the concrete walkway. His partner did the same. One of them said something in Indonesian and directed it at David. Shortly after they got moving again David heard a creak, the kind a rickety door might make.

His nerves were on edge. It reminded him of the time one winter evening years ago, in what seemed like another life, when Alameda County deputies stopped him minutes after he had made a modest drug purchase. The memory flashed through his mind and it did little to calm his nerves.

He recalled that the two ounce Ziplocked baggie filled with white chunks was in the inside pocket of his brown leather jacket. It was a terrible place to keep it, especially with the prominent bulge it made on his then slender frame. But he wanted to get far away from the Mexican venders as fast as possible. Hiding it in the pouch he'd installed behind the glove box of his new B2000 required three or four minutes and the nimble use of a screwdriver. That would take too much time.

He was seventeen at the time. He had an older buddy, Sam Zamrzla, along with him for protection. Sam was a tall skinny nine-teen-year-old with long, wavy, light brown hair outlining his pointy pockmarked face. Any cop would have considered the two seated together in a new car probable cause.

They had taken side streets on the drive from the Hayward drug house thereby avoiding the main drags often populated by bored cops. David drove down Lewelling Boulevard, over the tracks, about a mile more then stopped at the red light at Mission. He had to turn left toward the freeway on-ramp. An Alameda County deputy sheriff car appeared out of nowhere and pulled in close behind them. David absentmindedly glanced in his rear view mirror, saw the cop, then stupidly ran the red left turn light. The cop pulled them over and with lights flashing waited for backup. Within minutes he was surrounded by four cruisers.

The cops jumped out and took position all around while the one who first pulled them over ordered the two teenagers out of the car. He leaned inside the open window and grabbed his microphone. He shouted a command over the loudspeaker. "Get out of the vehicle, slowly."

They did. Rubberneckers slowed as they passed by. Some pedestrians gathered to watch from across the boulevard by the dilapidated Rocket gas station.

"Leave the doors open and walk in front of my car. Keep your hands out of your pockets."

They did that, too. The cop tossed the mike onto the seat of his car.

"Take off your jackets and empty all your pockets on the hood," he instructed.

They followed his orders. The costly cocaine was now on the hood of the police car, the baggie probably poking out of the inside pocket.

The streetlight overhead was dark, shattered by a tossed stone, or maybe shot out by a modern gunslinger. But the headlights of the police cars as well as their brilliant spotlights lit them up as if they were stars in a Broadway performance.

His trusted friend, Sam, was stoned as usual, his eyes bleary from constantly smoking pot. While buying the dope the Mexicans had offered them complimentary shots of some expensive bourbon, which David declined, but Sam accepted. He downed three in quick succession. David hadn't smoked any pot that day and was stone cold sober. But he was more than a touch lit up from sampling a few lines of the cocaine, which likely led to him blowing the light. He tested a touch with a kit, too, and concluded it was somewhere around eighty percent pure, as good as it gets. Its gripping impact on his mind and body concurred.

"Please place your hands on the hood," the cop commanded, this time in a more gentle, almost friendly voice. He pointed at Sam and tapped the passenger side of the car's hood. "You, with the hair, on this side. You, the driver, on the other side."

They did, each of them palms down on the hood as rough hands got ready to swarm all over their clothing. Two of the cops patted them down and found nothing interesting, except Sam's Zig Zags. He tossed them on the hood of his car with the rest of the scattered pocket litter.

"You been smoking pot?" One of them asked Sam.

"No, officer. I do not smoke marijuana," Sam replied. "It's bad for your health."

"You sure stink like pot."

"It's my cologne."

"Sure it is."

Afterward David stood by picking his fingernails while Sam began whistling some idiotic tune observing the performance through glazed eyes. They watched while one of the cops searched his car. He found nothing interesting. Four additional deputies stood by on the sidewalk watching the scene, too. It was about fifty degrees and a bit breezy. The chill only worsened his trembling.

David's brown leather jacket was flopped near the cruiser's buggy windshield, covering one wiper blade. He knew as soon as the deputy reached inside the pocket it would mean cuffs, a trip to Juvenile Hall followed by a few days in custody, a week at the most. After he turned eighteen the record could be sealed. It would be like it never happened. That was the risk. He considered getting busted an annoying speed bump, no big deal, although miraculously he never did. He had twenty-five grand and another ounce of coke hidden in a heater vent at his apartment, yet the thought of losing two grand worth of fresh white and being out of business awhile worried him the most. But he was nevertheless scared, even terrified, his heart revving somewhere close to his red line.

After rummaging through Sam's coat, their wallets, and scanning through the tiny pictures on their flip phones the cop who initially pulled them over spoke for the last time. "Grab your things and go. I'm going to give you a warning for running that red light. Good night gentlemen." Without another word he returned to his cruiser and took off. The rest of the cops scattered in different directions.

"I can't believe he forgot to search my jacket," David said to Sam as they jetted up the freeway on-ramp. "I just can't believe it!"

"Whatever," Sam replied. He pulled a joint from behind his ear and lit with a struck match. Then he slid a CD into the stereo. "Let's listen to some Zappa."

David had told that story a hundred times. He decided it was time to tell it once more, this time to Shannon, if only he lived long enough.

The memory vanished but the fear increased as a dark hand protruding from a tan sleeve gripped his shoulder. David turned some and the hand gripped tighter.

"What's he want?" David asked the young woman. She had reached the top of the stairs but hadn't quite reached the dimly lit door. She was still close by. She stopped and turned.

"He wants you to go with them into the garage out back," she said. "I'm supposed to go inside the house and fix tea for everyone."

"Okay," he said to her. He found it strange that these people would drink tea at a time like this. He realized both of the tan-suited guards were standing right behind him, close enough for him to smell the hand gripper's spicy breath. He called out to the woman for confirmation. "I'm supposed to go with them now, right?"

"Yes," she said with a smile. "You go with them. It has been very nice meeting you, Doctor Reseigh," she said.

David could've sworn she added more movement to her hips than usual as she stepped toward the front door.

"Hey, you. Get moving," the tan suit gripping his shoulder said. His English wasn't quite as polished as his white leather shoes but he got his message across quite well. David did as ordered. He now knew what sailors went through when they walked the plank.

CHAPTER FORTY-SEVEN

The other of the two tan suits grunted something at David in a stern stereotypical security guard tone. It wasn't in English but it no doubt meant get moving. He now stood before the slightly crooked wooden garage. It may have been the next building scheduled to be remodeled. The right side swinging door was open about a meter. One of the tan suits gently pushed him through it. His stoic lack of expression was etched into his face, a permanent feature, as fully developed as his monstrous biceps. His partner was no different.

David stumbled into the garage. It was dark, the floor concrete, the space inside lit only by an open bulb dangling from the ceiling. A heavy hardwood dining room table was in the center of the garage. A mower, shovels, rakes and other yard maintenance equipment were scattered around. The one small window in back was covered in black plastic.

The table, now a utilitarian workbench, had long ago lost its grandeur. Both shipping crates were on the floor in front of it. Two men were busily prying here and there trying to dismantle each of them. Long crowbars strained against the deep nails. Four chairs surrounded it. Three were empty. The imam sat in one and smiled.

He stood when David entered the room. "Doctor Reseigh," he said. "How good it is to see you again."

"Good evening, Imam Hasbullah."

"Come inside and have a seat," the imam said. It was more like a command than a request. A board atop one of the crates split apart. Muscular arms thrust the crowbar at it for another bite. "Let's have a visit while we observe the opening of the crates you've kindly delivered to us."

David wasn't sure exactly what was inside them. It was clear the people surrounding him believed otherwise so he chose to keep his ignorance to himself.

"Thank you," David replied as one of the men popped the top off the solid crate he was attacking.

The two tan suits stood silently outside. Their shoes were barely visible through the tall gaps at the bottom of the swinging garage doors.

The imam spoke to the men in Indonesian. One of them replied fast with a string of syllables unintelligible to David, followed by a big smile. His hands drummed a quick tune on the side of the crate he'd just opened. One of his hands reached inside and pulled out a few wads of two hundred euro notes. The yellow bills reflected bright against the single light.

"David. You are a national hero," the imam said.

"I don't feel like a hero," David said as a loud crack from the other crate filled the garage.

"It is open," one of the other men said in English, his stony face unchanged. He extracted a copper pipe and placed it on the table. He removed another and placed it by the first one. But the third one gave him pause. He gripped one end of that short copper pipe and set it back in the crate. The pipe was as wide as the container and fat, about three centimeters in diameter. He frowned at David, the unkind expression clear to all. Then he studied the pipes remaining in the box a moment. "It's filled with these pipes. But some of the pipes are filled with something. Imam, please leave the room for your safety while we examine them."

"Come, quickly," the imam said to David as he stood. "We must leave the garage. That crate may hold explosives. These men will probe deeper. If it's a bomb they'll dismantle it while others drive us away from here."

One of the four escorted David and the imam out of the garage. As David took a step outside he glanced back just as the man pulled the heavier pipe from the crate. The end he saw was plugged with wax, like a crude pipe bomb.

The two tan suits outside encircled the imam and moved away fast, instructing David to follow them. One told David to stand behind the nearest of the two SUVs. He had taken six or seven steps that direction when the garage door opened a crack. The creaking noise caught everyone's attention. A face appeared wearing a shocked expression. The door opened a bit more as the face of the second of the four men appeared. He spoke excitedly, but not loud, in Indonesian. He was waving his arms crazily at them, apparently calling them back into the garage.

"Wait here," a tan suit said. He jogged to the garage and went inside. As he ran his light coat flapped opened and David saw the handle of his holstered handgun. It jabbed him in the ribs the first few steps. His right hand reached back and steadied the handle the rest of the way.

A moment later he came out and summoned the imam back inside. "Gold. Some of the pipes are filled with gold coins. There are hundreds of them."

David's nerves calmed back to idle when the imam invited him to help count the cash. He was given the job of counting the many packets of pink, five hundred euro notes.

The copper pipes inside the crate contained precisely one hundred rolls of one ounce Chinese gold Pandas. Each roll held twenty coins. Including the cash, the delivery added up to the equivalent of thirty million US dollars, plus or minus some depending on world currency markets that day.

"When you return to San Francisco tomorrow I would like you to stay close to the land line in your office," Imam Hasbullah Ali said. It was nearly time to send him back to his hotel room.

"I'm flying back tomorrow?" David said. It was news to him.

"Yes. I'll explain why. We are consolidating power much faster than we ever imagined possible. I'll not share specific details now, but if the military government disintegrates much more we're going to announce a governing Islamic Revolutionary Council on Sumatra, maybe as soon as this weekend. If that happens we may have one more favor to ask of you."

"More smuggling cash?"

"No," the frail imam said with a smile. "The seeds you've sown have sprouted and borne more fruit than any of us had hoped. This time we may ask for you and your professional expertise."

"As an environmental advisor?"

"Something like that. I'll know more soon and keep you advised."

"I'd be interested in helping the new government in any way I can," David said.

"We all appreciate that and thank you for what you've done for us. The entire nation needs to thank you. I hope some token show of our gratitude will be forthcoming soon."

"We're actually winning, aren't we?" David asked, smiling a bit when he realized he had used the plural pronoun, "we."

"Yes, we are winning. The true victor, however, will be the rainforests. All of them."

"After this, I do hope so," David said. His watch read eight thirty. "Imam Hasbullah, since there's not much more for me to do here, I would like to go now and rejoin my two colleagues."

"Yes, soon. One more thing. There has been a new development you need to be aware of. There's something I need to tell you. As you've learned, your friends are now in Kuala Lumpur."

"That's what I understand."

"They are fine," he said with a soft smile. "We took good care of them. We provided them with plenty of travel money and first class tickets, too. The stakes were getting very high, especially when we found out about the crates."

"What about the crates? Why didn't you just grab them if you thought there was so much money inside?"

"We have friends all over this city, but none working at Simmons. I'll tell you what happened. When an associate told us you had stopped there to drop off some equipment yesterday we investigated further. We discovered that you had dropped off a solar unit there. We also found out that two small crates had arrived at Simmons two days ago. It was addressed to them, but deliverable only to you for use on some natural gas project not far from here. It was quite clever. We concluded that your cash supplier wanted to be certain the smaller shipments generated results. When he was satisfied he would release more. And he did. Then the crates sent to Simmons' were released to you. Did we get it right?"

"Yes. But even I didn't know about the Simmons' shipment until this morning.

The imam smiled. "You knew before we did. We didn't find out about them until late this afternoon. We presumed they contained money, but we weren't certain. It would have been a wasted risk stealing two containers of drilling equipment. So rather than seize the crates ourselves we decided to let you deliver them to us. It would be quieter that way."

"Smart."

"Anyhow, back to your friends," he said. "The situation was getting too dangerous for Shannon and Gary. Army agents were known to be continuously present in the hotel. They continuously occupied one of the rooms. We suspected they were monitoring guests, possibly the three of you."

"My room was bugged?" David asked thinking of the intimate moments he and Shannon had shared the past several nights.

"We don't know that for certain. And furthermore do not inspect the room when you return there. Act and behave as you would have without knowing this information."

"I'll try."

"Please do. Even worse, their presence was making things complicated for us. What if one of your friends accidentally blurted out something regarding the money while inside a bugged room? The risk had become intolerable. This afternoon a decision was made to change their travel plans. One of our operatives called the airlines and arranged it for them. The flight they took was originally booked solid with forty-seven standbys. We paid a small bribe and two first class seats opened. The cover story we invented was simple. Gary fell ill and required an escort. Shannon became the convenient escort."

"What'll I do tomorrow?"

"Sleep in late. Enjoy your breakfast. The air is clearing so enjoy a late morning run. While you're jogging wear a loose-fitting shirt and be sure to wear your document pouch. While you're out running someone will hand you your plane tickets for the four p.m. flight to KL and some travel money."

CHAPTER FORTY-EIGHT

David's Thursday afternoon flight to Hong Kong with a stopover in Kuala Lumpur was uneventful. The Indonesian exit control officer didn't bat an eye as she chopped an exit stamp into his passport. Roving Malaysian officials armed with low-slung automatic rifles ignored him while he waited an hour to change planes in the airport's tightly secured transit wing.

It was late evening when he landed in Hong Kong. The Chinese immigration official only asked him for the purpose of his trip.

"Shopping," David had replied. The ten thousand US dollars he carried made a substantial bulge in his front cargo pocket.

She stamped his passport and called for the next passenger in line.

Once outside the official inspection section he glanced around. A familiar voice shouted out loud. "David!"

It was her. He shouted back. "Shannon!"

They met like a head on collision and openly hugged in the crowded terminal.

"Hey," David said. "Dig this. It's sure been awhile since we've been free to hug in public."

"I didn't mind the Muslim custom. It was a bit fun saving all of you for later," Shannon said. "Maybe those Islamists are on to something with their thing about banning public displays of affection."

"Hey. What about me, Gary?"

"Gary who?" David asked while gazing into Shannon's eyes. He broke free a moment and shook Gary's hand. Then he turned and hugged Shannon once more.

"Good Lord. I'll leave you two alone and go fetch us a cab," Gary said.

The taxi was a compact red sedan, like most of them in the former British colony. All three sat in back while the taxi whisked them to their Hong Kong hotel.

"Red paint on the outside, green paint on the inside," Shannon said. "This taxi reminds me of Christmas."

"Seeing you two is better than Christmas," David said. "I hope the revolution lasts that long."

"The international news is calling it a terrorist revolution."

"Terrorist, my ass," David said. "For the first time in four hundred years Indonesians have a decent shot at reclaiming their land and, most importantly, forming a lasting nation in harmony with nature."

"The military leadership dissolved the MPR while you were on the plane," Gary said. "According to the BBC news Direct Action rebels now control Borneo and Sumatra. Plus the Free Papua Movement has declared independence in West Papua and Papua Provinces. Sulawesi is expected to fall today. The government is on the ropes, David. It's struggling to retain power. Soon all the old government'll have is Java."

"Yeah, but Java's a hundred fifty million people. That's almost sixty percent of Indonesia's population."

"They'll soon join with the rebels. You'll see."

"The guy who met me at the airport and gave me my new airplane tickets told me Direct Action had invited all the rebel factions to a big unification meeting near Pekanbaru. It's probably underway now. They want to drop the term Direct Action and form a rebel government. They've proposed naming it the Islamic Revolutionary Council, or IRC."

"All my life I've been a supporter of religious and cultural diversity. But I never would've thought I'd be rooting for the radical Islamists," Gary said.

"Oh, Gary," Shannon said. "Embracing the concept of cultural diversity doesn't mean you have to approve every social system."

"Shannon's right," David said. "Just because you and I may disagree with some of their cultural norms doesn't mean they don't have a legitimate right to safeguard their traditional social and religious practices. And from what I've learned lately they're nowhere near as wild as they've been painted by the western media. At least on Sumatra they're everyday people, a bit more religious and patriotic than some, maybe. But from what I've experienced they're good, decent people."

"Well I'm certainly impressed with how organized they are," Shannon said.

"From what little I could gather during the hours I spent with them, Direct Action has supporters everywhere," David said. "They were able to do an incredible amount of damage to the military in a matter of days. And as soon as their allies on the other islands received the green light all hell broke loose."

"So we've been reading," Gary said. "Now the US wants to organize an Afghanistan-style invasion."

"Against two hundred fifty million people? Good luck with that."

"The US has made crazier military moves than that in the past century," Gary said. "But the US military only does what it's told to do by the military industrial complex. It's all about profits. So who knows what might happen next?"

CHAPTER FORTY-NINE

Civilian government in Indonesia had ended hours after the Dumai bombing when the president declared martial law. Fearful of their fast eroding power the besieged military had made desperate calls for international assistance. Western corporations crushed by the stoppage of the palm oil trade lobbied hard for an international force to occupy key ports and destroy the terrorists threatening to seize power. Mining and lumber interests joined in lobbying on behalf of the government's call for help.

Singapore, Japan and Australia joined with a number of energy hungry European countries in supporting the creation of a United Nations peacekeeping force. The countries involved in the invasion force had extensive economic interests involving the export of forest products and minerals. All of this economic activity had been based on relentless deforestation.

Neighboring Thailand, Burma, India, Malaysia, Brunei and New Guinea all remained neutral. The document outlining the invasion was quickly crafted, modeled after the agreement guiding NATO and allied forces when they carried out the botched occupation of

Afghanistan. Fearing the fast consolidation of power enjoyed by the rebels, in four days it was signed to by representatives from twenty-seven nations. The invasion force would assemble and get underway within days unless the military leaders of Indonesia showed clear signs of defeating the rebels.

With the widespread popular revolts against the army's response to the bombings, fighting that many feared would become an outright civil war had ignited throughout Indonesia. It started the night of the initial port attacks and soon engulfed the entire archipelago. The battles were more widespread than back in the fifties and sixties and some were becoming equally brutal.

Armed anti-foreigner gangs waged systematic attacks against anyone believed to be employed on corporate owned oil palm tree plantations. Since few plantations were owned by Indonesians that meant palm oil production ground to a halt. Then came the push back. Within a week one million oil palm trees had been cut down. But the true scope of the loss of life leaked out when a rebel document revealed that ten thousand loggers, miners and oil palm tree workers had been killed since the Direct Action attacks began back in May. It was a terrible toll, but nowhere near the half million killed in the upheavals a half century earlier.

This time it wasn't a communist led uprising, like the ones back in the fifties and sixties. Although leftists played a significant role in organizing workers to participate in the week-long general strike the rebellion was largely open to all. While life in Jakarta and throughout Java continued pretty much as before, in the rebel held lands such as Sumatra, only critical sectors of the economy including hospitals, grade schools, public transportation and food production remained fully operational. Fuel scarcities worsened, pushing drivers out of their poor mileage personal vehicles and onto small motorcycles, bicycles and buses. Most other workers honored the request by Direct Action to not report to their jobs and instead work to support forces loyal to the rebellion.

What happened this time differed from the past rebellions. This time supporters of the rebels included all sectors of the population. Rich and poor, students and farmers, even radical Muslim groups toned down their rhetoric and joined forces with secular liberals. Political and social differences were subordinated to the prime objective. Stopping deforestation and ridding their nation of foreign economic domination came first. Police officers and freed criminals convicted of petty offenses battled side by side to defeat army units remaining loyal to the government.

Four days after David arrived in San Francisco and a week after the martial law declaration, an initial landing force of twenty thousand predominately US soldiers had arrived in Singapore, ready to roll across the Strait of Malacca to their intended landing spot south of the port of Dumai. Other western forces were scheduled to arrive within days to militarily silence the rebels fighting on other islands.

On that day two Singapore Navy patrol vessels fell under attack by underwater divers armed with high explosives. The vessels were sent to the sea bottom by former Indonesian navy divers while anchored just off the coast, only a few kilometers from the rocky shoreline near Dumai. No lives were lost among the fifty-six crew members each carried, but it was fast becoming clear that occupying Indonesia would be far more costly and difficult than the invasions and military takeovers of either Iraq or Afghanistan. The land invasion, which was expected to be a fairly simple operation, was put on hold.

Direct Action, by far the leading political force in the uprising, refused to compromise on the twin issues of deforestation and foreign economic domination. This, they declared, was the critical unifying element bringing all Indonesians together as one, regardless of religious or political disagreements. Harming the nation's forest treasure would simply no longer be tolerated. Politically this was a brilliant move. Massive anti-war protests broke out in cities across North America and throughout Europe. This further served to erode the enthusiasm of the nations responding to the request for assistance from the ruling authorities.

Just as importantly, the US led invasion force fell apart when the EU nations that had earlier joined with the usual initial enthusiasm pulled out of the coalition.

With rainforest resources dwindling the council followed the lead of Peru, which had recently banned newsprint media. The reason Peru had made this move was that the pulp used to make newspaper originated in the western Amazon basin. It was one of the leading causes of that nation's deforestation. Rebel-held areas in Indonesia followed that Andean nation's bold move when supplies of pulp and locally made paper ran low. With most news read online few complained.

Meanwhile the IRC, now made up of representatives of the key rebel groups, passed several guiding resolutions. A constitutional assembly and an elected people's assembly would come later. Each resolution carried the power of law in liberated territories. Most importantly the interim leadership agreed to set aside their political, religious and social differences and focus on defeating the weakening military dictatorship. Secondly, they agreed to continue applying the death penalty against anyone participating in further damage to the rainforests. But by now the word had spread. And with the oil palm tree plantations out of business across most of the nation it was rarely enforced.

A number of lesser agreements rounded out what was called the Ten Point Manifesto, including the freedoms of speech and assembly. Although print newspapers would soon be outlawed due to their harmful impact on the forests, digital press and Internet freedoms would be guaranteed.

With a ninety percent Muslim population it was obvious that it would be a Muslim-led republic. Attacks on minority religions would not be tolerated and would be addressed in accordance with previous criminal law.

The protection of primates was on the top ten list, too. With an estimated thirty thousand orangutans remaining in the wild, and the extinction of all wild primates looming ever closer, a severe penalty was needed. It was decided that a ten year prison sentence combined with twenty lashes would be issued to anyone convicted of killing, harming or threatening them or their habitats.

With most of the nation's navy now allied with the rebels due to widespread mutinies, foreign navies were warned to not intervene. With two Singapore Navy ships sent to the seabed no others challenged the warning. Only Java escaped the rebel attacks against air bases. They had successfully neutralized the military dictatorship's air power.

On Sumatra, Borneo, Guinea, and on most of the smaller islands across Indonesia, the army had by day ten switched its loyalty to the rebel camp. Hundreds of high-ranking police officers and civilian public officials replaced corrupt and unpopular army brass. The tainted army officers were summarily stripped of rank and retired. Their ill-gotten wealth was seized, appropriated for use by the revolutionary government. In lieu of facing prison, most were sent off to work on assorted forest renewal projects.

The council decided to offer air force and army members still remaining loyal to the old regime a full unconditional amnesty. It would protect them against prosecution for any offenses committed during the period of unrest. The full integration of the military would occur by the end of the second week when Java finally fell. At four a.m. on the morning of June tenth most of the air force planes on Java flew to various bases on Sumatra and Kalimantan. The Sultan Syarif Kasin II airport in Pekanbaru was packed with fighter planes. The entire air force had pledged its loyalty to the Revolutionary government.

By noon that day the army had capitulated and a bloody drawn out civil war had been averted. Army officers and soldiers were invited to reapply for their old positions under the leadership of the newly formed, but greatly downsized, Revolutionary Guard. Most did, but few were accepted. Over the past fifty years the Indonesian Army had existed for the sole purpose of guarding foreign interests and curtailing domestic unrest. The RG's mandate was to safeguard the rainforests and the revolution. It was an entirely new direction for that nation's military.

The IRC received a needed boost when the EU biodiesel mandate was scrapped. It had required that all diesel fuel sold in its member nations contain from five to ten percent palm oil. The end of palm oil based biodiesel, one of the most environmentally destructive policies in modern history, was mourned by few. Market demand for palm oil disappeared overnight. Wilmar and Neste went bankrupt. Other than the top executives and stockholders in the international palm oil corporations, few complained and their cries for help went unanswered.

For Indonesia a bright new day had dawned. By the fifteenth of June few fires raged and the air over Sumatra was mostly clear. Although the clearcutting had stopped, the damage to the rainforests and peatlands would continue until the last of the flames had all died out. Many of the fires in the peatlands would continue burning for months, the persistent ones even longer. But with demand for palm oil no longer there and the market for hardwoods and wood pulp decimated the financial motive to cut trees had ceased.

On June sixteenth the rebel leadership received a boost when Russia formally recognized the new Indonesian government. By July first, seventy additional nations had done the same.

CHAPTER FIFTY

B ecause the tone and tenor of the revolutionary rhetoric was clearly anti-foreigner, observers were stunned when an American scientist was invited to become the rebel government's first chairperson of the newly formed Ministry of Forests. His record as an environmental activist was irrefutable, but because he was an American citizen no one could understand why he was chosen. He had been to Indonesia several times and had worked extensively with rainforest advocacy organizations, including the million-member Indonesian Peasants Union. They strongly supported his selection. The founder and leader of that organization, Henri Sarigi, once called deforestation the root cause of poverty, lawlessness and hunger.

Outside Indonesia the most widely accepted theory was that they wanted to showcase a token foreigner in a prominent position in an attempt to quell growing allegations of institutionalized xenophobia. An American scientist in such a position would serve that purpose well.

It was nine in the morning Monday, the fifth of June. David had just returned to San Francisco the day before. He had been in his office since seven dealing with an assortment of mundane financial matters related to his trip to Indonesia and the operations of his office and organization. At the moment he was online reviewing the office's unusually high electricity bill when his office phone rang. It was Azka. He was the one chosen to break the news of David's nomination. It was going to be a very busy day.

He told David about his nomination for the top-level office in the revolutionary government. Azka first congratulated him about receiving Indonesian citizenship. Interestingly, David hadn't even applied for permanent residency, which was generally a prerequisite for citizenship. But there were often exceptions.

He asked Azka to thank the IRC for their trust and faith in him. Azka told him he would. "And tell them I accept," he said. Since citizenship was generally a prerequisite for anyone holding such a high office in any country, that initial move was an important technicality.

Azka explained how to access the business class e-ticket for his flight to Pekanbaru via Hong Kong and Kuala Lumpur. The flight was scheduled to depart from San Francisco International Airport at ten that night. David's new employer was adamant about him accepting and starting work the next day. Crossing the International Date Line meant he would begin Wednesday morning, Indonesia time. They'd even purchased business class seats on each of the three flights it took to get there. This journey into the unknown reminded him of the terrifying walk to that side garage six days earlier.

His nomination for the cabinet-level office was approved by the unanimous vote of the fifteen-member ruling IRC. He flew back to Jakarta to accept the appointment and got to work. In his Skyped acceptance speech he invoked the name of British Admiral Thomas Cochrane. Two centuries ago the admiral had been recruited by the Chilean government to lead that nation's navy during its war of independence against Spanish colonial rule. Doctor Reseigh included that name when he pointed out that history had a long list of foreigners fighting in revolutionary movements.

"Indonesia has until just recently been continuously occupied by foreigners since the colonial era," he pointed out in a Skype conference. "In fact this time it's not only Indonesia's riches they've been after, it was much worse. For the first time corporate forces worked in unison to destroy this nation's very lifeblood. This country has been occupied by foreign economic forces for over four hundred years. I pledge to you that I'll remain in office until the rainforest once again spreads across the archipelago. I'll continue to fight against anyone harming one tree or one animal or one bird indigenous to this great nation."

His first act of office, which he requested as a condition of his appointment, was to recruit high school and college students to cut down every last oil palm tree in the country other than those existing on locally owned plantations prior to 1985. This demand was written while he was on his flight to Pekanbaru, where his executive offices would be located.

The Jakarta Post granted an indefinite leave of absence to one of their field reporters when David appointed Azka to be his executive secretary. Azka soon became more than that. All day long the two close friends worked side by side as Azka continuously translated conversations and official documents. Azka insisted that David learn his newly adopted country's language as soon as possible. Within a month David was able to carry on a basic first-grade-level conversation. In three months he was nearly fluent.

David and Azka had calculated that three hundred thousand workers would be required in order to cut down the vast majority of the twenty million acres of oil palm trees growing throughout Indonesia. Ninety thousand acres, roughly equal to the production in 1964, was allowed to remain. Tens of thousands of unemployed loggers and plantation workers were recruited to perform the task. They began the eradication project on June sixth. The process of allowing the forest to reclaim the land would take time, likely decades. The initial goal was to return the forest to its 1990 level within ten years.

The damage from topsoil runoff was shocking. In some mountainous areas the soil had been washed away, leaving a wasteland of bare rock. The reforestation project clearly faced a severe challenge. But it would be much easier to initiate the reforestation process now rather that trying to bring the rainforest back to life long after it had vanished and the fragile topsoil had washed away.

Existing mining operations were nationalized and allowed to continue. But no additional land clearing permits would be granted. When the forest clearing and mining were at its peak, little of the wealth generated had trickled down to the vast majority of the population. Therefore, when ended the economic damage to the population as a whole was minimal.

Since Sumatra had been the first of the larger islands liberated from foreign and military rule, and Jakarta had yet to be captured, Pekanbaru became the nation's interim capital. With their political base strong on Sumatra the oil palm tree eradication operations began in Riau Province on the day Reseigh arrived, partly as a test, partly because he was available to supervise and direct the operations. The destruction of the rainforests had finally been stopped and it was time to start the recovery.

He had a late morning coffee with Gary, who had taken BART from Berkeley into San Francisco. Gary and his crew of graduate assistants had already started his Sumatra water and soil study. By August he had submitted the study for publication. In a few months he would find out if it had been accepted. Meanwhile he accepted David's invitation to join him in Pekanbaru to continue to study the streams and rivers of Riau.

"I've been told the government has arranged for me to move into a house in the suburbs," David said to him. "They sent me pictures. It's rough, but you'll approve. It's small, on stilts, about a thousand square feet with three bedrooms. The imam's even loaned me two of his bodyguards. One of them will accompany me at all times. I suggested they prepare for daily bicycle rides."

Shannon, who had originally intended to vacation in San Francisco for another week, changed her plane ticket to Ireland via London for the same evening David flew to Pekanbaru. Her British Airways flight was at nine. His flight to Hong Kong, at ten. A daypack and his laptop would accompany him on the flight. Getting that ready took fifteen minutes.

But it took him forty-five minutes to properly pack his four-year-old Look 695 road bike into a cardboard bicycle box. A week or two is one thing, but he couldn't imagine leaving for an indefinite period of time without it. So the bike just had to come along, too. Indonesia would mark the seventeenth nation where he'd ridden his prized nine thousand dollar, carbon-framed bike.

Shannon sat at an office table and organized her photographs and notes from the trip. David attended five straight hours of meetings. He took a late morning break to jog fifteen blocks from his California Street office to Chuck's where they met for an hour.

Chuck was delighted that his seed money had produced such spectacular results. He told David that an additional two hundred million dollars was available to help fund the revolutionary government, but to keep that information to himself while he worked out the details regarding how to move the funds, if required. David told him he didn't think that much would be necessary, but an ace in the hole never hurt.

As it turned out, the revolution consolidated political and military power so fast David decided none of it was needed. Therefore, none was requested. Nevertheless, Chuck applied that money, and more, to establish a billion dollar trust fund to help restore the Sumatran rainforest to its natural state. Not only that, but on the fifteenth of June the first of a lifetime of promised monthly trust fund checks was electronically deposited into David's bank account. Rather than begin the payments after he died, Chuck made an arrangement to start the payments immediately. The ten thousand dollar deposits would accumulate there until David decided what to do with the money. For now he would do nothing.

With David's rushed schedule he and Shannon only had a few minutes to speak while at the airport prior to their departures.

"This past week's been like a non-stop car race," Shannon said. "I was thinking, David. Since school's out on Friday, the twenty-eighth of June, would you be interested in taking on another assistant?"

"But school starts in September," David said. "It'd only be for six or seven weeks."

"Maybe not," Shannon said. She thought about her plan to visit with her parish priest. "I'll take care of a few things and plan to be in Pekanbaru by the end of the first week in July as long as I can get seats on a plane during the summer rush."

"I wasn't too wild about being away from you for so long. Thank goodness the imam has a knack for finding open seats on airplanes."

"That airline connection of his may come in handy," she said. "In the meantime I'll apply for a sabbatical."

"But what if things go wrong in Sumatra? What if the revolution collapses for some reason?"

"That's even more reason for me to be with you."

"That would be wonderful," David said. "Bring your bicycle. The first thing we'll do when you arrive is go on a ride."

"How sweet. A bicycle ride in Pekanbaru. That means you really do love me, don't you?"

"Yes," he said.

She kissed him on the forehead. "You are such a sweetheart."

"I'll let the IRC know about your plans. I imagine they'll want to be aware of such things."

"We wouldn't have to get married or anything like that, would we?"

"Maybe. But I believe they have some loopholes when it comes to that sort of matter. So they'll probably grant us some cultural consideration."

"I can't wait. But you have so much work to do."

"The tough part lies ahead. The destruction of the rainforests in Indonesia has finally been stopped," he said. "But now we'll have to figure out a way to reverse the damage. That's never been done before on such a massive scale. The best way may be to keep people away from it and allow the trees to reclaim the plantations on their own."

"Time will tell," Shannon said. "I sure hope Sumatra and the rest of Indonesia don't go the way of Easter Island. It's so depressing. At times I wonder if there's no stopping the mass extinctions and ecological devastation humans are causing."

"We have to face the possibility the revolution may not succeed," David said. "If that happens the rainforests on Sumatra are doomed. We may even lose them across all of Indonesia. It's possible, maybe even probable, that in fifty years or less humans'll go extinct after consuming every last gram of nutrition and burning the last speck of fossil energy on this round petri dish we call Earth. But I swear to God I won't allow it to happen to the Indonesian rainforests, not on my watch, and not without a fight."

CPSIA information can be obtained at www.ICGtesting.com
Printed in the USA
LVOW06s2134160714

394720LV00002B/202/P